I0714706

Other books by Thomas McGonigle

In Patchogue

The Corpse Dream Of N. Petkov

Going to Patchogue

St. Patrick's Day: Another Day In Dublin

The Bulgarian Psychiatrist

In Bulgarian

Диптих Преди Умиране

Diptych Before Dying

Предсмптните Биденир на Никола Петков

The Corpse Dream Of N. Petkov

Empty American Letters

the Bulgarian novel

A BOOK FROM BULGARIA WRITTEN IN THE AMERICAN LANGUAGE WHICH PIVOTS ON A SINGLE VIOLENT DEATH OF AN AMERICAN WOMAN LIVING IN UPSTATE NEW YORK, USA.

Thomas McGonigle

(late of Patchogue, New York, USA,
Sofia, Bulgaria and Dublin, Ireland)

SPUYTEN DUYVIL

New York   Paris

Library of Congress Cataloging-in-Publication Data

Names: McGonigle, Thomas, author.
Title: Empty American letters : the Bulgarian novel / Thomas McGonigle.
Description: New York City : Spuyten Duyvil, [2022]
Identifiers: LCCN 2022027686 | ISBN 9781956005738 (paperback)
Subjects: LCGFT: Biographical fiction. | Novels.
Classification: LCC PS3563.C3644 E47 2022 | DDC 813/.54--dc23/eng/20220623
LC record available at https://lccn.loc.gov/2022027686

Anna

jaoks

Thank you

and good morning. добро утро! Gnaydin.
Dia dhuit ar maidin.
At first there is possibility: Welcome… but that
word is ominous, there is the silent complement: and
be gone with you.

Seni gormem imkansiz imkansiz imkansiz
ruyalarim olmasa
—Zeki Muran

nothing more illegitimate than to bring
chronological scruples to a work and…
—E. M. Cioran

КНИЖАРНИЦА
·ЕЛИН ПЕЛИН·

Reader, and there is never a reason to write unless one expects to be read… I could find an ear, for sure, any ear and pour all of these words into that receptacle and have done so but such an ear will surely die and then…

Reader, you should know, what follows is concerned with work and a journey around Bulgaria and why a few people are not with me and Piret as we make our way in June as we went from Sofia to Strazhitsa, to Veliko Tarnovo to Varna to Plovdiv to Sofia, to Pernik.

Warning:

(—)   …is saying, the trailer was a mess: there is blood all over everything and dog feces… her two dogs have been locked in the bedroom and that is awful but the rest of the place is splattered all over with blood and in the bathroom there are towels soaked with blood… that is where they find her in the bathroom… Linda has tried to stop the bleeding… the police are really very good, the state Troopers, and talking with these homicide investigators and while they didn't answer all the questions…

Quoting an old document:

…and if it is to be another seventeen years before my next visit: the place is Istanbul but I am tempted to think of other cities, as if the actual city mattered—a change of mood you will notice, a hint of optimism, seventeen years, another visit, I will be … my life nearly at its end—if my parents as a model—possibly dragging along some awful child, who will not want to be here, I could probably sell him or her if there is still a market for white children, would anyone be the wiser, when back in New York City—though the irony is, I will have come back here only a year later with the woman who would be the mother of the son I am to be traveling with and now I am on my way to … and to think—in another—years: … how many years older? …

The absence of those people gnaws at our journey, never stopping us in our proverbial tracks, never goading us on, but always shadowing, even on cloudy days... never speaking to us, but always forcing us to speak of them, aware always they are listening and would hold us responsible for every word we use or did not use when talking about them though to be sure they are not ghostly figures, not figments of imagination but humans who would surely be nailed to the earth as recorded in the registries of births and inevitably the date of their departures is prepared but held in detail, as is said, within the bosom of...

Setting out, but first it is necessary to record the authority for the words which comes from the actual walking the streets of New York City... either it is the wound in the side of Christ or the demand of Thomas's to stick his finger in the wound of Christ before belief... but upon the appearance of Christ, according to John in the New Testament, Thomas did not put his hand into the wound, something that would be impossible if you follow this walking about Manhattan, this thing I call my walking life which is my walking day for I am also walking in...

I am sure of it when I am finally awake. There must be a destination and a departure point because there is no hangover of fear when finally awake. If there has been no departure point, no planned place of arrival, the awakening would have been consumed by uneasy feelings leading quickly to...

I know the architecture of the dreams: glossy pages of their intended realization and the smell of newsprint on which they finally do appear alive for a day and then yellowing, soggy with the damp, heaped up at the curb Friday night.

No dream. This day in and day out of walking. Five days a week. My Walking. Uptown is where I do my walking, up there where people are serious and about their business, down here below Fourteenth Street and above Chambers Street, business is hidden away and no one labors in public. This is the nature of how things work and it works for me, this person who is now awake ready to walk again though he had walked all night in the dream.

Nothing remains of the walk of my dream. Nothing remains some might say of my walking Uptown and they are probably right on most days but this is not one of them.

a

…in the Paleolithic. This implies, on the one, a belief in a "soul," able to leave the body and travel freely through the world, and, on the other hand, the conviction that, during such a journey, the soul can meet certain

—A History of Religious Ideas (Vol. 1) by Mircea Eliade

b

(everything is a problem)

c

They would always be separated from one another by a deep gulf of happiness.

—*Three Travelers* by Marie-Clair Blais

-1-

Never not been in love with M——, written in the head, and written down in a copybook while stretching out on the bed in the Howard Johnson's in Saugerties.

Upstate to Saugerties where the mother and father died, now so long ago, not a trace of their own time or of those years remains except in a mind driving around in the town, out past the house or what I know as being *their* house on 9W north of town.

-2-

Get off the highway and check into a motel. Go down the hallway to the ICE AND SODA. You need a credit card for the Coke machine. At the front desk you ask if there is a grocery store nearby. The girl says go out of the parking lot turn left go about a mile and you'll find one, it's in the middle of the village.

The sun has gone down. You drive into the town. You find the grocery store but it's closed. An old guy says, they closed early today. Do you know where I can get a bottle of soda or something? There is a gas station that has a shop a mile or so along the road. It's 24 hours.

The front door of the shop is propped open. There doesn't seem to be anybody around. You get two Cokes from the refrigerated wall and decide not to get any potato chips. The cash desk is by the window when you turn back to pay. At the counter you notice something: a guy is on the floor, face down. There is a smell. You turn and start for the door and as you step outside a police car turns into the yard. You tell the cop getting out of the car, something is wrong. The guy in there is on the floor.

Today I am writing to share some very
troubling news: our budget shortfall
which I announced in the earlier memo
has now grown to $3.9 million

-3-

The aerial toll-houses…should not be a matter of public debate or discussion as it is believed that it may be detrimental for the inexperienced… Has ever a statement been made to not goad a person to throwing themselves into or away as the case may be… these "places' where the soul stops on its forty day journey, awaiting

-4-

…to be so alone as to wonder what is coming after and is there really an after and that is the moment when It is said: he is dead. Or, as some now say, he passed… which strangely is more accurate in defining this what we are trying to talk about… that something passes along and there is a lot of to-ing and fro-ing as to what is about to happen.. . You could think it a small holding pen where the schedule gets worked out for this path through either out there or into there or who knows where… and that is probably closer to what we are getting at… the throwing up of the hands: this ain't where I thought I was to be taken to when

София

I left the train at five o'clock in the afternoon and find love

-5-

You're the only person I know who went to Bulgaria to spend time traveling around.

-6-

Get the dates right: September 1967-April 1968
                              May 1973
                              December 1973
                              July-September 1984
                              July 1990
                              January 1993
                              June 2010

-7-

—Your child would be forty years old.

—Would by now have had children?

—Would still be in your lives or your life?

—Would be having mixed feelings about the two of you but you would have begged out of that *two of you*?

—Would have been hard enough for you to keep all this straight and how to remember how hard it had been and how alone you both felt?

No, how alone you feel and even just walking around in Sofia didn't help as too many days are given over to not remembering—all these years in fact when no one before Piret ever asked what you thought, been thinking, while you know, says she never remembers or thinks about that time (she has even lost her Bulgarian) or that place about which for some reason you keep talking, which I don't understand, she says, you've lived now so many years in other places, as HAS she, though she's never gone back there.

—Why would I go back there, she asks in a sharp voice, tell me that! Did your grandparents want to go back to Ireland, a place that had puked them up and across the Atlantic as twelve year olds to work as servants, never saying… and glad to have the work, mark my words.

—Imagine them saying they wanted to go back to the old country!

None of this would be happening if he did not notice a series of paintings on the outside wall of the church within the Rila monastery …

-10-

Another plot for a detective story: first half of a book about characters that leads to characters in the second half but no real connection between them so reading the story, you have to read the whole thing hoping to get the complete picture but to no purpose as you learn the lesson that sometimes there are no connections, a necessary but uncomfortable lesson for heading out to the street in the evening, tonight even, or any evening.

-10a-

Linda Nelson dies a redundant useless death in upstate New York.

Linda has been in a terrible predicament. As it is, she lives in a trailer in the woods, never being able to afford going to restaurants or participating in a cultural life (as in theater and concert performances, etc). VERY sad indeed.

-11-

-What happens when you die?
-When a person dies?
-To go on a journey for forty days.
-The obvious Biblical allusion… how many are there?
-But this is no Christ or Moses or God who…
-On a wall of the church in Rila Monastery a depiction of the 40 day journey of the soul from the moment of death until the particular judgment.

-On the streets *necrologues* for the 40 days: did the person make it to heaven, purgatory or hell... **can you detect the Catholic intrusion?**

-Let's drink to that one at the *grobisha* in Sofia.

- Pour many a man a drink into the earth and himself to be gone long before the spilt glass...

-Don't be too generous as the earth has an unlimited thirst.

-How frustrating the long arcades of compartments for the ashes...

-What a terrible attempt to instill sobriety at last into the central Sofia Cemetery.

-No bench to sit on, no over-arching trees, yet overgrown shrubbery all about.

-No one is coming along to linger in front of these busted open ash containers...

In the Orthodox countries there is sometimes at the gravesite a bench with a little table and often a storage box where people leave behind the food they have not been able to consume as they drink, eat and talk about the person who is not there.

On the 40th day the soul reaches its judgment, having been dragged through its previous journey as the life is always described in the literature…

-6-

Lidia is pregnant, the technician says.

She has diarrhea and sees himself walking behind a child for 21 years.

Lidia sees her body torn apart, grown fat, bleeding from places she didn't want to be aware of.

That night, she eats two plates of hot peppers, drinks a third of a liter of hot slivovitz and four cognac glasses full of gin.

She pukes on herself, on her pillow and wants to…

In the morning, she is still pregnant, angry at my and her mother's ignorance.

A week later the doctor scrapes the beginning of something from her womb.

The next day we see *ZORBA THE GREEK*. She wants to practice her English and there are so few English language movies in Sofia.

This is in the Kino just off Dimitrov Boulevard.

-X1-

****   here we must allow a blank and while once-upon-a-time the word *soul* could have been used, today the word might make many uncomfortable and in truth even he is unsure exactly what the word might mean and while he has no objection at any level to the word it is not part of his vocabulary when he thinks of what was about to go traveling for forty days according to the Orthodox Christian tradition.

-17-

Do you have regrets about your past?

Well, history is history—whether it's bad or good or criminal, it doesn't make a difference. An act, a deed, remains part of history forever. You can't change a story, just by blathering on about it, and make it into something other than what it was.

Rochus Misch (Hitler's bodyguard in the Bunker in Berlin, 1945).

-18-

The journey is as real as those paintings on the outside wall of the church in Rila, aspects maybe of the old philosophical debate: the oldest in the West anyway, the idea before the physical reality or is the idea depended upon the physical reality for its own shape?

21

-18a-

What happens when a person dies?

-19-

So, to forty places, some which are visited more than once, as life is like that and this trip did partake of that previous making a way into and upon the earth. No order in mind before the listing.

With no guidebook at hand.

Wasn't it in the *Canterbury Tales* a line about everyone being on the road these days, always getting about for some reason or other and it wouldn't profit anyone to ask too closely as to the why.

So, as to let everyone in on the places possibly to be taken to, there is a listing but that is no guarantee of the progress of the journey since it would mess with the freedom of the—does one dare throw in another complicating word—*angels*?

Patchogue	Strazhitsa	Paris
London		
Dublin	Kyoto	
Douglas	Sofia	
Helsinki	Pernik	
Venice	Vienna	
Istanbul	Bellport	

22

Corner Brook   Malvern

  Mattituck   Amsterdam   Washington, DC

Jamaica, VT

  Beloit   Chicago

Mexico City   Muncie

  Menasha   Toronto   Lourdes

     Havana

  Saugerties   Hermosa Beach   V a r n a

Port Jefferson

  Copenhagen   Roanoke

Berlin   Rovaniemi

  Veliko Tarnovo   Edison, NJ

Sofia   Patchogue

-23-

Strazhitsa. Just saying the word takes me away and that is the first step down a path, the preacher might say.

To be taken away, as even once again, as I am, to a lakeside restaurant on the outskirts of Targovishte, which is to avoid talking about what is happening in Strazhitsa which has a far more calamitous meaning within the life of this soul, a disaster equal to the one befalling me in Patchogue...

-20-

When first in Strazhitsa and having been at the station in a snow storm, along with Medy we are taken to the house of Medy's mother and brother. The streets are outspread fingers of a hand disguised by the snow but that there was a plan to the layout is beyond my reckoning.

Today, in Strazhitsa, those fingers curl into a fist with bruised knuckles and scraped skin, streaked with dried scabbing blood.

-21-

Strazhitsa (Bulgarian: Стражица, pronounced ['straʒiʧsə]; also transliterated *Stražica*, *Strazhica*, *Strazhitza*, etc.) is a town in northeastern Bulgaria, part of Veliko Tarnovo Province. It is the administrative centre of Strazhitsa municipality, which lies in the eastern part of Veliko Tarnovo Province. The town is located in the central Danubian Plain, not far from the Balkan Mountains, 45 kilometres northeast of the provincial capital of Veliko Tarnovo.

The town was badly damaged by an earthquake with a magnitude of 5.7 on 7 December 1986. Strazhitsa has an art gallery, an Eastern Orthodox church dedicated to the Dormition of the Mother of God, as well as a museum of local history. Strazhitsa's name comes from the Bulgarian root *strazh* (страж), meaning "guard".

-25-

My father walks from a bar in a small shopping center just south of Saugerties. Simmons Plaza. Behind one of the buildings there is a bar which served a little lunch. He is there and is on his way to the car when he is struck with his end. Judge Cody, who lives across from him on 9W, notices the car and the ambulance when he is driving past and is able to identify the stranger who it seems had a heart attack or something—Cody says he is pretty sure it is a heart attack as your father's face is discolored—and D.O.A at the hospital in Kingston where the attendants do not steal his watch or the money in his pocket. The undertaker finds the watch on his wrist and mentions it had been over-looked at the hospital. This is in August. Only the neighbors next door to the south come to the funeral parlor.

-26-

Piret sees a man standing about two feet from the front of the car. He had not been there a moment ago. We stop on the main road after having driven down from the new church up on the hill in Strazhitsa. He came from nowhere, she says in a voice letting on she did not believe what she is saying. One never knows what can happen in strange...

I do not know how I get home—rather to the house where I am staying that night when Medy and I are in Strazhitsa—from the bar I sought out after seeing *The French Connection* in the movie theatre in the *Dom na Kultura* that had been put up by the БКП Българската комунистическа партия. There were two other people in the theatre and I counted both of them as the lights were going off and they were still there when the lights came on. I am the third person sitting in the balcony. Unlike in Sofia they did not sell tickets for specific seats.

Before the movie starts there is a long commentary in Bulgarian explaining the film we are about to see. This is a rare honest film, the commentator says, about what life was like in the capitalist United States of America, about the ruthless life which people experience there on the so-called paved-with-gold streets, though most reasonable people would conclude the streets of America were in fact paved with the blood of the exploited and beaten down members of the working class who exist in constant fear unlike the workers in the People's Republic of Bulgaria.

Piret is very wise to be afraid of the man she sees standing in front of the car. In Strazhitsa, as I am walking about in the town, I am telling her of seeing the hauled up body of a pig that had been slaughtered. Scattered about on the ground are a variety of containers filled with its blood. For some reason they had been remiss in estimating the quantity of blood and I thought sure they did this many times before, but such a killing I guess never prepares a person exactly for what is likely to happen. From the acquisition of the piglet until the moment of its killing the creature gradually became a member of the household so of course no one could ever consciously provide for the quantity of blood as that would add a sense of premeditation to the killing and the near cannibalism of a creature who had endured as being part of the family through the days, weeks, months of its living close by—separated only by the thickness of a wall that was no greater than the thickness of the walls that separated each member of the family—I know the people in that house would be eating with a fundamental transgressive enjoyment at the remains of the pig for what remained of the winter and part of it would still be present in the house long after the killing.

The man Piret is seeing had probably not been born when I am first in the town though it is very possible I am seeing his father in that bar or in the little shop next door where I buy a folder of postcards displaying the life of Vladimir Ilyich Lenin as there are no picture postcards for the town. The young man's father is gone. The young man walks by. He is not even looking into the car. The Lenin postcards are in New York City. *The French Connection* is available on DVD.

-96-

HISTORY PROFESSOR DR.LINDA NELSON ALSO PASSED AWAY IN RECENT DAYS. NELSON IS PERHAPS BEST KNOWN FOR HER WORK IN RESEARCH AND TEACHING EUROPEAN HISTORY, ESPECIALLY RUSSIAN HISTORY. NELSON ALSO TEACHES SECTIONS OF US HISTORY. LINDA NELSON DIED AT CANTON-POTSDAM HOSPITAL, SATURDAY AT THE AGE OF 60.

-27-

Men die nightly in their beds, wringing the hands of ghostly confessors, the Man of the Crowd.
—Edgar Allen Poe.

-28-

The cycle of pig killing is fixed into the lives of families in Strazhitsa and while Medy's brother does not have a pig to fatten—he is too nice for such, Medy's daughter tells me in New York—he and their mother are recipients of meat from slaughtered pigs owned by families to either side of them. People feel an obligation sometimes to share what they have been blessed by, Medy would explain to her daughter, though increasingly that is becoming rare in Bulgaria.

Medy does not eat slaughtered pig when she visits her mother and her brother. While not usually sentimental, Medy claims to eat the slaughtered pig meant to take into her body the sounds the pig made as it died, as the blood gushed into all those household pots and pans. Of course one hears all the time in Sofia that foods do not taste the same as back before… and I realize since people no longer participate in these rituals which are described as cannibalistic, what people are complaining of is the loss of intimacy that eating such as a pig provides…

**On the first aerial toll-house,
the soul is questioned about the sins of the tongue**

-29-

Piret is still frightened by the man who stood in front of the car by the time we stop at a small restaurant by the side of a lake. Not wanting us to sit in a small room it is fortunate the restaurant has a large patio from which we can look at the lake. A bus for school children is just being re-loaded with its passengers. The kids had not sat at the patio tables. She points out the solitary children, those who did not have the ability to attract friends or acquaintances or who had successfully repulsed all intimate encounters during the school year and even on the summer journey they were not to give up their solitude for the transitory pleasures of having a best friend while visiting the Black Sea and now they only had to get through the final leg of their journey, Veliko Tarnovo.

Cops, it is often said, in once-upon-a-time bars like The 55 in New York and even in the Bambouka in Sofia, are an international fraternity and you could say the same about school children and from our point of view even if these kids are in high school they are still kids and as such are pretty much the same no matter where you are observing them, once you have seen beyond the momentary presence or absence of hair, the clothing, kempt, unkempt: all those trivial features masking similarities… but, those solitary kids with the eyes always focused on something not immediately in front of them, who are not listening, not touching, not being touched, not being…

-30-

Naturally, the man Piret has seen in Strazhitsa should make an appearance in this restaurant which cooks fish caught in the lake or raised in pens in the middle of the lake. There is some distinction between caught fish and raised fish but my Bulgarian is not good enough to distinguish between the two and my tongue could not tell the difference in order to clarify as Piret orders a wild fish—Piret should have said caught fish and as a result the waitress questioned Piret as to what she meant by wild and Piret put her hands into her armpits and moved her arms imitating a bird as in free as a bird though the waitress didn't seem to get the distinction or is it a distinction foreign to this waitress who had grown up in a country where birds are not seen as being free though that would take both of us or the three of us if I included the waitress in this flight of linguistic elaboration.

I order a raised fish and the waitress smiled at the sudden simplicity.

The versions of the English language in Bulgaria are ever remarkable and it has long been mentioned about Shopka's salad which was a favorite detail often brought back from menus read in Bulgaria along with the stories of being robbed, assaulted , defiled in some way or other. The desire for great linguistic purity is always remarkable in people who rarely read a book but thought of themselves as great travelers, connoisseurs of wine and pickles.

-30-

A picture is taken of the lake. Someone parked a mobile home near the shore and it is a necessary detail to avoid the too easy acclamation of this being a very beautiful place to have lunch by and a place where Piret could congratulate herself on having avoided a fate looking to say the very least to her as we were stopped in Strazhitsa as not being something that would be easy to talk about back in New York City, even to those long jaded by friends' misadventures when venturing out of their beds in the morning.

Now, we have Piret talking about the man who stood in front of the Mercedes we were driving and while it unfortunately did not come with tinted windows, at the very least it would receive a tiny bit of respect... once having escaped the possibility of being robbed because we are driving an expensive car we would have the advantage of driving a car that would suggest it would be a mistake to do some harm to the passengers and driver as obviously these are people for whom inquiries would be made. If we had been driving some non-descript car there is always the danger it and the people inside could be made to disappear.

All of this goes through Piret's head in a disorganized sort of way and I take no credit for bringing any clarity, as always the photographs of destroyed Mercedes automobiles are ever vivid with the imagination supplying gruesome evidence of eviscerated torsos and severed limbs.

Nothing, so far, but who can be sure, seems to have happened in Strazhitsa and you have been alert to the presence of a photograph—not of anything that has been mentioned and you have wondered what purpose it is to serve… though now, we are dealing with this man.

This man.

This man is standing in the parking area and begins to walk towards the patio, walking by the part of the restaurant where people order directly into the darkness within, not a symbolic darkness by any means but in contrast to the brightness without and the clear light of the patio.

Standing, walking and about to step up to the patio and find a seat, easy enough, as we are the only people still at lunch and he sat…

Piret is sure it was the same man and I am not disputing her as she is sure it is the same man who has stood in front of the car in Strazhitsa.

Not that it would compare with the moment on Hristo Botev Boulevard in Sofia—in the fading September light—as the poem would have it, when I stop and ask into the window of the kiosk... but that came...

There is not the need to remind me of that, Piret is saying. You have your story and you must allow me to have my story. Already I have noticed how you are taking possession of what happens to US and please hear me capitalize the word US both with my finger drawing air letters and underlining both of them with a slash of my flat hand rabidly moving from left to right wondering if I was to do the same in the Hebrew would an Israeli slash from the right to the left?

We finish our fish both raised and caught and sampled each other's fried fish agreeing there is no difference but we are not experts in the matter and decide we would take up this matter with Filip in Sofia as surely he would know the difference.

This man seems to have something on his mind as is often mentioned in narratives and it is well that Januarius MacGahan is still current and well-read in Sofia both in English and in Bulgarian so my claim cannot be questioned by anyone familiar with such situations. It would have been better if what happened has been really dealt with in Strazhitsa.

Piret is waiting in the car while I visit the new Orthodox Church on the hillside above the town. Built after the earthquake, built after the celebration of the atheism of the town's people by the previous regime, two old women are moving about in it making sure I do not help myself to anything. The newness of the church did not invite candle lighting, did not suggest lingering while the bright sun from the wide open door opposite the door I had entered from the path to the road seemed to blow apart the church such that one could only want to escape, leaving me with some hesitation as to stopping for a soda in the town center.

We both notice the bus station which is more convenient than the train station which remains hidden to our foreign eyes so we make do with the bus station which seems to Piret demanding only departures but one could never be sure buses would actually leave the town while I think the bus station is the perfect portal by which to enter the town and one would step down from the bus with a modicum of anticipation but it might be quickly tempered and stiffening the resolve of the newly arrived to make the best of the situation since the next bus is not available for some time.

In Sofia we have not concerned ourselves with train travel since we are only going by train to Pernik but that is another story.

The man—of an age such as he could have been in the bar—makes no effort to speak to us. I have the impression he is just waiting for me to offer up my *azim gavoirie malko Bulgarski* and my pathetic attempt to transcribe my battered Bulgarian should provide a chuckle, as is once said, to those in the know. He will smile and raise his hand in a sort of greeting.

Does a man leave this world or does the world stop arriving for a man?

That is the beginning of something Piret fears, a something she has no plans to encourage. As the daughter of Estonian refugees she long knew strangers did not bring any sort of news that is likely to... but she cut off this train of words with a sigh saying more than any paragraph could establish. Not wanting to have any part of being addressed by a stranger bearing or not bearing news of any sort... she simply says, If you want to stop at Madara we should be leaving now. There is no special emphasis placed upon the final word of her sentence. No need for such intimidating tactics.

-29-

I am not one for taking hints is a well-established trait. I usually don't get it and in the Strazhitsa winter by the time I am drinking my third *malko studeno mastika* I am well on my way somewhere. The conversation is about a relative of one of the Bulgarians sitting at the table who has a relative in Canada. There is the traditional discussion of the Bulgarian head nodding when the words yes and no are said and the idiosyncratic habit of doing the reverse of what is the practice in the United States and for some reason this man is trying to argue that Canadians—according to his relative who has come to Bulgaria for a visit the previous summer—have taken it into their collective heads to adopt the Bulgarian version of head wagging as a way to differentiate their country and their people from that place due south and somehow—the connection is and is still lost—the conversation lurches to the idea when Canadians flush their toilets, everything went south...

Not having an opinion on this matter it seems I am seen as being provocative and it is suggested I preferred to have violent intercourse with beasts of the field and it is a well-known fact, your mother is a willing sex slave to a cohort of *negatifs* who dropped from the trees all over the city of New York, having fled their zoo, escaping the clutches of the Ku Klux Klan which this man maintains is in control of the city of New York in alliance with the *yevrytzki*.

Again, having no opinion I suggest we should have one more round of drinks for the road.

The next I knew, I am at the door and Medy is in her fur coat and night dressing gown saying something very quickly to the man who is as he says and I understood: the *Amerikanski* has been saved from drowning in a sea of mud which is the road down which he was wandering as the gathering of the philosophical society broke up in the bar, though I am pretty sure I am supplying the orientation of the society which is in actuality a brief meeting at the *partizan klub* which has been extended as it is concerned with how they are to celebrate Soviet Bulgarian friendship careful to avoid painting green the two hands meeting in the eternal space of that strong as tempered steel ... but the rest of the sentence remains unfinished as someone lost the page on which the remainder of the message is written...

In other words these men got me drunk and are happy to let me go off and drown in a muddy street in Strazhitsa. They well knew how strong the mastika is and how it would work its magic in getting rid of their visitor who is annoying beyond any reasonable...

Medy says, you have to be careful: it is not part of the Bulgarian mentality to wish well upon people. They know, as the cliché would have it: no good deed goes unpunished so why start?

-29-

But the man is still of interest to Piret and he is never far from our conversation as we went looking for Madara which is essential for the going into Bulgaria.

You of course have been into Bulgaria, Piret says, as we prepare to finally leave Strazhitsa, if something like that can ever actually happen.

Naturally, Piret should have known better since there are some places you can never leave once having been to them and the town of Strazhitsa holds one by the what could happen, by the what which does happen and the allure of all the still unknown *ulitza* to be explored where live the unemployed atheism instructor from the local *gymnazium*, the sign painters who no longer are called to decorate the public buildings for the recurring communist feast days, the drill instructors for the marching students who are always lending their caressing strength into the multitude of ever beating youthful hearts, the monitors of enthusiasm—as certain members of that organization which is not talked about as there is no need of such—but which is always present, to ensure the protection of the masses still developing the correct consciousness, even at this moment when they are said not to need such... but ever present they are... and everyone in the town knows who is who and who is who is never for a moment let to go to forgetfulness.

-41-

THE DEATH OF THE FATHER

*

In those days I lacked the strength necessary for curiosity.
"The Used Book Dealer"
KOLYMA TALES. Varlam Shalamov.

*

Feel the pleasures of a normal man.
Ian Curtis. JOY DIVISION

UPSTATE AGAIN

The cop tells you to go in ahead of him, keep your hands where I can see 'em.

He says don't go anywhere.

You're standing there holding the two bottles of soda.

That isn't what is meant to happen. A guy arrives not really in a new town, rather just a motel up at an exit, across from the Gulf Station, a Wendy's, a Denny's… nothing special about any of it. He is not really sure there is a town or even a city nearby. These exits have become places hard to define. People who work at them must get to know other people who work at the same exit. Maybe they change jobs, strike up conversations about the weather, the car breaking down, how to get things done. Another guy asking for a grocery store is just another guy and what he is asking for ain't odd or anything, so just a guy, a white guy, she is sure of that… not very old, not a teenager, but old and not young.

He is saying to himself, you need to stop to rest, stop for gas, to pee, to eat but you never want to stop and think, sit at a picnic bench in the middle of a deserted dog run with the trucks coming in behind. The sun beaten smell of dog shit. The parked and parking cars. The children getting out rushing to go along with their parents into the rest stop and one kid lingers behind and he is told to hurry along or we're leaving you behind, Mister, if you don't want to be left behind.

On the television set above the gas pump: Gas Pump TV: a woman from Wisconsin is talking about her daughter who went missing 15 years ago. I try to stay positive but in my heart of hearts I know she is gone. The way I figure it she drove her car to this parking lot. Someone called her from another car and she carefully set her soda down on the dashboard of the car and that was the last anyone knows about her. I can't imagine anyone would want to hurt her but obviously someone did because she isn't the sort of girl from what I know of her who would just disappear like that and not get in touch all these years. Now she is a grown woman but how could she have hardened her heart or allowed it to be hardened by whatever must have happened to her after she—I would use the word disappear as that is the most neutral word I know but it is hard to even say that word as it has at its center the fact she is gone from sight all these years and that is the worst of it. If she returned it would be surrounded by a vast hole but I would hope what I feel for her would allow us to…

-32-

In the shopping mall south of Saugerties on 9W, Simmons Plaza, the man in the END ZONE Wines and Liquors says he remembers the bar back there… but the shops now are all different. I don't remember what it was called back then. I think there was a Grant's but they went out of business and then a supermarket of some sort and other stores… that is a long time ago. I was just a kid so didn't pay any attention to stuff like that... you know what I mean?

A man with a little movie camera is walking from the car to where the bar was or is and then walking from where the bar was or is to where he imagines the car is parked.

Did his father fall forward or backwards or did his legs just give out and he sort of crumbled to the pavement, as you read in some novels when the writer can't figure out how a person falls to the ground?

His eyeglasses are not broken, so it can be assumed his body just eases itself to the pavement and his head tilts backwards and if the glasses came off as he is falling he would not have been able to see the sky and if any consciousness remains he would not have been able to see the faces looking down at him but if they remain on I wonder in a way that can have no answer: did Dad see something though would he have been able to say anything more than I am looking at the sky and now the sky is blocked by a face I do not know... his eyes would be closed behind the glasses as they were when he was in his casket.

Nobody likes to be reminded of irony so I did not draw attention to the name of the liquor store and my purpose of being there in Simmons Plaza. The man did mention when I am trying to remember the name of the stores, there was a Victory Market and something else.

One goes the other goes. No one is keeping track of things like that.

When I am at the funeral home to go over the last details, the funeral director is picking my father's name out of the letters in the large fishing tackle box making sure he spells it correctly. No one wants to leave with his name misspelt and it is something people never forget.

When we come for "the viewing" it seems he is the only act on then, though there is room for other names in other "chapels."

As we are leaving the funeral home for the church in the morning the receptionist is taking down the pushpin letters of his name returning them to the storage box.

-33-

When a person dies the soul goes on a forty day journey along a celestial—for want of a better word—highway and stops along the way.

On the first aerial toll-house, the soul is questioned about the sins of the tongue.

The second is the toll-house of lies

- The third is the toll-house of slander
- The fourth is the toll-house of gluttony
- The fifth is the toll-house of laziness
- The sixth toll-house is the toll-house of theft
- The seventh is the toll-house of covetousness
- The eighth is the toll-house of usury
- The ninth is the toll-house of injustice
- The tenth is the toll-house of envy
- The eleventh is the toll-house of pride
- The twelve is the toll-house of anger
- The thirteenth is the toll-house of remembering evil

- The fourteenth is the toll-house of murder
- The fifteenth is the toll-house of magic
- The sixteenth is the toll-house of lust
- The seventeenth is the toll-house of adultery
- The eighteenth is the toll-house of sodomy
- The nineteenth is the toll-house of heresy
- The twentieth toll-house is the toll-house of unmercifulness

-33-

It is hard to get a cat back into the bag even when discussion is to cease about certain things. The tattered pieces of brown paper are reminder enough. Have you ever tried putting an eggshell back together once it has been peeled from the hardened egg?

-33a-

IN SOFIA

don't worry about when before or after… does it matter? The possibility of a child…

-34-

As we are walking along Solunska, Piret says, your child would be 42 if he had not been killed. Do you ever think of that? Would he or she ever come to Sofia to see the place of the conception? Does Lidia ever think of this?

These days are very warm in Sofia so that there is a slight haze through which we walk…

-35-

We are stocking the journey. Planning, getting ready. Steeling the mind …

MADARA

-47-

Piret and I find Madara. A cliff with some sort of carving into the stone from way back then and arguments as to who, what, when…

Piret did not see anyone who is following, who might make trouble, who wants something. A destination I have not been to. There is an admission and then a long hike to the foot of the cliff and the caves that are used as shrines. Two tour buses are parked and the people from them are deciding on walking up the too many steps and they have seen all this sort of rubbish as the English voice says looking over to the booth with the postcards, ceramic objects… but I could use a beer…

The trees provide cool shade for the walk and when at the top looking up, the carved man on a horse is more there because they say it is there and then in the fine print it is revealed: you have to be there on a certain day, a certain hour…

So, Piret says. I get it. It's old. Old and like all the old stuff you need a vivid imagination. What's wrong with going to ruins: just piles of stones and people being dragged around them with a commentary you can't usually hear and only to find out what you don't know and never will know and what's to be learned with piles of stones arranged in artful patterns, *by time*.

-36-

Whether it was a boy or girl, man or woman, it would be nearly impossible to imagine walking around Sofia with Piret and this man or woman. The grammar does not allow me to avoid deciding between a man or a woman, a middle aged adult in any case. Piret thinks it would have been a boy but she is more interested in the fact that the child would have been close to her own age and would have been a combination of the two of you.

As she is telling me this, I thought, it has to be a girl and I knew the reason for it is I had traveled with Elizabeth— *once upon a time* in Europe—who is my daughter, when she is twelve when we would be looking for my brother who had disappeared from my life when I am still in the unremembering grip of babyhood. All of that was too complicated to explain to Elizabeth back then as my parents are long dead and in many ways my life has been apparently one with the simplicity of growing up in Patchogue and the children have become used to the tending of my parents' grave on Good Friday on Long Island after which we go to Patchogue to drive by the house where I have lived and then there is no mention of a distant brother, long gone but now alive in Europe.

This daughter walking in Sofia will not have made me a grandfather. She does not know why. It never happened. It never seemed to be the right moment with the right man. The miserable life you inflicted upon me by allowing me to be born, a sin beyond forgiveness so maybe just another argument for the Old Testament torturing God but I will have nothing to do with such thinking, she is saying, since that makes it all more important than it is. You can find a way to justify anything and so are indifferent to our four feet hitting the pavement and what could have brought us to walking along Vitosha, which I have no memory of ever visiting though you say I was brought here in those early years before the transfer to the promised land of America.

I often feel I was one of those Jews who wandered around for forty years and never made it to the Promised Land or something must have happened as it sure is no promised land by anyone's standards. I heard enough of the years in Dublin and then finally the getting to America. Dumping me into America after that room we three lived in while you are finding yourself in Dublin. The sheer selfishness of your life, of her life who is not here and who has never ever come back to Bulgaria! If I could only understand how she could have moved to Fargo, North Dakota, far from the pathetic drama of you discovering what you call your life and once there she avoids all those delicious ethnic celebrations Americans are so fond of throwing. How I love the complicated Polish names being transformed into Smith and Brown. How I long for that blessing. It is no mystery, at least to me, that she did not revert to her Bulgarian name but how I wish for to forsake the Irish name she inflicted upon me.

And now you want to catch up! Find out how I am doing! Discover there is no real abyss in the center of our lives and why don't we spend the rest of our lives filling in that pit which you just claimed didn't exist! You might as well erect a sand wall against the ocean proving how strong you are. You ain't no King Canute about to send the waves packing but there you are sitting inside your shit-eating grin of how powerless I am as the waves filed up the slippers …

You might as well try to stamp out your shadow! You want me to be friends with your new wife and then there is the mother of your other children and who else is going to ooze out of the woodwork of your mind? We can walk along and see what might have been yours and what might have been mine and what might have been my mother's but there is nothing there at Vitosha 52. They even smashed a new entrance into our palatial apartment to be. Without asking you or me or my mother. Imagine. Another unclaimed fortune down the tubes as they say. A perfect commentary on your life. Next, you'll be telling me about a map in search of buried treasure and a future undreamed of which will make everything okay.

Nothing can be made right. A mistake and that mistake compounded for forty-two years, I will say before you can take responsibility for any of it. Hands are dealt out and

them's the cards trying to soak up the spilt milk of your
love and lust.

How you could even think to walk me to Vitosha 52?
What am I supposed to feel? Am I supposed to believe you,
am I supposed to fill in the picture, draw myself a nice
picture of what might have been when nothing might have
been as you well know and which you hear yourself say
going to the Bambouka when you are in Sofia back then,
back then.

Of course that place does not exist and your only proof of
its existence is some self-published memoir by a Bulgarian
now retired to die in the squalor of his imagination in the
Bulgarian countryside: the only place grimmer would be
western North Dakota.

Do you remember telling my mother she should get
out of Fargo and go west, go west but she countered your
suggestion with: do you think I have grown a dick between
my legs and am dumb as the boys sent west by a crackpot
New York editor when he wanted to empty the city of all
those eager young men full up with energy and wanting
really only to die of something more than boredom.

The Second is the Toll-House of Lies

My mother is not as stupid as you have made her out to
be. She took courses, got degrees in the required useless
subjects so she can count herself *a real American* though
with the good sense never to return to Bulgaria, the scene
of your repeated folly as one visit should have done it for

you but back you come worse than a dog to its vomit.

This voice by my side, as we walk along Vitosha Boulevard, by the clothing stores, one after another, the strange restaurants that sickened one before entering, is as unrelenting as well it should be since I am on my way: lies, slander, gluttony, laziness, theft, covetousness, usury, injustice, envy, pride, anger, remembering evil, murder, magic, lust, adultery, sodomy, heresy, unmercifulness.

It was not for me to answer, I came to understand, which might sound like a way to avoid what has been said. The rules of behavior while visiting the Toll-Houses are not very clear. Probably they were nailed to a tree in the old stories after the fashion of the day but the print is obscured by the weather of what is over-looked and poorly remembered. All too often, as is said, if only I had...

MADARA HOLDS PIRET FOR A WHILE

Until the guy opens his mouth, Piret is attracted to him, even if he is probably smelly and hasn't had a bath in the last couple of weeks. He is playing a shepherd's flute and I guess the music is traditional but we both only heard what sounds like the hic-cupping women singers and this is the music that can be what the great caped men played who once again can be seen coming down from the hills pushing along the sheep—like moving tents—shepherds disappeared during the communism, it seems, but now across the hillsides they move, specters almost of something that once had been… he has a few CDs for sale of his music… just like the guys in the subway in New York, not missing a beat, with a plate in front on the ground for spare change…

Piret is wondering if he has a big dick, I bet he does… all long and smelly, do you think he is circumcised?… I wouldn't be able to guess but does it matter… you're right he is just too smelly… and he didn't have many teeth though bearded and you know it is essential: the sad eyes and those deeply carved wrinkles across his forehead, almost as if you could use them for slicing his skull, his skull, with face attached in some mystery of preservation as we saw in the Mutter Museum in Philadelphia where someone took a human head and sliced it like a pre-sliced hunk of cooked ham, the head just resting there with flesh, bone and brain matter fanned out accordion style.

Piret didn't want to stop in any of the villages that we drive through after leaving Madara. She is saying, you are always thinking lightning is going to hit you for a second time and this new story is going to envelop your life once again... you keep hoping you will remember the name of the woman in the fish restaurant, who at first said she was from Targoviste but when VV asks more closely [a foreshadowing of a future meeting] she says she came from a village—a real *selo* girl, you could say: *Buhovci*. Every day to come to the lake to waitress and hearing, at least, you have a job unlike so many these days and without a job, what are you going to do, now that there is...

Not to venture into the political since everyone has an opinion, now once again though who was it? Ernst Junger? who said, Piret says, opinions don't matter, that is all they are: opinions. We should only be interested in what people believe. Then, you have something to talk about, something to kill for or die for or console yourself with when it all falls apart.

Piret usually does not quote. While she has a perfect memory when it comes to who was sitting where in her first grade classroom and their fate year by year as time went on, quoting was not usual and made a person uncomfortable. Surely, she is not shoring up the ruins with the scattered comments coming from my mouth?

PIRET PLAYS HOUSE, she thinks

I wonder, as we pull off to the side of the road—in the middle of nowhere (whatever that might mean when you have a map spread out on your lap) she is saying: if I had simply said, I am staying here and sat down next to the musician. What would the man have done? A youngish foreign woman, you'll grant me that, blonde hair and not an unpleasant face and with tits, as the men usually say: more blonde than the Bulgarian blondes or a more believable blonde woman, not Swedish as I did know how to say *Amerikanska*...

What would the guy do? This isn't the busy season or the season has not arrived yet as we didn't see very many people up there looking into the caves, looking up at the side of the mountain... just this man playing his flute: older than you, but I have never liked young men, so that is not unusual. Did you notice his black and white vest was clean as was the white shirt? His trousers were a little shabby, maybe I don't want to know what has happened there... his cheeks are clear and his brown eyes are sweet, almost...

An adventure as a sort of revenge against the paucity of daring in my own life: how unfair it would be to this man... plotting to ruin his life or maybe it happens all the time?

I would have been—just my luck—one of those girls, one of many who has the same idea because if I have the thought it can't be that uncommon. Isn't that how it happens in the world? There is no such thing as an original thought. That's what the professors are always telling us... it is how you order them, how you express them.

I sit there for a few hours and then follow him as he walks down the path to the parking area and then along to where he lives. It is not too much of a dump. There will be a nice dog and he will have fruit trees and he will point to a photograph of a young woman and say what I know to be what he is saying, his wife, жена ми, and she is dead, мъртъв, he will close his eyes and look up to the ceiling.

Thank God. I say to myself as one doesn't want to share a bed with *his* wife. We sit on the little porch. He gives me a glass of red wine. I say *nazdravie*. He smiles and says *nazdravie* to me.

Our lives begin.

Of course the life together goes on for twenty years at least. He dies and I go back to America and find everyone else is now dead and no one is there to listen to my tale of what I found living in the mountains of Bulgaria with a man who plays a flute of some sort, the name of which I will have learned and my English will be frozen in whatever year we are living in right now and all my points of reference will have long been forgotten... but I could choose on the other hand to imagine I would live with him for twenty years and still be the same age I am right now, still know all the same people I know right now and tell everyone of my years of living in Bulgaria with Racho, that is the name he has to have since you said that was his father's name, and since he is dead no one will confuse my Racho with her Racho when the commentary comes to be written.

I want to imagine my coming back to New York and you are there to meet me. You must be, even as you shake your head at the unlikely possibility since as the publisher of this book announced not long before his own death that your death is already there waiting for you and just how painful that is for me to think of.

I have grown very thin in Bulgaria as I am walking every day up and down the mountain with Racho and we live on fruit and yogurt and I built a garden and his magic thumb is a far more productive appendage than that dick of his and he would have taught me something and I would have lost all interest in visiting any big city and could never be lured to Varna… wasn't it enough for us to have gone there for those few days..

But that is another story we will get to right now as you might say.

I grow used to the world as coming to visit us or rather visiting Madara and what a cross-section of humanity in particular on certain days when the strangest people came with their eyes toward the sky and seeing things only they could see: if only you could see what I see, the gift I am seeing, the English ladies would repeat like little parakeets.

Racho didn't like the mystics: they are cheap. They like

to travel and feel things but they didn't drop any money into his dish.

At night, Racho always turned me over and sexed me right and good making me stay in the bed as he says it was good to stew in the secretions of our sexual activity. I know it sounds really weird or maybe I got the Bulgarian all confused with other experiences in my life.

Racho is dead, I would say and you would ask did he have a nice funeral and I say he was buried wrapped in a blanket and I didn't allow anyone to take a picture of his dead face. I wanted only the memory of his sweet brown eyes to be my reminder of the man I spent twenty years with on the mountain side near Madara. I have no photographs of Racho. Tourists would pay him so they could take his picture. Sometimes they would promise to send him one, but as the years go on: it never happens. Moving the stuff around in my mother's house the photographs of my father in his coffin were once again revealed. They seem more disturbing than if I had photographed him walking from the toilet to the bathroom when he was sometimes naked.

Didn't you say, at one time kids would say: *I want to live fast, die young and have a good looking corpse?*

The Third is the Toll-House of Slander

(a reminder of who set us on the tollway)

From:libill@jjay.cuny.edu
 Subject:Overdue ILL Item
 Date:Thu,3Jan>Anitemthatyouhaveborrowed:
 Title: The relations of the Yugoslav government-in-exile with
the UnitedStates,1941-1944 /
 Author:Nelson,LindaLorraine.
 Due Date: 11/25/2010

To:Inter-LibraryLoan
Subject: RE: Overdue ILL Item
    This book was a long time ago returned... why are you
writing to me now?

From: libill@jjay.cuny.edu:
   I am sorry this message was sent to you. It was
completely an accident. I apologize again for our error and the
inconvenience.

TO: Inter-library Loan:
   Thanks for note you actually reminded me how long I have
been working on a book that pivots around the violent death
in Upstate New York of the author of that MA thesis ... It had
been and remains an important bit of information ...

From: libill@jjay.cuny.edu:
   Dear Professor. Thank you for your understanding.
Please do not hesitate to contact me if you need any further
information or materials from ILL.

-37-

And on this day, Vitosha Mountain is clearly visible in the distance as it rarely is these days and as it is rarely seen in years before as we walk to the culture palace put there by the daughter of the former communist boss as a showcase for 1300 years of Bulgarian culture.

Fronting the palace is a park and just before it an area of fountains and shops, mostly shuttered.

As good as any place. Years before without your mother but with thoughts of Lidia I sit in the rooftop restaurant with Medy's best friend who wants to know everything about the life in America.

I talk about American distances, inconceivable as we sit in what is thought to be one of the best cafes in the city. The hundreds of miles endured on a whim and not thought of as being more than a going down the elevator to the ground floor in this monument to Lyudmila Zhivkova who has a grave in the central cemetery guarded by two soldiers in antique uniforms. These distances and the subway in New York City, the deserts and the mountains... of course this woman knows there is New York and there is Hollywood and what lay between would be hard to discover. Telling them, it is all very far away seems to be sufficient and leaning over the low wall edge of the restaurant I could see fifteen stories down the fountain spraying water about a display of shiny silver balls arranged in a mystical proto-Slavic pattern, someone told me about, as Zhivkova who is responsible for this culture palace has made it fashionable to listen to every sort of medium, every aged woman who hears voices, every authority who could link the curlicues of Bulgarian grave scratching with similar markings in Ireland, in Mongolia, in Mexico. All of which seems to ring true though no one in their right mind would passionately long to travel to any of these places unlike the more practical romantics who long to die in Paris or Zurich while re-enacting revolutionary episodes...

-37-

Another year goes by: the fountain has been turned off, looted of its copper pipes and even the bulbs of the overhead public lamps have been stolen by people who have no need of such large bulbs but stealing is now a habit without purpose and more years after that some of the pipes have been replaced when money arrives from Brussels and, and, and: the wheel is got to running again.

I told Ginka, Medy's friend, if she came to New York I would take her on the ferry that went across New York harbor. She asks me why we would do that? It is the best way to see New York, to see what makes New York special. I don't need to know New York is special, she says. You did it with Lidia and you did it with Medy. If you have done it with them you don't have to do it again.

Pictures are posed in front of this vast building built for all time, a reminder of what has been accomplished even though Zhivkova is dead and what has she done for any of these women who do not listen to nattering old ladies or travel into the mountains to listen to the Bulgarian soul as the fog lifts in the early morning?

My old women are now all just dead. Medy is dead in New York and her best friend is dead in Sofia. This no longer young girl is telling me: as full of the shit as ever and ever, you might conclude this singsong recitation which evokes no sympathy in me, I can tell you. I have heard it all before and from those better practiced in the art of befuddlement, an amateur of this art you are.

I am no tour guide, I am telling Piret as we walk into the cultural palace, as I call it, still, I am sure, some will silently say, you would, not having been here through the changes, which can't you see with the semi-naked girls rubbing against young men dressed in black selling—God knows what they are selling—though I am telling in what I am sure is a reiterating know-it-all tone of voice: they had concerts, theatrical performances, a night club, bowling alley, a shop for traditional Bulgarian music, a place to buy newspapers from the fraternal socialist countries, small coffee bars, large coffee bars, restaurants both formal and informal... and now?

The elevator taking us up to where the restaurant is run by an old man who does not question me about why I want to go up. I say something about the *gori* restaurant and he says something and when we get to the top he says, *kaput*.

Of course he could have said it without taking me up to the top floor but he is an honest man who knew one's eyes are more truthful than either the mouth or ears.

Didn't you notice I wasn't with you? Piret is asking where had I disappeared to and no, I didn't want to go up that elevator, no way are you getting me into an elevator in this building. I'm not a pet dog for you to lead around.

The broken tiles, the boarded up shops, the weeds growing between the cracks in the pavement, the old men sitting on straight back chairs watching and watching, the vast darkened spaces of the ground floor inside the culture place: whatever had this place been?

Shut up, the daughter would say to me. You can claim you never told your children to shut up as it is one of those phrases that destroyed the imagination or is that just some sort of rubbish you picked up when better parenting was on your agenda for the seconds you gave of your precious time to that task, time away from your constant maudlin, depressing commentary on your fast track to the grave. All you did is serve up do-it-at-home fast food and out of the apartment as fast as you could go back to…

Can we get something to drink, Piret asks. One of the real improvements in Sofia these days. The Coca Cola is served really cold and made with the right mixture of syrup and water. I know it is a trivial detail. Piret likes the varieties, sour to sweet, of the cherry juices. In the sun the old men are sunning their broad backs. One of them will say, the sun is the only free thing left in this country

I DON'T WANT ANYTHING YOU CAN GIVE ME
I AM ONLY INTERESTED IN WHAT
I CAN TAKE FROM YOU

VARNA. STALIN.

INTRODUCING   <AGAIN>   LINDA NELSON.

Varna has been called Stalin, but that changes in the 1950s. I wonder if there are jolly songs being sung in the early 1950s as young Bulgarians went off to Stalin:

In honour of the 70th birthday anniversary of <u>Joseph Stalin</u>, taking into consideration the request (or "request") of the citizens of Varna, the Council of Ministers issued a decree to rename the town. Thus on 21st December 1949 Varna became Stalin and a monument of the town's patron was erected at the entrance of the <u>Seaside garden</u>. Time passed by and at their 1956 plenary sessions the Communist Parties of the Soviet Union and Bulgaria admitted still another mistake and the recent town name was regained. For those in the nostalgic mood, however, the old streets of Varna still keep drainage covers made in the town of Stalin.

Now, that is a subject of much interest since in this journey we did go to Stalin. Just as we had walked cross *Plastat Lenin* in Sofia and walked along Georgi Dmitrov Boulevard so we came to Stalin and stayed in a villa to the north of the city on the *Cherno More*.

Thomas **Tom Mcgonigle**
Online Obituaries Online Death Notices ...

McGONIGLE, Thomas (Tom) - Suddenly but peacefully at his home on Wednesday, 18th August 2010, Tom aged

67 years (electrician), a loving husband and soul mate of Josephine, also a dear brother and uncle. Funeral service to be held at Carlisle Crematorium on Wednesday, 25th August at 1:00p.m. Family flowers only, donations if desired to the Great North Ambulance Appeal Fund, c/o Walker's Funeral Directors, 80 Wigton Road, Carlisle. Tel. 01228 515650.

-44-

And before one is accused of morbidity... in 1971 at Columbia University, Richard M. Elman had his students write their own obituaries and the obituary of one of their classmates.

NOTE: a tiny bit of flexibility is required of the reader who has been travelling through Strazhitsa and is now again on the move.

-45-

When we went walking in the Seaside Gardens in Stalin, looking out to the sea as one inevitably does, a desert of longing—a linguistically inconceivable conceit if you ask me—since and I have only been together in Bulgaria in the months before and after the winter so Stalin is only a thought, a memory to which can attach the little seaside figurines of a cartoon sailor complete with pipe stabbed into his mouth and a body made of angular shapes suggestive in an approved cubist design. Medy has a friend with an extra room and they would go there for two weeks, mother and daughter, independent of the usual collective holidays of his classmates and their parents.

The gardens extend for miles in front of the city but as the years have gone on they were broken into, as it were, by holiday hotels, by restaurants, now no longer only for the communist elites but for those with a need to loll in public as young people fed these mouths with food and drink.

Like Buñuel, Piret suggests, maybe it would be better if people ate in private and did other things in public since they could charge admission for those formerly hidden away spectacles. Why is it that Europeans want to be seen eating in public in the most derelict parts of New York such as on the Bowery where they seem to really enjoy the homeless and semi-homeless drug addicts lingering and who in turn are watching the Europeans at table...

-46-

Before we got to the villa, which sounds grand and suggestive, we stay at a hotel set down in a plot of land in front of a vast housing block.

Obviously, someone paid someone who paid someone and who paid someone: to sprout a hotel.

But the housing block is also looking to the sea…

We are just visiting for a few days.

Passing through.

What are we expected to know?

Walking, after getting "settled in," across the highway and into the Seaside Gardens, just walking, walking as thousands, millions have done over the years…what's so special?… the pine trees, the random street lights… the mass of faces… just walking and Piret is waiting, of course, for the man from Strazhitsa who is always deemed ready for a re-appearance but not in this evening stroll you will be disappointed to learn.

Just by memory, Piret's memory, creating those memories to take back to where we came from and then the trying to tell someone of where we have been, this summer, though most are just as happy to stop with: and we went to Bulgaria for two weeks, drove around a bit, went to the seaside, went to the mountains and flew home by way of Milan.

Being struck stupid since resisting: when I was here in 1984 without a sentimental reason to re-trace the steps, the pauses at looking out there: the moon across the sea and all the rest...

A few days as a reward for having been for a summer in Sofia at the Slavonic Seminar, so taken to the Black Sea at Albena and into Stalin by bus for a few hours. Have the taste of the group activity. Now all together let's hear it for the bus that didn't break down, for the cheap restaurants that didn't make anyone sick, for the *Night of Talent*, the sing along, the countryside going by, passing there beyond the stained windows... the Norwegians, the Germans, the Swedes, the Russians, the French all of them linguistically involved with the Bulgarian language only from a linguistic point of view... much talk of adjectives, verb forms and shifts of meaning: collecting a language since at home they study philology but here is an American who is beginning her work on the Bulgarian woman in 19th century, which never became a thesis and sent her over the edge and dead on the first day of classes... years later, like the guy who throws himself in front of the train just as rush hour is beginning... a pretty blonde girl from California, then in Mississippi and then Upstate...   dead   and   dead.

LINDA

But crossing with the memory of just last week or it can have been any week coming back at night across New York harbor on the Staten Island ferry and looking down at the cotton-looking wake created by the ship, so easily one can slip into the bright white, startling bright white churned water, for everything is swept away—behind into the dark: how long would it take?, yet the sure immediate regret as letting go, no swinging back up on deck so swallowed up by the cold of the water and the struggle and then...

LINDA NELSON

And of course you know I have taken up the name.

It is probably not safe to be speaking of the dead. They are gone and nothing remains except the words we speak of them or if they made something these objects remain tied to them for as long as someone...

The dead are dangerous, not because of health issues or some such pedestrian reason. The corpses are buried or burnt. The physical is done with. Dangerous, still, because we the living envy them. They are done with it, this it, in which we still find ourselves.

What stops us from immediately joining this or that dead person...

Such is called on to the page by Linda Nelson.

As we age we collect the dead as lines through their names in our address books.

They populate our memories in a far more vivid manner than when they are alive.

How can you say such disgusting things?

There are still areas of the so-called life that are unsettling.

-75-

Linda Nelson wore glasses. She had a disorderly life, a husband somewhere along the line, boyfriends. From Nebraska, to Kansas to California, to Bulgaria to Mississippi, to Upstate New York. Things not working out Things getting in the way.

-48-

Linda Nelson is fucking the Bulgarian assistant. They disappear. She comes back either drunk or satisfied. It is going on all the time. Making connections. She doesn't like the smoke or the meat. She says she is the very last hippy and has just moved to northern California. It is never drunk AND satisfied. The guy can't handle both. Just my luck, you could say, she says. And all you can do is get drunk. It's worse than Nebraska when it comes to things like that. But I need to learn the language and he wants to practice his English so I get him to talk Bulgarian with me and I postpone what he wants as long as possible. It happens and it is okay in a way and then I talk English with him. And then he wants to get drunk and do it again. Some of it goes a long way I can tell you. He thinks he is some sort of man of the world but he has never been out of Bulgaria, though he tries to pretend he has traveled but he hasn't. He has the strangest ideas but all Bulgarians have strange ideas. You get used to that quickly. You know what I mean, I am sure. He's sweet in some ways but I can tell it could go either way if the circumstances change, even a little bit. He thinks I am still married so at least he doesn't think I am about to take him back to The States. It gives him a real sense of power to make it with a married American woman. If he only knew, poor deluded man.

-51-

You always learn too late, Linda is saying, a man is never a way out of anything—one day—when we went over to the supermarket to watch the African students stock up for the weekend—you remember; does anyone remember—the Slavonic Seminar is out there in *Dervinitiz*—the university residence area, *studenski grad*— halls for lectures and classrooms: a statue of Karl Marx in the economics section, far from the city center, high rises into which the government stacks the foreign students—from those countries Bulgaria is told to be interested in... the students are those who couldn't get into the American, English, Irish, French, German, Italian, Swiss, Swedish, Canadian universities: the bottom of the barrel and the Bulgarians try to keep them out there, away from the city center for too many obvious reasons and these students know, all of them, usually the hard way, but then what are they to do, this is a chance and there are Bulgarians from the countryside but these are not there as this was during the summer so the only people in residence are the foreign students, who usually couldn't go home as there is no money or way: once you got on the plane for the People's Republic of Bulgaria you stay for the four five six years and then go right back to wherever it is you are from, no lingering is allowed and there is no place for you in Bulgaria and no Bulgarian would allow a *negatif* to ever place a hand on them… I knew much of this from and Linda has tried to talk to some of the students but they didn't know what to make of any American who would willingly come to such a place and so we are watching the Africans who saved up their dollar grants and splurged every weekend we were there on liquor to get themselves good and drunk on Friday, Saturday and Sunday: drinking enough, Linda said, to float a battleship and a few of them have tried to come to the disco at the dorm where we are all living and from nowhere, she says, these guys came and just grabbed them really hard, pushing, shoving and hitting them behind the knees with long poles which they carried it seems for that purpose: leaving no marks… she has never seen these guys around during the day so it must have been *them* and you know who I am talking about: there is that guy who acts the fool but who was it said he is really in charge and you notice that he did not go through the line in the cafeteria and just sat at the table and the food is brought to him and it didn't look like the stuff we got which is really pretty good and his was even better… but you have to be looking for things like that…

But we are watching them filling the carts with the Bulgarian versions of rum, whiskey and rakia: they didn't waste time with the beer or wine…they go right for the real stuff and there is nothing worse than Bulgarian rum or whiskey… my husband would bring home once in a while a bottle of Mekong whiskey some guy gave him who was shipping it back home from Vietnam...

-57-

LINDA DOES NOT GO AWAY

But the poor African students... how they rained the bottles down from the balconies all night, if you had ears to hear it... I tell you, ears to hear who had saved up their money to drink their way through each and every weekend or at least it seems that way from the noise coming from the blocks as bottles rained down smashing on the sidewalks below.

But as with memory there are no real connections, whatever that might be, between the paragraphs of Linda Nelson's conversation or rather near monologues against what has happened to her and continues to happen to her.

-57-

Nebraska is just nowhere, Linda is saying, I well knew. The guy I married was leaving and I had no other way of leaving. He was a medic in the Navy but he wasn't heading for Vietnam for some reason, a reason I never knew so I went along with him to Germany, the coldest place imaginable in the winter near the East German border, waiting for the Russians to come. They were to hold the Russians for one or two days until they could bomb the shit out them, he said, or I think he said as we never talked once we got to Germany. My husband left me on my own and I left myself alone. I didn't do anything to myself. I wanted to do something to myself but I couldn't go to the base doctor and I didn't speak German so I couldn't go to a German doctor. So, I waited. Not that I would do anything drastic. I felt, I felt… that is what I said to myself, in the past tense, mark me, I said it in the past tense: I did not say I feel.

Days of greyness followed by days of greyness and rain and then snow and then greyness and sometimes some sun but not too much. I took the train once to Italy.

On my own.

On my own I went to Italy.

On my own I came back to Germany.

We went back to The States and I kept going when we got to Nebraska. I had saved some money and I went to California. I wish I could remember what I told him.

He was hurt that was for sure, for all of a week, my brother wrote me, and my Ex was married again within a year.

I was on my own with an Ex. For all I know he's long dead and unmourned by, I am sure, the batch of kids he had off the woman who had my Ex all to herself. Who knows what happened to her. As if I care or could care or would care. I do not protest too much. My brother left Nebraska for someplace in Pennsylvania, another godforsaken state I can tell you. Have you ever looked at a map?... two big cities and all that land filled up with tiny villages stuffed with people who will do nothing but live and die. I didn't want that so I went West and fell into Bulgaria. You go east and got off a train. Same accident different continent, different circumstances but you end up at the same place: why did that or this happen? I am not going to trace it all back to a mother who put her right breast first into my mouth rather than her left breast... isn't that always a temptation, drag one's decision back to something happening a long time ago and walk away from the mess staring up at you from the sidewalk .

***

"In stories, it's possible to withhold the worst, defer the unpleasant, and even cancel the ending, no matter how logical it seems. Mimicry intimidates more than one soul and turns his little tale into a hodgepodge of verifiable truth, although truths erased by the final period."
BEACHBIRDS
S.Sarduy

***

-53-

LINDA NELSON IS ALWAYS PRESENT, I HOPE
Linda Nelson is speaking, from Bulgaria to Potsdam, New York, Upstate, really Upstate, beyond the Adirondacks, just before Canada. Far away, really. And before Upstate I am in Mississippi nowhere...
But you go where you are called. Beggars can't be choosey in this environment, as they always say, these part

time or non-tenure track jobs… use you up and you move on… when you are young you hold on to the possibility of something happening…

I will get the time to finish that damn thesis and then my life will change.

I am sure it will. I can no longer repeat that sentence to myself as it comes back at me as if I am now doing the dreadful underlining by nutty people who leave up visions on supermarket notice boards.

I AM SURE. Just if… everything is not so far away.

Being from Nebraska, I know what being far away might mean… Nebraska is the center of only one thing and that is those bombers flying overhead waiting for orders to go to Russia to drop the bomb. Didn't you say you knew a girl whose father was a bombardier on one of those flights? A large blonde girl, you said, but she went and married a friend of yours when you weren't looking. The strangest things got said in Sofia. I say something. You say something. And then?

Nothing prepared me for the frigid intimacy of teaching. The standing in front of a classroom with the guys undressing me and the girls commenting about what I wore and when I made the mistake of wearing the same outfit two days in a row: it is hard to hold their attention to the Missouri Compromise: even if I talk about the blood flowing in Kansas… the dead, the dead and they look at me and I know they didn't know where Kansas is, not a one of them knows one state bordering on the state of Kansas: I dare them to do it as didn't you ask people to name a couple of the countries bordering on Bulgaria and while no one could ever tell you any of the countries, once upon a time, I thought you were impossibly arrogant about it but here I ask a simple question about America.

Doesn't everyone know the line: it ain't Kansas anymore? Was I being unreasonable when I suggest they buy themselves a map of the United States? A student writes an evaluation of me, while I am a very warm person I did not respect her and her fellow students.

Some people scare up their nerves after years of teaching but that is not the way it is for me. Just walking into a classroom, some of the heads turn in the direction of the person walking into the room—that's the way it has always been, there is an animal curiosity, in particular on the first few days of class but not anymore, really. It is something you notice because very infrequently a student will look up from whatever is fascinating them at the moment on one of their electronic devices and you will suddenly be startled by seeing a human face looking at you as you come into the room. The fear begins at that moment. Is this the crazy person or the guy or girl who knows everything or as is more usual nothing at all but thinks it is totally un-necessary to know anything before opening the mouth to give the heartfelt and deeply rooted opinion on you name it.

When I first began to teach, students would always turn to the door when the teacher or professor walked in. That too is disconcerting but I do remember being one of those heads turning as the professor walks in. It is almost comical and I am sure someone made fun of the students for being so attentive. Things are different now.

Do I blame students?

Do I hold up the victim for vilification?

Do I regret falling into this profession, so remote from Bulgaria?

My routine: three times in the morning I repeat myself: hour after hour for three hours minus ten minutes on the hour. Then I say one thing once. Three times I repeat a lesson on European history. One time I speak about American history. They have us doing this three times a week to get in the required minutes the state mandates. The people mandating the hours have never ever been in a classroom since the moment they left *all that behind*. I put students to sleep and do not complain unless someone is snoring, too loudly. There is a tiny pleasure in watching the eyelids slowly descend. Is that what I will take from my years of teaching?

-54-

LINDA

Notice the glasses do not stay in place on her nose. She is frequently pushing them back in place. Placed on a ripped open paper bag is a large container of takeout coffee and next to it a plastic bottle of freshly squeezed fruit juices with a label in sans-serif type: ENERGY FOCUSED.

This makeshift paper tray is unsteady since the slats of the bench on which it rests are separated by about an inch of space and are slightly irregular from wear and tear. On another corner of the bag is a still waxed paper wrapped half of a home-made sandwich. It is a peanut butter and jelly sandwich because the jelly mixed with peanut butter is smeared on the inside of the paper as the sandwich was probably at the bottom of another paper sack which is not visible. In her left hand she holds a half of the peanut butter and jelly sandwich that has been opened and is being held in such a manner that her hand does not touch the bread but is separated from it by the folded back waxed paper.

When she is picking up the container of coffee she touches the fruit juice bottle which wobbles and she hurriedly puts down the opened half of sandwich to catch the bottle so it does not fall from the bench and the sandwich in the course of this action almost drops from her hand but she catches herself: the coffee container is returned to its place, the fruit juice bottle does not spill and she has now finished eating the second half of sandwich but at the corner of her mouth is a little dab of grape jelly which she misses with the napkin and her tongue has not detected it. She will not notice the drop of jelly that found its way to the front of her dark blue shirt which since it is a little large had a number of natural wrinkles which would have concealed this accident except to the most scrupulous eye.

Those eyes are much more common than she at first thinks but that is still in the future on this day which is cloudy yet just before the first chill of winter's a-coming in. On the bench next to her is a plastic bag from the supermarket. Since it looked like rain she has an umbrella there along with the European text she is using for the introductory course. That bag is holding in place two napkins she has almost forgotten about until she moves ever so slightly and her body pushing the bag loosened the napkins which unfold as tiny crumpling parachutes heading for the ground which is disfigured with crushed cigarette ends, some lip-stick smeared, to complete the sordidness of where she finds herself: having lunch, waiting for the next class.

MADARA

-55-

Forcing myself upon him, is what I had to do, Piret is saying. It was so far from the way I am normally meant to be. It is a whim that goes over the line for a moment and then I stay, minute to minute and to the hour to the half day to the whole day to the night and then the next day. I refuse to enter into his head. I did not imaginatively rummage around inside where motives wrestled with rats for all I know or care. In my mind my mother had died. You died. The house in New Jersey had died. Yet I could not escape the irony of knowing this is one of the oldest American delusions carefully delineated by the professors at Sarah Lawrence: those experts on American delusions and as they look out at us or at me, they knew they are dealing with delusion incarnate.

Linda Nelson should have learned a few lessons. But that is now far too easy to write and so elevating these words into becoming a sort of bucket of shit being dumped upon her: I told you so, is another way of putting it.

An easy lesson. Have a backup plan, even one you might never need to use. Though before that comes the toughest lesson of all: be fortunate. There is no substitute for it, a temporary holding action for sure and eventually everyone's luck runs out and as they say, *by then I'll be six feet under.*

Everything after-the-fact is easy. Vast numbers of experts running around, who are always perfect and know everything even as they admit an awful lot of stuff just slips out of the mind, falls by the wayside: dropped the ball on that one but next time, next time.

> Today I am writing to share some very troubling news: our budget shortfall which I announced in the earlier memo has now grown to $3.9 million

You try, you really try, Linda is always saying and even she is tired of hearing herself saying this, you try and you try and then you try again and the years roll out and the summer is a pause, not even time for the collecting of a single half a thought. You have the feeling and you are of course right that the photocopying machine will not be working, just when you really need it and you didn't make the usual allowances: I just can't be perfect all the time.

And then the secretary says there has been a screw up with the paperwork, we have to do it every semester you know that, and we had this girl this summer doing some of the paper work while Isabel was on maternity leave and only Isabel really knows how to fill out those forms so we tried to do the best we could, you know how it is around here?

But Linda knows no one cares beyond the room where she is listening to this woman telling her the pay checks will be delayed by a few weeks, but not to worry you can get an advance, I am sure you know that—you have been here long enough and know the ropes, by now, now, don't you, though I am sure it doesn't get any easier but not to worry everything works out or it doesn't as the comedian is saying on the television: and it doesn't and they have a show now for people who seem to have a knack for falling into impossible situations where nothing ever goes the way it is supposed to... which is really just too much stuff to think about and that is the last thing I can deal with: how to get the cable to work since it went out last week so I am not even in contact with *Law and Order* which is crap I know but it is re-assuring crap where even when terrible things somehow some sort of little good comes out of it for that hour and there they are again the next night getting into another awful situation, maybe even worse than the one before and again they don't remember a damn thing episode to episode and the only one who remembers any of this is the person watching but, but, but how awful it becomes when the cable goes out and you have to call the cable company and they try to do what they can but they will have to send someone out to check on the connection since there seems to be something wrong and yes, there is something wrong... and before you say it I just did, really did send in the check for the month and please don't cut it off it has been one of those years: Yes I am sure you have been hearing a lot of this.

Again, she says now to herself, one of those years—and I am a grown up woman who is supposed to be able to take care of herself and I have been taking care of myself for many years

This plan does NOT include or envision layoffs of full time staff or faculty

with no thanks to anyone, thank you, I can say with some tiny bit of pride though where did this pride really get me? No way can I go down that rotten path. I am not complaining.

But just, if once, once again, could I catch a break as they are always saying when the cops pick them up—my friend Albert was telling me this—I was just trying to catch a break, what's wrong with that, just one break and the cop looks at the guy with how many times have I heard this, I gotta tell you, ain't nothing new under the sun and the breaks are for those who make their own breaks, surely you know that, being a college professor and all and I try to tell him I am not a college professor like he thinks and then that abyss opens up and you know you have lost him—the cop and even my friend Albert and you yourself are lost having gone down that path once again... dear Linda, Albert will say over a cup of coffee, decaffeinated all around, they say it so glibly, them's the breaks and them's saying it have never seen anything broken, I can tell you...

-57-

Breaking the narrative so back in Sofia

Both of us see the guy and I take the picture aware I am sticking my dick up his ass. Not having really the Bulgarian language I am preserved from having to explain this sentence to him. He would have been happy with the sound of some coins falling into his dish set there on the little stool, him sitting on that guard rail of the pedestrian bridge going over Boulevard Bulgaria as we are walking to the palace of culture having come back from walking up to where the newly rich live in Sofia.

A glance turned into a photograph of a human detail which goes against my own tendency to never take pictures

82

with people populating the scenery. I never wanted my picture taken by the Europeans and Japanese and who knows who else walking around now in New York looking for the real New York and they seem to like to take pictures of me being a messenger hauling my cart up and down the steps to the subway…

So, this guy has ended up inside the Bulgaria, Piret and I walk through, playing his *kaval* in the bright sun on a pedestrian bridge over two boulevards now loaded with traffic. And there is the expected commentary: how things have changed after *the change*.

> *Part-Time (Adjunct) Faculty:* I have asked Provost Bowers, working with the Chairs of our Academic Departments and Vice President Richard Saulnier, to take a close look at the schedule for spring 2011 (and beyond) to determine whether we can consolidate sections and postpone course offerings in ways that would reduce the expenditures for part-time faculty.   The schedule developed by Provost Bowers and Vice President Saulnier will be reviewed by the FPS and the Provost's Advisory Council. Provost Bowers will also review all reassigned time for the spring semester to determine whether we can reduce adjunct expenditures through a judicious reduction of reassigned time.

-58-

Dear Linda, Albert would say and has said even on previous weekends: you just don't know how things are going to turn out.

She has heard what he says. She knows the difference between the past, the present and future. There is more of the past and far less of the future and not much of a present.

It is a simple truth when you are sixty. My mind is quite clear on this no matter what you might think. Didn't you yourself tell me the present seems to go like the snap of the fingers?

Of course Albert has said it and when he has said it he knows and says he knows you, Linda, know it too, so what else is new?

She blows across the open coffee container as she doesn't want to burn her tongue. I just couldn't take that right now. No matter how many winters I am here… the darkened cold days and the nights but they want to take it all away from me.

Albert sits across from her. One detail: his hands are resting on the table top. The fingers are entwined and the right thumb tapped against the left thumb or it could have been the left thumb tapped against the right thumb. We used to sit like this in third grade, he is telling her. The teacher went up and down the aisle making sure our thumbs are not talking as she claimed they were if she saw them doing what I am now doing. Wouldn't it be better if you were done with all this walking up and down the aisles? From what you have been saying, there ain't much difference between that third grade and what goes on in the college. Don't get me wrong… but really what is the difference when you come to think about it?

I am not counting moving thumbs. I am trying…

She is sure Albert did not hear what she was saying and now later she could not remember what she *has* said. It is like that now, more and more. Vaguely, she knows what she has said, said it to herself, trying to get the kids to…

Arbitrary Insert to Help the Reader

Frederik is writing: As always nice to hear from you, my dear friend. Sorry it takes time for replies. Concerning Linda Nelson, I remember her very clearly, but never met her again. Faintly I seem to recall that I borrowed her dissertation (On Bulgarian Verb aspect, or something like that) but am not sure.

I remember, total recall, one hot evening in August -84-, when Linda Nelson came back with that black (Afro-American) professor, Kevin Nalin I think his name was, specialist in Serbo-Croatian, not Bulgarian, if memory serves me right. They had dined at a Korean restaurant, or was it Vietnamese? Any case, heard that the prof died from AIDS some years later, a colleague in Oslo, Norway, who followed that path some time after, was obviously privy to the fact.

Frederik, as always, has some things confused and others… but here is Linda's voice in a note to the article, Education, Association Activism: Bulgarian Women of the National Revival Intelligensia (1850s-1870s)

62. This is a point on which I differ with Bulgarian historiography which denies the connection with world women's and feminist movements, viewing the associations in a specific national context; see *Bulgarski zhenski suiuz* which states that the *zhenski druzhestva* "are purely ours," (85), and Paskaleva who denies feminist intentions, stressing the uniquely Bulgarian nature of the groups.

While

61. The fate of women's associations is an open question at this writing (1992). During December 1989 splinter groups of the communist Bulgarian women's committees formed, but the current socio-economic conditions have apparently rendered them ineffective. At the present it is difficult to obtain accurate information on conditions in Bulgaria

***It is likely she wrote the contributor's note: **Linda L. Nelson is presently completing her dissertation on "Nationalism and Gender Identity: The Bulgarian National Revival, Women's Consciousness, Women's Activism." Her other research and publication areas include Yugoslav history, gender studies, and film studies. She is currently on the faculty of the Center for Liberal Studies at Clarkson University, Potsdam, New York.**

Linda Nelson is an editor of SCHOLAR, PATRIOT, MENTOR, Historical Essays in Honor of Dimitrije Djordjevic. Published by East European Monographs, Boulder.

END of Arbitrary Insert to Help the Reader

MADARA cont.

-59-

You can't steal Racho from me, Piret says. He is my kaval player. He is my Bulgarian musician. Yes, we walk by that guy and you linger to take a photo of him and next you will be giving him thoughts and then sentences and you will find him a street in Sofia where he can live and you will drag in what you know about how people live in those houses over near Hristo Botev Boulevard because that is about the only other place you know anything about and you will have him in the room Toshko lives in with his mother... am I right... and you will have to find some complicated way to avoid telling us about all of this without sounding like a stupid journalist who has been in Sofia for a week and is now the resident authority on all things Bulgarian for *The Guardian* in London.

No, that kaval player stays on the bridge forever. If I had wanted to bring in Toshko and there will be time for that, there is always time for that. But we both saw that guy on the bridge. He is really there and we have a photograph of it though that is no longer evidence anyone in their right mind would accept. We walked up around the back of the Palace of Culture which is cracking and ageing—as if it had been worked over by a war or something—though it only went up what around 1984 or just before which now in Bulgaria is back then, as they say, before *the changes*.

You could say everything in Bulgaria is BTC and then

ATC. And now my voice changes, as you say when you have had just about enough of the past and what you know of the past is okay since we are not walking through the past except in your mind…

Anyway, I did come here when this was new and people dressed up to go to the cafes and the restaurant up on the top of the building and there was a bowling alley which was very expensive…

So what?

I never saw a guy like the kaval player. It was not allowed. On one of the streets, right near Botev there is a guy with a bathroom scale who charges a couple stotinki to get yourself weighed. You give him the coins, get on the scale and he looks down at the number and not bending up tells you your weight. You could ask him to repeat the number and he usually lowers the number by a kilo. He knows his market, it could be said. I wondered where he got the scale from as they didn't sell things like that in TZUM, back then. Just a way to avoid this going back.

-60-

Linda goes to McDonald's some nights, more nights than she likes to remember, but she goes there. She always parks the car and goes into the restaurant to order the food. The service is slow in the evening as most people use the drive-up window. That is something she does not do. They were always changing the sequence of steps—it seemed, though she could be mistaken—for the ordering, the paying, the picking up and there were always cars behind her, impatient cars, she could think or imagine as even in Potsdam people were rushing about and she was one of them, caught between the two colleges, so the rushing from work to home to shopping to…

Always the same three things: a regular hamburger, small fries and small coffee. She asked the kid to put the milk on the side as well as the sugar. She took extra napkins from the dispenser. Tonight the lid of the coffee had become a little undone and the wrapping on the hamburger was slick with coffee, which got on her fingers and which she then wiped with the napkin though the stickiness remained.

The position of the parked car meant she was looking into a car filled with a large family eating supper. Next to that car was another car, of course, and this time a lone man was drinking, she could see, from a milk shake. Milk shakes made her gums ache but she had to be really careful with the coffee because sometimes it came out so hot it burnt her tongue.

The coffee cup was on the dashboard to the right of the steering wheel. She had torn the paper bag to get at the French fries, on which she did not put any ketchup. She probably should have but the little packets of takeout ketchup always tore in a direction she could not really control so to avoid that sort of mess she had her French fries without ketchup. She took a bite of the hamburger and then put the hamburger down on part of the ripped open bag.

She felt very tired and was aware just barely of her head

between the palms of her hands and ever so gently she lowered her head so that her forehead rested on the top of the steering wheel.

Was she the corpse of a man rubbed out as gangster, shot from behind and head jammed against the steering wheel?

The newspaper photographs insinuate themselves into our minds but how dated that must sound if she said it to the students. To mention a newspaper was like talking about a black and white movie… if I had mentioned a black and white movie they thought I was talking about race relations back in some far time.

Now, it is a far time ago since she walked into the McDonald's: a millennium had gone away and soon it would be time to get back to her place. She did not say back to my home. Apartments are not homes, I am sorry, she would say. Maybe it is the particle that remains from Nebraska where even in Omaha only a few live in apartments as the very word apartment has a similar quality to the phrase, he was sent to a military academy to get straightened out. Normal people did not live in apartments: something had gone wrong, somehow they didn't fit in. Is there anything sadder than seeing curtains in the windows of what is an apartment above shops just off a main street.

Just beyond the lights of the parking lot the Bulgarian word *vechera* came back to her. As dark here as in the mountains outside Sofia. One or two or three of the colleagues knew what she was talking about, though the talking had now stopped ten years ago. There is no way to work Bulgaria into surveys of American history even during the years of European immigration since for most of that time Bulgaria did not exist as an independent country. Even knowing this removes her from the conversation on St. Patrick's Day. I am from Nebraska. My name is from Nebraska, as plain as that, you could say without the redeeming aura of austerity attached to the plain style of the Amish or Mennonites.

In a McDonald's parking lot!

-61-

When you are dead you're dead. Something only a living person… the failure of language to prevent such sentences.

MADARA again

-62-

Piret was saying the guys in those donkey carts near Madara, near Strazhitsa frightened her and made her afraid and bothered her and scared her and why do people have to use such things… and no matter what you say about some people still not having the resources to use other means for getting around or moving their stuff: there is nothing romantic, there is nothing that can convince me I was living suddenly in a Russian novel and no amount of snow and no being wrapped in a great cloak and no matter that the young man was nice and you were sitting next to Medy, can make me think anything other than how primitive:

this is in Europe after all and Bulgaria is in the European Community and it still has people getting about on donkey drawn carts or more like broken down horses that someone probably stole and don't tell me those were dark southern Bulgarians, they were gypsies or Turks and even if they were Bulgarian and even if they are gypsies or Turks that is still not an excuse…

LINDA

-63-

Cremation. 02 01 2010.

-64-

Certificate of death. To repeat the words. Certificate of death. As a way to stay alive.

Toward LINDA

-65-

Piret and I drive Upstate in bright sunshine on Sunday, stayed overnight in Saranac Lake in a dark room at the Best Western, had an Italian dinner at what might have been an old restaurant but as we are leaving the waitress says can you believe it this used to be a Burger King, the guy who owns it owns another Italian place out on the highway as you come into town…

In the morning after a night when I fucked Piret as hard as I could with her sitting on the edge of the bed after she had sucked my dick for a little bit while kneeling on a pillow between the beds and then I fucked her hard as she said to do it harder, do it harder and she looked very sweet and compressed with her tits sliding around as on a scrap of pink white ocean, and then she said to do it from behind for a while and then in the morning I bought her a yogurt and some bananas from the supermarket, a Grand Union, while she was getting coffee from the Dunkin Donuts… and last night I told Piret I had been reading the chapter in the bio of Stevenson about him living in Saranac Lake when he was trying to recover from his lung ailments and the weather had gone down to forty below…

Then we drive to Potsdam through the hilly forests which looked a lot like Arizona if you subtracted the trees as the emptiness of the roads and the lack of houses…or, rather, how the houses were interspaced and far between… occasionally a little village with a cemetery with modest stones on a hillside, and as we got closer to Potsdam I stopped for gas at a Valero which I think of as some sort of California gas station since I remember stopping at them in California and there was one with a plaque saying that Jimmy Swaggart has gotten caught in the motel just down the road in Indio and how it ruined his career being with those prostitutes…

In the shop I bought myself a soda and was talking to Joseph, the guy behind the counter, a white guy and I asked him if he went to SUNY Potsdam and he said he had and made an MA and was unemployed and he knew Linda though he didn't have any classes but he told me about her professor friend but he himself was a member of the ISO the Independent Socialists Organization (as he carefully spelled out the abbreviation) and I avoided arguing with him about much of anything and he was giving me careful instruction to find the college and when we found the college: in a very large administration building there was a guy at a desk in a big office who said he didn't know Linda Nelson but had gone to her funeral to support the department but I didn't know her and he knew about the cuts though the irony was that the money was found and they rehired everyone.

Upstairs the colleague of Linda had an office door filled with radical notices and a message about his book about an East German communist intellectual and I found in the discard box : POLITICS: WHO GETS WHAT WHEN HOW and at random I opened the book and found these words on page 155

> The problem of readjustment is plainly connected with
> the level of general insecurity, which is a function of the
> way in which environmental changes are interpreted as
> inflicting indulgences or deprivations...discontented into
> the provoked alarmed ambitious and haughty...

After the college, we went along to Garner Funeral Home. I rang the bell and a woman came to the door saying no one was around but could she help me and I explained I was trying to find out if Linda Nelson was buried... she didn't know but she could call the funeral home manager Corey who was away and he told her how to find the info in the files and found the file and a man came in, her husband, who was the driver for the ambulette company which was connected to the funeral home in some way and they copied the CERTIFICATE OF DEATH... while he was saying he drives people around and just came back from Long Island a nine hour drive bringing a woman from one nursing home to another, all that way she sat in the wheel chair... what happens to people these days...

The woman showed me around the home and the viewing place, a very large room with folding chairs and all ready, the guy who runs it is very handy with his hands but the place is now part of a chain it hasn't been independent for a long time...

We found the house out in the woods from the address on the CERTIFICATE OF DEATH, a two story porch house and behind it a mobile home on cement blocks.

This is where she lived—and died, I have to imagine it was in the mobile home... but I don't know for sure... a great space of lawn surrounded by a bank of very tall trees... no one about but a warning about a dog, no mail in the mailbox...

Then we drove back into the town to think about what we had seen or what I see...

Certificate of DEATH

Not a single scratch had she made on anything we had seen...

Back in the town on the main street in the arts council shop a customer was telling the girl behind the counter there were farms around here that didn't get electricity until late in the 1950s and a lot of people never had American television until the late 60s and before that there were only Canadian stations and we grew up watching *The Beachcombers.*

Series overview
The Beachcombers followed the life of Nick Adonidas (Bruno Gerussi), a Greek-Canadian log salvager in British Columbia who earned a living travelling the coastline northwest of Vancouver tracking down logs that had broken away from logging barges. His chief business competitor is Relic (Robert Clothier) (whose actual name is Stafford T. Phillips), a somewhat unsavoury person who will occasionally go to great lengths to steal business (and logs) away from Nick. The series also focused on a supporting cast of characters in Nick's hometown of Gibsons, often centering around a café, Molly's Reach, run by Molly (Rae Brown), a mother figure to virtually all the characters in the series (including Relic). Molly had two grandchildren living with her, Hughie (Bob Park) and his younger sister Margret (Nancy Chapple).

Was it about Canadians in Florida? No, in British Columbia… but you get the picture..

We drove back to the city by way of the roads passed the various lakes and small towns...

Nothing remains of Linda Nelson...

As far as I can tell.

-66-

So the details: Linda is fucking some guy in Bulgaria at the Slavonic Seminar and nothing remains except a scrawled detail in the diary I am keeping, as if it means something... even then I know I am just piling up crap for someone to throw away when I...

Right back to me again.

In the driving Upstate, there is just the driving. Piret does not ask why I am doing this. I guess she understands and it is a day away from the office though she is always connected to the office with her worry since things are never finished at the office—there is always something unfinished.

Not having known where Linda Nelson lived, not knowing a single person who knew her other than a German professor in the History department, not having as they say a clue and there are only a few hours in Potsdam.

No scenery, none of the nature. The Fall. Autumn Dying leaves. Already a little chilly. Is that enough. Bright sunlight. Only a few cars. A holiday after all.

LINDA NELSON IN SOFIA, BACK THEN

There is another moment in Sofia at Restaurant Krim. They have all insisted on going out one last time. There are too many languages being spoken and people are careful of the time and they have so many things to do and there is only the experience of having been out at *Dervenitsa*, what a way to spend the summer, a long way from what matters. The waiter takes his time getting over to the table. I try to tell them about what Philip has said: there is no reason why the guy should come over to ask what we want. He knows who is important and he knows we are not important.

The dirty table cloth has been turned over a few too many times. The table wobbles a bit. The place is crowded. The Russian Klub is one of the oldest restaurants. They now own it—Balkan Tourist—whatever that means in socialism. Linda sits opposite me, across the table and… one waits for a sentence, a question. The Dutch girl is talking with a Norwegian boy about his studies and all the work he has to do when he gets back to Oslo…

Linda is talking about graduate school exams. She is getting too old for such things. You know they are serious and really matter but you have a certain distance from them because you are not 22, but this distance is of no help since there is no way around them and I am not a genius whose name is being shopped around as someone everyone is looking forward to meeting or wanting to be part of the contribution I might potentially make to the field.

But what does it really matter.

I can hear her tone which is not available to the Dutch or Polish girl.

We sit and wait and wait. The menu is a large leather bound book with stamped red ink seal with a scrawled signature at the bottom right hand corner of each page from who knows what official.

The waiter finally comes to the table. You do not need the menu, he tells us. I will tell you what is available. No vodka, for a start as one person asks for vodka. We have beer. We have Coca Cola. We do not have. We do not have. We have this and this and that is it. Fred says, it doesn't matter since it all looks the same both going in and coming out. It will be a piece of some sort of meat in a bowl of liquid and on a large plate there will be fried pieces of potato. There is no bread…

Suits me, Linda says. I do not eat meat. I'll have the potatoes.

The waiter returns with a green plastic bowl in which six pieces of paper have been folded into triangles. There are also six forks and six large spoons.

He must have forgotten the knives, Linda says. But at least we have napkins.

-68-

HARITTENA BELEVA WILL NEVER GO AWAY
so he says

"but she has nothing, nobody, and no one will mourn for her (and what's death without tears?)" The opening sentence of *L'Herbe* (*The Grass*) by Claude Simon.

-68-

I could not find where I believe Harittena Beleva might have lived. Street names have been changed now a number of times. Even remote small streets.

In December 1973, in the winter, in Sofia I meet Harittena Beleva. She has tan eyes and sings in the choir at Aleksandur Nevksi Cathedral.

-70-

LINDA IS SAYING, a real screw-up, you're thinking, I know you are, she is saying as she waits, again, for the secretary from the department to come out and bring her into the college. Last night she knew something had happened to the car, again, she is saying, I am really sorry about this and I really appreciate it, I know it is out of your way and I wish I could ask you in but everything is such a mess, you know what I am saying, I am sure, there just isn't enough time in the day or night to keep up with how the stuff just piles up and I am behind again with the student grades and I should have sent in the attendance roster, but I have to thank you for covering for me since I told you all the students were attending which is remarkable but as you well know term-to-term things change and now things

100

are really hard in the economy so maybe students will be a bit more attentive, though I don't expect that much really because there is this timeless quality to walking into the classroom... term after term, as you might have noticed, though you just see us stagger into the office and for some reason you always have this wonderful smile on your face, you make the room glow I think I might have written on Secretary's Day: none of my colleagues give much thought to you, really, maybe because they have not ever been in your chair... keeping track of such a bunch of screw-ups though this is not one of those shows on television where they collect a bunch of "lovable or annoying" characters and fix them with a laugh track... that reminds me the cable went out again and I just didn't bother to even call the company. I can think of it as saving some money at the very least and I don't have time for television, anymore, and not even back in Nebraska did I watch television, really though even there already back in ancient times people filled up their lives with repeating plot summaries of the shows they had seen last night, *my shows* they even said as if they owned them by paying an hour or 30 minutes of time for them so I guess you could say they did own them, after all.

-70-

LINDA IS STILL SAYING, then, you guys are just so wonderful, really and if only you guys were running the show our lives would all be so much better which is probably more a hope than reality, I know, because the world swims in versions of hope and dream and year by year there is a little less of what I think of as that hippy spirit. Remember I told you I am described as being and even describe myself as the last hippy alive... boy, did people laugh when I said that which is better than this guy in Sofia saying, when he went back here from Bulgaria with his Bulgarian wife to live in northern Wisconsin and he is teaching school and these long haired guys are unloading some sort of truck and all the kids rushed to the fence and began chanting hippy, hippy, hippy and you could almost feel the ropes in their imaginary hands... which he says is his first thought but then he tries to revise that out of his description because it didn't fit into his politics, as he is always shifting around realty to suit what he thinks is his politics of the moment. He hasn't liked hippies as he is a little older and so is protected or just didn't get it but he didn't mind the sex that came off being around these hippy kids in New York City which just has to have been a pretty pathetic bunch of kids as hippies can only really be out in California but then I have to stop myself as Charles Manson shows up: you remember him, don't you?

-68-   (Harittena is)

Whether she knows it or not, Lidia's mother has abandoned the rooms on Vitosha Boulevard. She would not be coming back to Sofia: by then it matters little really in which room she finds herself, and while not blind she has little interest in the room where she would sit day after day.

I stay in the front room—back then or is in mind doing this right now—for a few days at the end of August before leaving for Istanbul and finding *Dark as the Grave wherein my Friend is Laid* which has been there more than ten years. In a little cabinet are some seaside souvenirs Lidia bought when she went to Varna with her mother. The photograph cut from a magazine of Alain Delon from *Rocco and His Brothers* is still there along with a package of BROOKLYN chewing gum. On blank page of the book I write:

I seem to fornicate with cities I have been to before. There is that familiar rushing over the streets to be sure all the limbs are still in place, that the mind has not lied, for the hands seek out the recent constructions and renovations.

I have not found Harittena.

In the summer, in Sofia, it is very hard to recall the winter.

And I am in the mood for that sort of sordid pleasure, futile both at its best and worst with no one who might even listen to such.

Just sentimental, the Americans would tell me. Who do you think you are, Bulgarians would say. I did not open the windows at night as the room is cool and I did not want to be bothered by mosquitoes. The Americans are rushing back to where they have come from. I am nailed to this country now for so many years and no matter how I twist, how I try to pull myself from the exhibition plank...

-72-

This shit, **Linda said**, never did I think I would be still dealing with the same bucket, the same pile, the same sandwich: that first husband is an expert when it comes to the use of the word *shit*. He isn't much good for anything really, but he does know how to use the word *shit*.

-73-

Talking about the dead and realizing how the dead don't do what they are supposed to do since I want to be able to write: HOW TO KILL A WOMAN and shape this woman into a suicide or a woman whose death is a result of a letter that is sent out and which enters her body and mind and not knowing which is more important or less important though it sends her—as the romances would have it—to her death.

**On the ninth aerial toll-house
is the tollhouse of injustice**

-78-

Linda is: To get sick is not an option. If you get known for getting sick they don't ask you back. They excuse you once in a while, but if you get the reputation. I don't want that, so I get myself into the college. The kids don't care, and why should they.

104

To become interested in someone
To be a person of interest
To admit the person exists, separate.

(**Linda never** forgets a conversation that has been repeated, repeated in the way that you learn to decline verbs).

Can't go away.

One can't disappoint.

One can't go away.

Who'll take care of the dogs?

Who can understand what it is like?

Do you understand?

I'll see what I can do.

I really will see what I can do. It gets expensive paying these penalties to keep the plane reservation. It is just so embarrassing, now.

Do you know how expensive it is to board two dogs?

And they're getting old.

I just can't ask anyone to come over to the house two or three times a day to feed and walk the dogs and it's not just putting them on leashes and walking them around the property. You got to lift down the old guy because he can't get up and down the steps.

To get sick, **Linda says**, is not an option. If you get known for getting sick they don't ask you back. They excuse you once in a while, but if you get the reputation. I don't want that so I get myself into the college. The kids don't care, and why should they. They have their lives and have to live those lives. They are not paying tuition to hear a professor's problems and it is only the kids who give me that title *Professor*. The secretary for the department, the other higher-ups call me MS. The way they say it… miss. Miss. They don't turn the s into Z. They know I have missed the boat, as the more honest of them are thinking, but who knows

I (—**Linda**—) could go to Montreal, cross the St Lawrence, go to a foreign country, look at the river, going to a foreign country: read the local newspaper, try to figure out the routine, the way people go about their day.

There are times it felt like really going away. I have to say that. But then it came to an end. I would go in the Fall and then in the Spring just after Easter. But something happens and I…

Just don't go and I think I said to myself I'll go in the Spring and Spring was either late or early that year… you lose track of that, it seems… and I didn't go in the Spring.

-80-

In Mississippi—that seems like pre-historic time—and it is like living in the stone age, not the stoned age, which would have been okay but my hippy days are over, really and truly done with but I do and I don't miss them: stoned age… away from the stone age to Memphis or New Orleans.

In Memphis one had to behave.

In New Orleans it is not possible to behave. I gave myself away there, or at least I try to or tried to tell myself; give it away, or I try to tell myself and I just sat in some bar with another and another drink; those plastic buckets some guy was filling up.

Even with one of the oldest lines in the book: I got to watch my weight.

I'll watch it for you, you want another and the guy has a crooked smile, as if he is a little retarded and wanted to spell watch... for me and points to his wrist watch: watch my weight… 24 carats if a nickel…

-81-

A NECESSARY QUOTE: to skip it is to avoid the thought behind what has been read so far.

The sacred is what gives life and takes it away, it is the source from which it flows, and the estuary in which it is lost.

But the sacred is also that which one would not know how to possess simultaneously with life.

Life is wear and tear, and waste.

It vainly strives to persevere and to refuse every expenditure so as to be preserved.

Death lies in wait for it.

There is no artifice that is as good.

Every living being knows it senses it.

It knows the choice remaining to it.

It dreads giving itself, sacrificing itself and is aware of this wasting its very being.

But to retain its gifts, energies and resources, to use them prudently for all practical and selfish goals—as a consequence, profane—saves no one in the final analysis from decrepitude and the tomb.

Everything that is not consumed rots away.

Furthermore, the abiding truth of the sacred resides simultaneously in the fascination of flame and the horror or putrification

—From *MAN AND THE SACRED* by Roger Caillois

-82-

When I travel, **LINDA SAYS** and if you think going to New York City is travelling and I suppose it is, leaving from Potsdam though going to Montreal since that is a foreign city seems in some way a more natural way to say I have gone travelling when I went there but be that as it may—as some student will write from time to time—I have gone travelling down to New York City some time or the other and there is this guy standing with a group of guys way over on 57th Street around the corner from the Holiday Inn... I don't know why they are standing there... some sort of drug rehab: Black men with ID cards on chains hanging about their necks. I am waiting for the light to change. This one guy is saying in a sing-song preacherlike voice, *Things are fucked up, they really are fucked up and there's no telling when they ain't gonna be fucked up and there is nothing doing since things are just so fucked up but you know you're over a barrel and things are really fucked up and it's a fucking shame, a fucking shame.*

I wish the guy hadn't been Black, but that is what I see and hear and you never hear any voices in Potsdam when you go downtown, which is not really much of a downtown as far as things like that go and I don't go there anymore. I don't know anyone anyway down in New York City. The students seem to have friends down in the city and they have these bragging competitions to see who can get to the city in the fastest time, but no one tells anyone the truth when it comes to things like that.

So I say I have gone travelling and I don't go travelling now. I suppose I should miss it, the adventure, the uncertainty, the wondering whether or not, the new people, the places, the coming back and having to tell people what you have done but knowing most people don't go travelling anymore, and I don't even have to qualify that...

Remembering Dr. Linda Nelson
By: Audrie MacDuff

On Friday, January 29, SUNY Potsdam lost the beloved faculty member Linda Nelson. Suspicion arose when Nelson did not arrive on campus for her usual Friday classes, and it was later found that she had passed away in her home.

Nelson began teaching in the History Department at SUNY Potsdam in the spring semester of 1999 and has been teaching classes steadily ever since. This semester alone, those classes included Europe 1500-1815, two sections of US History to 1877, as well as Imperial Russia 1613-1917. According to an e-mail that was sent to faculty and staff from Galen K. Pletcher, Dean of Arts and Sciences, Nelson participated in the campus Literacy Assessment Project as well as in the Supplemental Instruction Program for EOP students.

Linda Nelson studied at University of California in Santa Barbara and was a PhD candidate with a dissertation revolving around the topic of Nationalism and Gender Identity. During this time, Nelson was awarded two research grants and was named a research scholar by the Bulgarian Academy of Sciences.

Amongst many other accomplishments, Nelson instructed classes at UC Santa Barbara, Santa Barbara City College, Moorpark College, Clarkson University and Mississippi University for Women.

Since her passing, History faculty members were asked to share their memories of Nelson. According to Professor Axel Fair-Schulz, "Linda was one of the kindest and most helpful people I have encountered in academia. Given that she and I are fellow European historians, we had many discussions, specifically about Russian, Soviet, and Bulgarian history. She shared her insights freely, and we frequently exchanged ideas, articles, and even films. I am particularly saddened that the last few weeks of her life were so clouded by the New York State budget crisis that very much threatened her security and livelihood... I will miss her comforting presence terribly."

Along with Fair-Schulz, History professor Dr. Tom Baker shared a few words about Nelson's contribution to the SUNY Potsdam campus, saying that "it is worth noting that Dr. Nelson always took the lead in collecting donations for the department to recognize Leslie Delosh on Administrative Assistants' Day (also known as Secretary's Day) and at Christmas. The fact that she took this initiative as an adjunct instructor is a measure of her thoughtfulness; it certainly was not in her job description."

It is evident from these comments that Linda Nelson was an integral part of our campus History Department. The cause of death has yet to be released and is currently being investigated.

PIRET IN SOFIA

Life is what might have happened, is what I am being told as I walk around in Sofia during the night Piret stayed in the apartment and later she is going out to meet some of the people we have met through the Former Prime Minister. Later, she tells me they had gone to a small coffee bar... it has five or six little tables and maybe two on the sidewalk in front. Two girls are working there and it seems difficult to figure out why they have two girls working in such a small place. However as the evening goes on each of the tables is always filled and there is a constant, really noticeable stream of men coming in and going out after brief conversations with the two girls who never leave the coffee bar, not even to go into what must have been either a storage room or toilet at the back of the room, and that is what the place really is, just a room...

Between Piret and the husband and wife have they enough English or Bulgarian in common to describe what is the actual business of the coffee bar, and surely there is another purpose to the place than what is on the surface, a surface that is not very deep and while I want to tell Piret what a guy once told me: what is the point of skating on thin ice when there is only an inch of water under the ice?

I resisted the temptation and sure she would have reminded me you have said that sentence in another context and isn't the guy who said it a connoisseur of watching pornography in Times Square in the middle of the afternoon back before they made Times Square into a place not very interesting to visit unless you are French or something like that—do you know there are French people who take a room in Times Square just to spend the night there to be able to walk around at all hours of the night and day?

-85-

(Not really 85 but an interruption so we can get back to the topic sentence in 84)

Louise still staring at the face, the mouth drawn into a kind of grin she had never seen before—but the doctor said that it was the side corresponding to the part of the brain which was no longer irrigated—giving her a mocking sarcastic expression, as if she had retired inside herself, withdrawn, leaving on the surface that grinning, mocking face like a superficial layer of impermeable, impenetrable flesh—

THE GRASS by Claude Simon

Until reading those sentences I had never found the words for the expression of my mother's face when she was in her coffin in the days just before Christmas in 1972.

So, walking along from the flat on Solunska to Vitosha and deciding not to go right toward where I had stayed all those times where I had been with Harittena: a snowy night and the snow still in the morning, December, so dark and closed in and so lonely why not admit it: heat broken, broken, done for and yet for a few hours with Harittena and a few other nights not in that cold room, colder even when together... the trams had stopped so it was better and no one has seen her come in since the rooms are on the ground floor and Medy sleeps soundly and did not see her at all...

-86-

DEATH OF LINDA NELSON

Where is the story?

The story

Linda hit her head on a piece of furniture and went to the bathroom to try to stop the bleeding, right? I think she hit the back of her head, LINDA'S brother is saying. Maybe she couldn't see the wound, her skull cracked, you could say, but how did it crack—the edge of a table, a chair, but how is her body sent in that direction coming back late on Wednesday after a long day of teaching—?

The mess around in the trailer.

-86-

The trailer isn't a double-wide like Milligan has down in Virginia. This is called fore-shadowing. The only time I have ever been in a trailer is back in 1970...) A double wide gives you space to turn around in but in Linda's trailer you couldn't turn around, it seems, though she is a small woman, it is still hard as she has so much stuff and that stuff is all over the place. She isn't much for neatness, didn't see any purpose to it.

Driving home, did she think of the trailer as home? Or *my place*? Back to where I live? But probably she thinks when she closes the door: I am here. But maybe not this night or it is and she is tired, really tired for some reason, but she knows the reason, really, though saying or thinking, tired for some reason is an easier way of going about it and not having to repeat even IN thought...

Her landlady is a nice woman but they don't have anything in common and can there, really, be more with someone you pay rent to each month. With each month, with the cash in the envelope or when remembered, the check in the envelope: I am her tenant and she is my landlord.

Linda L. Nelson, 60, Parishville

PARISHVILLE - Linda L. Nelson, 60, of Parishville passed away unexpectedly on Jan. 29, 2010. She was pronounced dead at the Canton-Potsdam Hospital

A memorial service will be held on Feb. 8 at 4 p.m. at the Trinity Episcopal Church in Potsdam with Rev. Christopher Brown celebrant. Arrangements are with the Garner Funeral Home. Condolences can be sent at www. garnerfh.com. Contributions can be made to the Potsdam Humane Society.

-86-

Never thought driving would be... when she is 16, thinking within **LINDA**, the driver's license is a way away from the house, away from the street, away from the town: away from them... but it is only later she has second thoughts... what a miserable daughter.. but that comes much later and like so many things another futile thought, another one to chalk up on the board as the chalk scratches and students snivel about the sound as the mother and father are now long dead in their boxes in the cemetery.

Driving away to college and leaving the car behind a friend's house because they didn't let freshman have cars, but meeting him so into the car to be a married woman. Then to California, driving away or toward it is never clear, but more driving.

More driving for everything. He did the shopping the first weeks in California and then he didn't do it anymore. Enough of that.

Here the drive is out of town, what a false promise; I got to go out of town to do even the simplest shopping. Over to Messenia to: Price Chopper... how would someone translate such a phrase into Bulgarian or French?

In the parking lot again. Park, so I don't have to back out of the spot. Turn off the ignition. Sometimes the pause between the key turning and taking it out of the ignition and put it... and then gathering... to be stunned by *the what am I doing?*

Back in the car after the shopping experience, as I hear it described without irony, without a snicker of letting the other person in on the joke, back from the shopping experience: trying to keep the milk bottle upright and the bread from getting crushed and again sitting behind the wheel, key in hand and again *the what am I doing?* But cannot linger, she hears herself saying without any words being spoken. Her friend Larry, from back then in Bulgaria, is thinking when does a person learning a foreign language begin to do that idle thinking in that language or do you always do the idle thinking in your first language and hope the words come out in the new language if that is what you want.

-86-

Another dead person, this Larry, bragged about being the only coloured guy who knew Serbo-Croat, as it is called then, before the split up of the language. And he didn't die from a blood transfusion, I know that for sure, **LINDA** would say.

And the strength is marshaled, as they write in history books... well, not really anymore... but maybe they should. She hears the milk bottle fall over in its plastic bag as the car takes her back to where she lives.

The house out front is no longer lived in. The landlady moved into town for the winter, but she is good about having a guy come out to plow the drive back to the trailer. Don't picture some cute aerodynamic futuristic creation, **Linda** has written to her brother. Up on the cement blocks and it looks like it has been here forever, as I seem to have been.

That brother of mine knew about getting away... as he says I moved papers across desks in ten countries and if you ask me to tell you what I have accumulated from that: this house in Hawaii that we want to get rid of and move to someplace like Arizona where the doctors won't kill you before your time.

Avoid the doctors for as long as you can. They creep into your life with the checkups, the blood tests, the suggested tests. They start to prescribe vitamins and other stuff they believe will prolong your life: every week or two weeks you sort out the pills you take each day into these little containers marked S to S. As you get older the container gets larger and the lettering gets bigger: you have started the retreat back into babyhood when everything you were given to play with was exaggerated in size so you couldn't cram it into your mouth. Avoid them because your life becomes a cycle of visitations and worry, no matter how distant you are from your own life those words, we'll call to let you know the results or *you* can if you want call to get the results.

That could be one of the reasons **Linda** didn't come out to see us, **Linda's** brother says. I really can't blame her since I don't know for sure. It's bad enough having to deal with your *own medical issues* as the phrase has it, isn't it wonderful how all our lives are now packaged up into handy phrases that become a substitute for any sort of thinking.

Linda didn't let her teeth go which is something good I can say about her. Growing up our parents dragged us through dentist offices. Teeth are what separate people or rather the lack of teeth. Maybe I should say differentiate people. Our mother would say, did you notice the teeth on… and once we were taken to a nursing home to visit some relative who must have meant something to our mother and I can't remember who she was or even if it was a she: but I do remember looking into the rooms none of which had doors and you would see these people lying in the beds their mouths were closed up, puckered inward since they didn't have any teeth anymore or the nurses had to take the teeth out of their mouths after they ate whatever it was they were giving them or maybe they just kept the teeth out all together to save time and bother. Their mouths looked like assholes, pardon the French… wasn't there a joke along those lines: in one hole and out the other and soon enough you can't tell the difference.

REFLECTIONS

And. With each year—though no one is ever really aware of a year passing as it actually passes—though looking back: what a terrible year and more rarely, what a happy year that has been—to mention happiness in the passing year is to jinx what might come as never are there two years running... or at least in my experience, but that is not what is being thought because all of this is for some sort of modern greeting card: it just gets harder to keep up with people, both people near and far away who have been friends, people known and there are no lines at the front door of potential friends, people if only one has met once upon a time... because: *why bother?*

I apologize for being so slow to respond. I do want to talk but am in the crush of the semester and a book project. I will be in touch by phone this coming weekend or the next.

From a colleague of **Linda's**

And. There are two matters: to have some sort of meeting of the minds, hearts, souls, whatever word gets invoked: how to tell a person about who you are and then they have to tell you who they are or you could just fall into some likely pit of a common interest: animals, the environment, politics but in each of these there are inner and outer well defined circles and you have as Audrey says: been parachuted in, much like one of those French resistance fighters dropped over a darkened field in France but since that allusion dates one so terribly, you get the drift… but who knows you might meet someone you can talk to when next you are at the clinic or in the line at the super-market. We have all heard stories about things like this happening.

And. Yeah, and that guy down in The City knows someone who will sell you the Brooklyn Bridge, really, cheap, cheaper than cheap and a bargain.

And. I have heard of an uncle up in Newburgh going into the bathroom after breakfast and dropping dead, right there, just like that. My mother says his wife had said, nothing out of the ordinary happened at breakfast. He just got up from the table went into the bathroom and she heard him fall. The door wasn't blocked by his fallen body. He just died. It was a heart attack and he is dead.

And. I heard, probably, the best way to go, no lingering, no paralysis, just gone, painless, though I still wondered why the guy had eaten breakfast. Yesterday as I was locking the door to go out: is this the moment when I die?... do people have these thoughts? Or are they so common that they pass over into the unspoken because something hesitates the mentioning it at dinner.

END of Reflections for now.

THE THIRTEENTH IS THE TOLL-HOUSE OF REMEMBERING EVIL

PIRET IS THINKING ABOUT PHILIP

Piret wants Jenie to tell her interesting stories about the man who became powerful for one year, lingering on in people's memory either as a good guy or as the reason for everything going to shit in Bulgaria and while it might be more interesting to hear about how he has allowed things to get out of hand and how he has survived, Piret wants to know what he was like before he is somebody who is aware she has noticed him, though didn't mention it when we are with him: people turn and look after him or when he goes into the restaurant people know who he is and even if they didn't like what he represents they didn't ever let on in any obvious way what they think of him because that might bring bad luck because they did know who he is and even if he is no longer in power he knows powerful people and you are a little guy who can't afford to have any enemies even someone you don't like and doesn't know you from a hole in the road and everything is still so tentative, so up for grabs.

Power is a strange thing, as anyone can say, Jenie tells Piret. A person does not become powerful. P was always powerful though he is not a member of The Party, didn't come from a big communist family, he has not been in the military, has not been in *Komsomol*. We have all gone to the same schools, read the same text books, had the same complex relationships with our parents... become involved with each other and then go in different directions.

P would say: naturally obviously. Of course.

I hope, Piret says, these English words capture his eyes

as they look at you after he has tried to explain something and you know he thinks he is right but he never makes you feel stupid or silly but he did leave you feeling helpless. I can't explain it better than that…

-89-

A scrap of conversation about **LINDA NELSON** with a reflection.

—That friend of yours sounds like she is depressed. I have known some people who have been depressed at times and then it passes.

—But what does it say to say: she is or she was depressed?

—Even that is too easy.

Every adjective is too easy. The sharpness of the nails positioning the exhibit against the neutral background of a sentence that goes along, well, so she is depressed, what else is new in this world where everyone ages, everyone has money problems, everyone has love problems, everyone, everyone: why should anyone care about just another depressed person? You have the experience of driving Upstate, out West and those little cemeteries: who do you think are buried there?

One of the advantages of getting your driver's license back: you don't have to look at the cemeteries that line the Long Island Expressway when you come out of the tunnel.

IN SOFIA

Sitting again in the park in front of the National Theatre, near the long closed *Bambouk*, near the long closed *Roza Café*, near where the mausoleum used to be, near where the gallery of Bulgarian artists is still showing Bulgarian artists, with the fountains working again, with the kiosks no longer filled with the piles of newspapers: the paper of comedy *STERSHIL* still published, but the familiar organs of the communists long gone and I often wonder why people bought them but what is so strange about that… people buy newspapers out of habit, out of hoping to learn some little things, even in New York City am I not right?

-90-

OR, how Thomas McGonigle found himself in a situation similar to **LINDA NELSON** since he had the same sort of temporary academic job at a college in New York City, unlike **LINDA NELSON** who was teaching at a college in Upstate New York

C o l l e a g u e s :

At the last department meeting, Joyce told us about the dire news regarding a new round of budget cuts affecting CUNY. Because of the possibility that those budget cuts would take effect before the beginning of the Spring 2011 semester, the administration has asked every department to place 15% of its course offerings on "stand-by." The status of "stand-by" means that a course is not open for registration, but is still on the books, should the need to open it arise (or, in this case, should the money to run the course appear).

In the English department, 15% works out to 67 sections. We may be given some or even all of these courses back, depending on what exactly happens with the budget. As of now, however, I have no idea how many of them, if any of them, will run in the Spring.

This is terrible news for our adjunct faculty, as the department simply has significantly fewer courses we can offer for them to teach. We are very sorry to have to say that we just will not have the same number of classes to offer adjunct professors, should we indeed lose all, or even some, of these 67 English sections. And yet, we want to be as fair as possible to all of our adjuncts. Therefore, for the time being, adjuncts will be limited to being assigned six hours of non-stand-by courses for Spring 2011, thereby allowing me to give more adjuncts at least one course.

Both Joyce and I wanted to let everyone know as soon as possible about this turn of events, so that: 1) everyone be informed about our collective budget woes; 2) adjuncts have time to make other arrangements, should they find that the courses we can allot are insufficient; 3) adjuncts understand why their Spring 2011 schedules may vary from schedules past.

I am sorry to be the bearer of such bad tidings. With luck, courses that are on stand-by will be reactivated, and I will be able to offer our adjunct professors more courses in the near future.

Best,

-91-

As **Linda** finds herself in November last year I find myself in November this year and as they say some things never change even as I try to remember this is my life and this is her life.

These letters arrive and when you ask for confirmation in person the boss says things don't look as bad as when the letter was sent and then a week or so later you run into the guy who sent the letter and he is telling you we can't promise anything as really things have not changed.

As **Linda Nelson** goes back to her trailer, her house on the cement blocks, the mobile home come to rest, where she drapes her coat across the back of the fat chair as she calls the one comfortable chair in the place, a great collector of junk: who knows what treasures have sunk under the cushions? There is the thinking of what to do and while she like I have been in this situation before a mechanism is also in place—the past is really no guide for the present, it provides no consolation to say, I have been through this before because as we well know the past is there: really just there and what can she, what can I do… she has taught at another college in the town but that is now some time ago and her contact has left… can she just go over to the other colleges in the surrounding towns: now, why can't she, why can she?

It has been said, Upstate has two businesses: prisons and colleges and of course there is tourism but they ain't looking for a woman of my age unless she wants to clean motel rooms and even there they ask for experience and are mistrustful of someone coming on to the team as being some sort of spy for the home office: or why ever would I want to do this? What is the matter with me and they see and dumbly I put down on the application that I have taught at Potsdam: what has happened there?

As **Linda** would wake up the next morning as do I saying, well, I can cut back on and I do have some money in the bank and as I think about it there is again a Remarque novel about a veteran after World War One living on his savings and watching each day as the money disappears and his death draws closer as there will be nothing when the last coin is given over…

-91-

I <Thomas McGonigle> cannot figure out how to force **Linda Nelson** to remember 1984 and while I have a few short notes from her:

Getting ready for Bulgaria is an ordeal.

I'll be in New York City for several days.

Your zip code wasn't on the IREX list and I intended to look it up but obviously forgot in the general rush of getting it together. A typical happening in my life!!!

I love NYC—could have stayed indefinitely if someone kept paying.

Sometimes I wonder what I really want—guess it must be a country life close to a big city with lots of foreign travel thrown in—at someone else's expense. Am I asking too much?

Greeting from a fellow survivor of the Letern Seminar— actually, I barely survived—came back with pneumonia!

I'm staying at the Hotel Empire—Broadway & 63rd.

Moved to northern California and am job hunting. The less said about that the better. Love it up here but hate job hunting.

Eureka, CA.

(I wrote to **Linda Nelson** and have a faded carbon copy— that long ago, a *carbon copy:* I miss Sofia a lot—wish I was there to go to the mountains if only could figure out... be glad you are academic and not a foot messenger.)

-92-

A Colleague wrote this letter about **LINDA NELSON**:

Linda was VERY alarmed about the fact that SUNY Potsdam decided to not continue their contracts with most adjuncts. As you know, **Linda** depended on her adjunct income.

She did not come to work after 2 days of classes last semester and was eventually found dead in her apartment. As far as we know, **Linda** fell on the ice outside her place and injured her head. She went inside the house and bled to death. Her landlady found **Linda** later on.

I assume that all the stress of the lay-offs etc. contributed to **Linda** being in a very rough state. She told me just one day prior to her death how scared she was of the future.

Meanwhile, several adjuncts have been hired back.

All of it was and is very tragic. As you know, I have very much appreciated Linda as a colleague and friend!

-68-

HARITTENA re-appears

He or she is when I count out the years, after what happens nine months before in December, 1973. Thirty-six years old, in this year. Did Harittena go to Rome before or after the baby came? Did her voice survive well enough to provide her with a career in singing?

Neither the child nor the mother is passed on the street I think...

I do not encourage Piret to visit Alexander Nevski Cathedral. We are close by, really close by as Philip wants to show her, his, parish church—*Sveta Sofia*—is that how you say it? and even kisses an icon when he goes into the church with us, a quick kiss and not remarked upon, as well as a candle for his dead parents.

I do not want to have to repeat the story of meeting Harittena, that watching her walk up into the choir loft, how she disappears and is not there when I go to look for her... the one night in the room on Vitosha. It is intolerable on such a day to think she has the fetus killed by giving into practicality.

She never writes to me. She has my sister's address. In Nadeshda, once, looking for her apartment but can't find my way around the apartment blocks. What would I say? And the answers to the questions: working in some sort of laboratory and sing for both the pleasure and the possibility of a scholarship to Rome, a person needs some hope and there is the chance of going to Rome as she knows a woman who did get the chance and she wasn't connected to anyone: Boris Christoff keeps up his connection to Sofia but likes the living in Rome, I only know his name and the opera always attached to his name *Boris Godunov*. Christoff lives like a monument in Rome, an alternative government, Harittena says. He is the only Bulgarian abroad, uncontaminated, and unsullied. If you could understand his voice, the sound of it, how it—how can I say it—as if his voice is a strong wire of electricity going right into your brain, that shiver of birth and death, can you say that?

I want to say you can say anything in English and I am waiting for Harittena as she has to get new pictures taken for some sort of revised identity card... there are these photo studios all over the place and you can see the extra photographs decorating or scattered at the base of the window displays: the newly sprouted moustaches... the shaved heads of the draftees on cameras never favors the subject.

Of course Philip said, as the joke has it: everyone is just waiting for the moment of being arrested. The commission of the crime is taken for granted.

Harittena wouldn't show me her picture.

Don't you prefer the human to the copy, to the shadow, to the indication of what was or is…?

I am standing before you, why would you want to look at a photograph of my face? Are you going to compare the two? I know you can carry away the photograph and you think you possess me through it, but that is as primitive as people thinking a camera is a soul stealer. Why not allow your memory to hold me, to possess me as you possess my body, once that night, and then we are watching in the *Sulza y Smyah* theatre a play by Gorki, but all of that… you not knowing a word of what they might be saying, but sitting there, being sure not to fall asleep… are not all these dimming memories better than some photograph and you will never have to compare the two at some later date…

-68-

Harittena, at first I am saying, she won't let go, but in reality, I will not let go though as the time goes by: less and less.

Aren't you about ready to walk along talking about how everything changes… and why should anyone be listening to you? Who cares if you have a memory? No one needs to know what's here once upon a time… unless they are trying to make a pile of money in some such way beyond my understanding.

131

Only the name remains, finally and that will be going soon enough.

I don't want her to get on the tram at *Plashtat Lenin*. We wait for one tram to go by. I am not to hug her. I can shake her hand. You never know who is watching. You can be sure someone is watching, you can be sure of... The tram arrives, screeching on the curve to the stop next to *Svetlya Nydelia*... She steps up and is standing at the back of the car. I would like her to be turned to where she has just been, but I can't really see because of the cloudy, dust streaked windows.

-94-

LINDA NELSON again

> I am seeing a guy I don't like.
> I am living in a place I don't like.
> I am doing a job I don't like.
> I am working with people I don't like.
> Linda is moving to Mississippi.

I don't think I am cut out for educating the future mothers of Tennessee Williams and William Faulkner or pay my dues to those particular temples. Without Memphis or New Orleans...

There must have been places in the trailer in the mobile home, in **Linda's** house, where she lives as she wants to live…

Places of what might have been…

A very arch way of…

Folders stuffed with pieces of paper covered with Cyrillic writing. No one could read it.

It all gets tossed.

No one wants any of it and in truth it is all just a mess, her brother says.

To see the ragged edges of the folders, I don't know when she stops looking into them or when she decides she can't do anything with them.

Surely, she knows there comes a moment but still you can't throw them away, **Linda** must have been thinking… and then there is mess from the dogs, over the years, but the stuff is still there and now it is even a bigger mess but no one can read any of it.

What must it have been like to realize she isn't about to get right back to the Bulgarian stuff?

Linda must remember when she jokes about how Americans are always starting again, even when they are in their 80s… we are always starting again, wiping out the past and getting on with it as they say in Nebraska. Everybody in Nebraska knows someone who has moved on finally, finally after a hundred years of trying to make a new start… and they end up down there in Arizona or some such place…

She must be thinking someday some way she might get a chance but she never talks to her brother about any of this or to any of the people she works with. While one or two of them might know where Bulgaria is no one really wants to talk about that far-away place and she hadn't much patience, anymore with explaining and gradually even she is aware of how hard it is to work up interest in that place that doesn't want her interest in their history.

Linda isn't like the naïve girl who wants to research a Rumanian village in Bulgaria and how Rumanian memory survives in Bulgaria… to even have to begin to explain to someone why that is a taboo subject…

Those pages in their folders, she must look at them or looked toward them and knows what is there: the pages of notes because it is hard to make photocopies… there are limits and permissions to be gotten and then the machines didn't work…

No one could know the sheer difficulty of working in Bulgaria.

And then there is the actual pages before her… written in a cursive penmanship in the 19th Century and then trying to find someone who she could talk to about this and there is really no one and anyone who might be interested is more interested in using her to get to the US or wanting to talk about the price of jeans or God knows what…

Those pages of her notes, those ladders never going up into the scholarly air of accomplishment, as might be…

Each time, **Linda** must think when I open a folder all I find is myself digging a hole into which I will be thrown:

how could I have ever picked this topic of women in 19th Century Bulgaria… always wives or sisters or mothers of who is supposed to be a more famous man… it is not an edifying situation, she must be thinking on a good day.

WOMEN IN BULGARIA. She is discouraged and then the sitting in Mississippi in a college for women worshiping at the shrine of Eudora Welty whose age has sanded off just how radical a woman she had been: but now she is a shrine…

Linda must look at her penmanship, at those notes… When did she…

THE FIFTEENTH IS THE TOLL HOUSE OF MAGIC

-96-

01.29.10

I am saddened to inform the campus community that Professor Linda Nelson, full-time instructor in the SUNY Potsdam History Department, was found dead in her apartment on the morning of January 29, 2010.

Linda Nelson has been an integral part of the History Department for nearly ten years and will be missed by colleagues and students alike.

The campus will provide the community with information about services as they become available.

Faculty are welcome to call EAP representatives Toby

White or Ada Santeferra at campus extension 2199 for assistance in dealing with the loss of Linda.

Students are encouraged to call the Counseling Center at 267-2330 or visit the Counseling Center at 131 Van Housen for assistance in this difficult time.

Professor Nelson's Monday classes are cancelled. Students taking classes with Professor Nelson should refer to the department web page at www.potsdam.edu/academics/AAS/History/ after 12 noon on Monday, February 1st, or contact the department secretary, Leslie Delosh, after that time at campus extension 2556 for information about classes.

On behalf of the entire Potsdam community, I extend my most sincere condolences to Professor Nelson's family and friends.

John F. Schwaller
President, SUNY Potsdam

-99-

Assisted living.

Assisted dying.

You have to know near the line of trees that ringed the far field near the trailer, near the mobile, near where Linda dies, they scatter her ashes and they mingle with the ashes of her two dogs that have to be euthanized. No one wants one of those grotesque funerals where they put the body on display. We have all enough of that. Let her stay where she has enjoyed living, I think, but of course am not sure.

Too many questions, questions that can't even be asked or formulated… back in Hawaii it all seems so far away.

There is a room here for her if she wants to come—the room has its own entrance so she could come and go when she wants to and she has paid into a pension that would have been enough eventually to live on and with social security… but one will never know… but she didn't… we have plenty of room and she could have gotten together her thoughts, but we are leaving to move to Arizona, to be near a doctor or a medical center that is not about to kill you if you go in…

-100-

Thomas McGonigle and Piret.

We don't go to Albena.

We don't go to Balchik.

We don't go to Nadeshda.

We go to Potsdam.

We go to Sofia.

We go to Varna and Strazhitsa and Targovishte, and Pernik and Plovdiv and Madara and Rila.

We see no path to heaven. The toll houses might have been operating or had they been closed for budgetary reasons or are operating—

We do not to Istanbul.

We do not go to… hell in a hand basket as I hear people saying at Pepsi when I work on the bottling line that summer… much as later, only recently, this woman is saying so loudly I can hear her up here in the room from the street: he is one sick fuck.

The Eleventh is the Toll-House of Pride

-72-

Linda's brother—six years older—is saying, the trailer was a mess: there is blood all over everything and dog feces... her two dogs have been locked in the bedroom and that is awful but the rest of the place is splattered all over with blood and in the bathroom there are towels soaked with blood... that is where they find her in the bathroom... **Linda** has tried to stop the bleeding... the police are really very good, the state Troopers, and talking with these homicide investigators and while they didn't answer all the questions they rule out foul play... there is just no evidence for it, they say but... Linda falls and hurts herself... she can't stop the bleeding... there has been a little wine drinking and she is last seen at her class on Wednesday and when she didn't come to teach on Friday they sent someone... so **Linda** is there for the two days... I don't know if she tries to call or if she calls or anything... there is nothing to save in the trailer—mobile home, really—everything is destroyed by the dogs and the mess is unbelievable and the mess is there before this happens... that's something I know for sure...so much of the stuff in her cabinets is in that Cyrillic which no one can read or is interested in... the books suffered a lot of dog damage... everybody is very nice and people like **Linda** very much.

Linda, you know, has an old clunker which she kept still complete comprehensive insurance on and I valued it at 25 dollars… it wasn't very reliable… she quit socializing, that was clear and I don't really know why she was depressed… I had bought **Linda** tickets to come out to Hawaii for Christmas and she kept postponing and buying postponements and in any event she didn't come.

We have an extra room here. It's almost a separate apartment… she would have been comfortable… I could have looked after her, get her back on her feet.

We scatter **Linda's** ashes over near where she buried her dog Duke, by that line of trees behind the field near her house… we also scattered along with her ashes the ashes of the other elderly dog she had living with her which was just too old and sickly… I had it euthanized… it is all just so ghastly: the mahogany coffin with the silver handles being buried and we discovered that with my wife's parents and **Linda** and I… with of our own parents…

Linda made some bad decisions.. I don't know what happened with her thesis, why she stopped, she never talked about it, it just disappeared and you don't… she quit socializing when she is down in Mississippi—she is always going to New Orleans and Memphis and when she is in Potsdam she is always going to Montreal and then **Linda** just stops.

TOSHKO is introduced

A nephew by a marriage that no longer exists so how to describe the relationship? A ten year old kid in a one room off Hristo Botev where he is living and sleeping with his mother keeping away from her on the far side of the one large bed which mostly fills the room where against the far wall of which are piled high suitcases on top of some sort of cabinet that could only be opened with difficulty in 1967 when Lidia and I go to visit them: he is just back from school in his dark blue trousers and white shirt, his mother *bustling*—is the best though old-fashioned—word for her actions as she tries to put together something for me to eat, honoured guest I was: she even said, *honoured guest*, though in Bulgarian the word guest sounds like ghost, or at least Lidia said she has been taking a course in English since English was the language everyone wants to learn English and at her job they have the chance, but she didn't keep it up as she has more important things... the one room, on the ground floor as you step into it directly from the street, with a light bulb suspended from the middle of the ceiling and a lamp in the shape of a palm tree brought back from Varna by Lidia's mother a year ago... on a little table near the bed... the window is covered with newspaper... Toshko is sent out to get bottles of beer and *Iskra* since having a guest means they have to have champagne... Lidia tries to tell her sister it isn't necessary, she doesn't have to go to the trouble, but Toshko has already been sent to the shop for the drink—and only years later did I realize his name is the diminutive of Todor—as in Todor Zhivkov, though that would only be something I might say or write as I am sure it never crosses anyone else's screen: that connection and it has nothing to do with the little boy bringing back a string bag of clicking bottles as I am going to the toilet which is an outhouse out back of the building: someone else in the building has the toilet…they had the privilege and Lidia's sister points somewhere or other and puts her index finger to her lips… the toilet is of course… out back and being careful not to fall and not seeing where I am going and so just peeing at the doorway as no way am I going into there.

-102-   cont. TOSHKO…

I should have asked for a candle or something but then I guess no one really goes out to the toilet in the dark… is this the night we have come back from the restaurant Budapest and stopped by on our way out to Nadeshda and Lidia says she is telling her sister about seeing this actor who made people laugh and he is drunk and everyone is laughing at his table, her sister then tells her something and Lidia says it is too difficult for her to tell me what she says: it is just a stupid Bulgarian sentence people say when you say this actor's name and people always laugh and they like this man because he doesn't have much to do with political things or that is how it seems… we have gone to the Budapest with Ivan who you might remember is that agent, which is a whole other story and we sit in a booth and the service is very quick: never do we just sit there waiting… they know who Ivan is… you can be sure of that, Lidia says… and here I am in this room with Lidia's sister who she says trained as a geologist and is married but didn't want to live in the country, no one wants to live in the country and so she lives like this, with some sort of job—a job that is never clear to me: and Toshko looks like he is just wanting to go to sleep and here we are drinking first the *Iskra*… and have to toast and I have to say *nazdravie* and then Lidia's sister wants us to drink the beer but Lidia says we have to take the tram and it is nice of her to invite us but she wouldn't go there if Toshko is not there since she feels sorry for him, he never sees his father who lives in the country as he came from the country and didn't like Sofia…

The Tenth is the Toll-House of Envy

-102-

Toshko smiles. He is a ten year old boy living with his mother in one room.

I never give him a thought in the remaining months of the then living in Sofia.

He is just Lidia's nephew, her sister's son and… am I sure he smiles?… he must have, surely or at least he smiles as we are sitting there and he didn't know any English and didn't venture any words… seen but not heard, a little boy, that's all… though aware of how did he sleep when his mother has a visitor and she did have visitors, I understood when Lidia is talking, about what her mother thought of the situation Elena has brought upon herself: why has she needed to marry?... what has been the point of studying if you are going to...

Five years later. Toshko and his mother are supposed to be living in Zemun which is across the river from Belgrade, Beograd... and I cannot escape books because when I am reading many years later *WORDS ARE SOMETHING ELSE* by David Albahari about his growing up in Zemun and I find the links on Facebook to pages about Zemun... the place exists as more than a street that I walk down... bright sunny day, warm, late April... hot in the bus and not remembering how I find the bus or which stop: but hot in the bus with windows that did not open—I know to be left off in the front of some sort of restaurant, which is closed and then I am to walk along the wide street I have walked along: individual houses set behind low walls, much overgrown front and back areas, and so walking along with a piece of paper on which Lidia's mother must have written an address and finding a house in which as far I can tell no one is now living and a man stops me as I come from the back of the property having looked to see if there is another entrance and I try to speak to him and saying Toshko, showing him the address and *ELENA* block lettered in Bulgarian by possibly and he nods his head both yes and no and I say the Bulgarian word *mykata* to describe Elena, Toshko's mother, and hope the word is understandable in Serbian and *sin* which again I am not sure if I am saying it correctly as the word for *son* in Bulgarian which again I have always heard as *sin* though the man puts his hand somewhere to indicate height but it's not the height of a boy but of someone taller than the short man who is telling me this… in the May, 1973… Toshko is no longer a little boy sitting on the edge of his mother's and his bed in Sofia but the man waves his arm as if they have gone away and he says the word *politzia* and has to say no more but then pats me on the shoulder in a way telling me everything is okay and as the saying goes:

For the life of me.

I cannot tell you how I am now sitting in a large room, a wall almost all made of glass against which shelves are arranged and on which pots of cacti are placed row upon row, some flowering… and the man is a lawyer who speaks *a little English* as does Toshko now though his mother does not and I understand this man is a lawyer and he is helping them with their problem, a kind man who Medy of all people found though she is in Sofia, found by way of sending money with someone who she can trust.

But Toshko tells me they say there is no worry now, something will work out...

Toshko and his mother left Bulgaria and the police have been around to ask his mother if she knows where they had gone and why they are not in Bulgaria: did they take her for being stupid, but she says nothing and nothing is all they will get from her, and all the good it did anyone, for Elena to go off to find a man to marry her and take her out of Yugoslavia.

I try to find Toshko in Beograd: but the bottles of beer from a kiosk at the open market, down the street from the Astoria, according to the receipt preserved for.... pivo, half litre bottles, brown glass, standing near an unpainted stall and aware of mud, being careful not to slip...

Are you drinking then?

Toshko says, in memory, I was going with him to where he is living with his mother, he knows the English word gypsy and says not to say tsygina... I'm not sure if it is a polite word or close to *nigger*, which it might have been or it could have been Toshko and his mother didn't want these people... they are *these people*... if you get the drift of what I am writing, in spite of... that I know some words in Bulgarian and to know the word for gypsy was to let them know I knew what most Bulgarians thought of gypsies but they are the only people who didn't care about the communists and for whatever reason, it is never more than a shrug of the shoulders why they should have given them shelter for many months after, though I know they put up with whatever regime is out there, as they thought of the place beyond where they are living at the moment:

HERE IS THE STORY

Somehow Toshko and his mother are picked up by the police in Zemun and quickly put on the train to be taken back to Bulgaria… near the Bulgarian border the train is of necessity going along very slowly as it is in the mountains.

Don't ask me how they know where to jump, but jump they do and make their way to a monastery—Elena crosses herself in the Orthodox manner three times—which shelters them and sending them on their way to where Toshko is taking me in the dark and would bring me back as you wouldn't know how to get back from what seems almost like caves though from the outside they are like cottages but once inside, the room is enclosed by and at the same time somehow we are inside huge bundles of clothes or something or other, suitcases of various sizes, round things wrapped in newspaper and tied with strips of cloth, piles of shoes arranged by size from baby to adult boots, all worn and creased by dirt, two skinny beds more like pallets forced into the heaps of… and there is a table with bottles and beer and a large bottle of Coca Cola for our American guest, and pieces of grilled meat and pickled red peppers and Toshko is asking: I hope he is asking what it is like in New York? how is Lidia?

<I had to put this here as a means of identifying my fake memory of what had happened: never did Toshko refer to Lidia by any other name than Lidi, which I have always

146

thought the name of a prostitute or lady of loose virtue from the Westerns, so I insist upon>

How do you like Beograd? You see Lidi, as he calls her, Is Lidi happy?

Lidia who he only knows, really, as his mother's sister but she is so many years younger than her sister, so Toshko is closer in years to who might have been an older sister... so a certain complexity, nothing unusual though the adventure seems so matter of fact, nothing more than what happens what you have to do when something happens what are they going to do: they are not going back to Bulgaria.

As we sit at the table people came and went... darkish people who smile and how imprecise and Toshko with his dark hair and large brown eyes, wanting but without enough words to tell me what he wants and and I know it is probably impossible to remain true to what remains and yet to indicate the room, that cave and I feel them looking to me, towards me, up to me for some sort of solution and maybe just my being there is the beginning though I have nothing to offer, nothing, except I had been in Sofia, I have married in the marriage palace, they see us off at the Sofia station, suddenly very hot with too many suitcases... just before Easter, one year, once, how do you wave back when you are leaving one life for... as we entrain—as in the old novels—for London by way of Venice, Paris, London... Toshko is seen in the proverbial corner, a hand raised, another hand against the sun, his mother crying... Medy crying...

THE SEVENTH IS THE TOLL-HOUSE OF COVETNESS

-73-

It is winter in Vienna. Harittena is in Sofia…

I walk around the winter streets always aware of Adolf Hitler walking along the Ringstrasse before what becomes World War One, by the Opera, by the Burg Theatre, maybe going into the *Kunsthistorisches* Museum… the chill, deeper than even in Sofia and surely colder then for this man, living in what are always described as flop houses, while I have a room with bed, chair, wardrobe, tiny window: a cell almost but as the plane flew from Sofia in the afternoon it is now night and at the airport, finding it on a listing, somehow to it, who knows where, now, no lobby… and next walking to somewhere and when I get to the office where someone tells someone who sends Medy an address: where Toshko and his mother would be… but as in that dream of travel, I am walking and walking along wide streets and avenues, trams going by in the middle, cobbled streets of… and I remember a massive building with no evident entrance way: a wall as to the sky since it is hard to lift the eyes from the pavement, making me feel *that* small and hearing my name… you know, what I mean, not knowing for sure anyone here, me, this guy mourning now the death of my parents, the death of, where is Melinda?, Harittena turns forever away on *Plastat Lenin*:::::::::::::::::: did not AH walk around mourning, knowing he has been cheated at the art

148

academy: we all know how to treasure our resentments: that constant gold in our pockets....

Speak for yourself, [a statement from an unknown voice] if you had learned more than how to count in German when you took some classes in Dublin at the Germany embassy on Merrion Square...

So, Toshko is calling my name and I have someone to go with into a café I have not been able to find, when later with Ruth back in Vienna: heavy crimson and black drapes about the entranceway, so you slide the palm of the your hand at the edge where the two drapes overlap and they slip back closing yourself and Toshko inside, finding two chairs against the wall, a mirrored wall which when turning to see the face looking at us from across the way with their backs to the large windows, beyond which people continue to walk along, we sit next to each other, which is probably a problem but no one says anything and Toshko knows how to order in German, unlike myself and I have a beer and some sort of cream cake... he is drinking Coca Cola and wants to look through the newspapers attached to wood reading frames, looking at the pictures.

Toshko, a kid, looking at pictures of cars and animals...

You can come to the camp, stay there New Year's night, leave your stuff at the hotel, you won't be able to get the bag over the wall, you can stay with me and my mother in our barrack, you can't go through the front gate, no one does, they go over the wall, you can see the path, the guards can see the path, no one says anything, why should they, we are not criminals, there are criminals, you have to be careful, we are all waiting, waiting, some people wait a long time, some people wait a short time, no one knows why, we have all sorts of people, from many countries, you do nothing all day, you fill out forms, you go to offices, you do this, you do that, things take time…

As long as you have money you could sit in any cafe you want. Your money is as good as anyone's. They give you an allowance. Some people spend their allowance on the first day. Better to have a good time at least once in the month than dribble it away for 30 days. We can go out there tonight, Toshko says and we do.

To Traiskirchen near Baden by Wien…

He leads me around the walled camp and sure enough as a letter writer might put it… the snow is stamped down and over the wall we go across a lawn following the footsteps, many footsteps, well traversed and Elena is sitting in a large bare room that could have held more than just Toshko and his mother, larger than their room in Sofia.

In the barracks, row after row of these long buildings with a long central corridor and rooms down either one side or on both sides of the corridor. This is a small barracks. There is a barracks for single men, for single women, barracks for people with children.

We are all mixed up here, in the next room a father and son from Romania, on the other side a mother and two children from Croatia, they say, you have to be careful of them, and across the hall some people from Poland…

People usually don't make it here all the way from the Soviet Union, it is too far away, I met a boy from Ukraine.

There are Indian people who have lived in Africa and then they were told to leave. It is sad to see people in Indian clothes—in the snow, they have never seen snow, they don't like snow, I want to ask them what snow is like, it would be interesting to hear them describe the feeling of snow, the look of snow.

-102-

The Sixteenth is the Toll-House of Lust

Writing about what I don't know and about what is not remaining.

Ignorant, but always within my name, the dumb ox, I am always saying.

151

Waiting for the rain of broken bottles, that's what someone calls it on Christmas and they tell my mother there would be another storm on the eve of New Year. People have been saving their bottles, they used some of them on Christmas, waiting and Toshko is telling me how they had gotten to the camp...

                      eventually my mother meets someone who knows someone who has passports we can borrow and which we are to give back to someone in Austria... it sounds... but late at night we sit in the middle of the bus and at one or two in the morning, the Yugoslav border guards don't really look... carefully, and all the pictures look alike... they don't care... it's just a job and if you were meant to get caught it is arranged so no matter what you have paid, you will be caught but nothing happens and we got to Vienna on the bus and there's an office you go to and they give you tickets to come here

                    what I didn't understand then or now: where did the money come from; is T's mother doing things that... but like Medy she now wears a cross on a gold chain and crosses herself in the Orthodox manner, as we talk or as Toshko talks telling me the story, crossing Toshko as he is speaking since he has told her what he is telling me, I am sure of that...

    and then you wait and wait

              we discover

    you don't know where you are going

no one knows where they are going

maybe some people know where they are going…

When it was Midnight: firecrackers, metal cans being banged, a bottle breaks, then silence: maybe another year… a folding bed was brought into the room from somewhere and I was told to stay there and we could leave in the morning…

Sometime, in the night I made my way to the toilet and the smell of vomit but for some reason the floor was not slick with as it had been at college back in Wisconsin on a Sunday morning.

In the morning they had pots of yogurt and slices of cucumbers from somewhere…

-93-

Linda L. Nelson, age 60 of Parishville, NY passed away unexpectedly on January 29, 2010. She was pronounced dead at the Canton-Potsdam Hospital. A memorial service will be held on Monday, February 8, 2010 at 4pm at the Trinity Episcopal Church in Potsdam, NY with Rev. Christopher Brown celebrant. Arrangements are with the Garner Funeral Home. Condolences can be sent @www. garnerfh.com. Contributions in her memory can be made to the Potsdam Humane Society.

Linda was born on July 29, 1949 in Lincoln, Nebraska to Harold T. Nelson Sr. and Rosita Sheahan. She was a graduate of Lincoln High School. She is survived by her brother Harold T. Nelson Jr. of Hawaii. She was an avid dog lover.

Linda's education from the baccalaureate onward was at the University of California, Santa Barbara. Her Master's thesis was entitled "The Relations of the Yugoslav Government in Exile with the United States Government, 1941-1944". Her areas of specialty were Modern Europe since 1715, southeastern Europe (Balkan states), women in the United States, and women in Russian literature. She was a PhD candidate in history at UC Santa Barbara, with a dissertation topic of "Nationalism and Gender Identity: The Bulgarian National Revival, Women's Consciousness, Women's Activism, 1840-1878." During her studies, she received two Dissertation Research Grants and was named Research Scholar by a board of the Bulgarian Academy of Sciences. Linda began teaching History for SUNY Potsdam in the Spring semester of 1999. Linda was a wonderfully flexible colleague, serving the Department of History through a variety of classes, and also occasionally advising students.

In addition to SUNY Potsdam, Linda held teaching positions at UC Santa Barbara, Santa Barbara City College, Moorpark College, Clarkson University, and Mississippi University for Women. During her graduate work at Santa Barbara, she was named Distinguished Teaching Assistant in the Film Studies Program. During her career, she made presentations at meetings of the Southwestern Social Science Association, the American Historical Association, and the American Association for the Advancement of Slavic Studies, and she was a manuscript reviewer for the journal Balkanistica.

Linda also shared her research findings at several campus events at higher education institutions. In 2000, she was organizer and co-presenter at a forum on our campus entitled "The Crisis in Kosovo."

-47-

I went back into Vienna and to the hotel and came back in the early evening and Toshko wants to show me Baden in the snow, he knows a place, but before that we meet in a café across from the entrance to the camp, a low ceilinged place filled with men hunched into groups, muttering would be the usual word to describe the human noise coming from the men, all men for some reason, about low tables with the nursing small cup of coffee and sometimes a small glass of clear liquid, early morning, getting ready for the next and next and next and from the day before that to one before that…

But the local train drops us in Baden, picturesque, it must be said, but the guy Toshko knew was not at the hotel restaurant where he works and no one knows where he has gone, people are like that around here, what can you expect, so we go along to this bar café club of some sort and young Austrian people look at us: you know the look: what the fuck are you doing here and I am thinking or trying to think my money's as good as theirs, and as we sit, we wait: that's what you have to put up with, Toshko says, is it like a sore thumb? I saw it in a cartoon at the film, a cat with a huge ballooned-up paw after someone hit it with a hammer, sticking up like a sore thumb… and I hear someone say: is he your American?

155

A guy, someone like Toshko, coming from Zagreb, can't go back, something happened, the police don't want me back, told me to go away, I knew what they mean, I was going away but went earlier than I thought I was going so it's okay being here where no one knows when they will be going... a skinny dark kid like Toshko, maybe a few years older... they don't want me in The States and Australia is too far away so I have hopes for Canada... there is someone here from South Africa telling us about what you can do there, but I don't want to do what they want you to do there...so, Canada is a nice place to think about...

Toshko's friend has better luck with the waiter and the friend is telling Toshko you just have to let money do the talking and money is the only thing a waiter cares about... he knows his customers don't want us here but I told him... and he didn't want broken glasses, how easy it is to hear broken glass!

Toshko would go to New York if Lidia would ask him to come. His mother will go to Australia, that was becoming clear... Toshko has problems with this man but his mother always has a man in her life and each one of them took something and when there is nothing to take they leave. She didn't see it that way, she tells Toshko, and some people learn in different ways, it depends on the person doing the learning.

This man is going to Australia and she is going with him. She would marry him to go to Australia. He is a man—that is all I can tell—Toshko says and laughs, but I am not telling you anything at all, but it sounds like I am telling you something. My mother likes this man, he is a little like my mother's father who you never met. He is a short man who is good with plants—that is my grandfather—he lives in the mountains outside Sofia, he was never bad to me or my mother but my mother's mother doesn't let anyone talk about this man. He is a drunk but now is not a drunk. I don't know how that can happen. He's my grandfather, you know. No one takes after him. He is just there and has a new wife and new children.

Toshko's friend buys a round of beers and then I buy a round of beers and I am ready to head back to the camp, but Toshko's friend has bought our listening to him.

-104-

Toshko would go to the US.

He will have a job in an optical supply company.

He would be promoted and told he has a future with the company.

He will hear about Unemployment Compensation for people who don't have jobs.

He will quit his job.

He will have to go on welfare thanks to Dick Bergin.

He will have a CETA job counting garbage trucks as they leave and then as they come back at the end of the shift.

He will meet a French banker who will marry him.

He will have his welfare case placed on hold as he is moving to Zurich.

He will move with the banker back to New York and

then to Paris.

He will fall into companionship with Bulgarians who tell him and he believes this that his banker wife is "ripping me off".

He will try to hit his banker wife who will divorce him with a cash settlement from her since she can't make him homeless.

He will go to New York, he will go to Australia, he will go to New York, he will go back to Bulgaria, he will have returned to Bulgaria. There will be something about a cell phone deal gone wrong.

STILL ON THE JOURNEY—BETWEEN WHO KNOWS WHAT TOLL-HOUSE—ABJURING THE FOOLISHNESS OF PAST PRESENT FUTURE TO SQUAT IN *NOIA*, BYRON'S AWFUL YAWN, ENNUI, TEDIUM, PEDESTRIAN CATASTROPHIC HEIDEGGERIAN BOREDOM: I know I know: the pretention yet

-104-

Toshko shall meet us at restaurant Hugo on Vitosha Boulevard in Sofia.

Toshko wants me to meet his friends.

I want you to meet my friends. You will really like them. You will see you will like them.

Toshko has maybe three teeth in his head and now talks barely opening his mouth... things have been tough, really hard, he doesn't have the number you need for social security or something like that in Bulgaria, still, he has been working, like they say, he remembers in New York, off the books and gets paid under the table, his friends go to Greece and buy stuff cheap to sell in small towns in Bulgaria, you can get really hung up sometimes, when things get bad—they do get bad—really bad, but my friends are really good guys and we help each other, they gave me a cell phone so I can stay in touch, but we can't live in Sofia... it is too expensive, like it is in New York I remember, but here we help each other:

I want to remember Toshko who seems to always have a pretty girl friend and then another one and something would happen—things are always happening to him—things that he couldn't explain—that just happen—she bugs me—he bugs her—we can't work it out—... he ends up living in a small place next to the Hell's Angels on East Third Street, they are really cool, he is always saying, when he is in that rock group NUMBERS, remember that.. playing bass as I remember.. Richie tells me—you remember Richie?—I wonder what's going on with Richie?— keep your mouth closed when I play as I have my mouth open when I play and we play a couple of gigs and things happen, I don't know what happens, that is a long time ago...

I want to remember Toshko without having to think of him as a dead guy, but at least I did not have to cross his name out in my address book: yet, since he is still among the living though it is unclear or maybe it is something I have to investigate: can the soul leave the body before it dies and goes on the journey… for the Biblically expansive forty days… stopping at the various way stations, I thought, could only be reached after the soul had left the body, but surely that is such a

limiting idea… sitting there downstairs in HUGO I know I am talking to Toshko but *he* is not sitting there next to me, is it possible to understand this without recourse to a language demanding the suspension of doubt when skepticism is the defining motor of each and every step now taken and this man whose aged face, and nearly toothless mouth recalls dimly the person in Vienna, in Beograd, in New York City: everyone has gone to a reunion and we see the remains of the young person there before our eyes: that instantaneous exercise in comparison and contrast.

Out in Patchogue they make up three inch buttons which display our faces from,20, then 30, then 40 and soon to be 50 years before staring in black and white right in front of us pinned to the chest of what remains but here in HUGO where there are too many waitresses and way too many managers it seems for the few customers but that is a familiar feeling in Sofia where most of the restaurants and cafes have other businesses than serving up food and drink: don't have the time to tell you why I asked to meet you here, but it's okay, Toshko is saying, but business has been very very slow and this guy got sick and that slows things down but there is something big coming along, I can feel it, you know what I mean, you can feel something and now is as good as anytime: how's New York?

I am telling him the building where he lived is still there next to the Hell's Angels and he is saying it is cool to live next door, they never bother anybody and do you go out to music, and I said I didn't anymore, all the old places have closed which is always the case and as you get older you don't know where to go and he says he didn't go out in Sofia because he didn't live in the city center but way out and it is hard to get into the city but he likes to get into the city but things have changed a lot and you can't get used to anything before it is rubbed away from you, do you have that feeling and Piret is looking at Toshko as if he had stepped off the line at the Catholic Worker, which I understand but she didn't have the picture of the little boy over there, off Botev

Boulevard, in that room and in Yugoslavia as it is then called and then in Vienna: how I wish I could go back to Vienna, but it wasn't there when I went that other time and now Toshko is about to walk out of the restaurant as he has things to do and can't miss the train or the bus, it is unclear how he is getting back to where he is staying, where there is neither phone nor internet so I guess I'll see you when.... he says.

See you, when I say, take care of yourself, I hear myself saying it and can't account for the words or voice though I can hear Toshko saying I just need a break, some sort of lead, do you have any idea, you know what it is like, man, it's real hard now if you don't know somebody and my friends I want you to meet my friends you'll really like them but they got hard lives to get on with and we are just trying to get by, you know what I mean, man, it's harder than it has ever been and I missed my chances and then they don't come around: I just need a break, a job, some sort of real job.

-104-

NEWS FLASH. The first real snow flurries of the winter. Of course Toshko is there in Bulgaria and there has been snow both in the mountains where he is living and in Sofia.

I realize I did know where one of those toll-houses was or is still located in Sofia, on the way out to the district Nadeshda. It is a tiny *skara biera* place on the south side of this very long road down the middle of which the tram

162

goes. There are five or six tables in one room and through a sort of window you can order *kebabchita* and a bottle of beer. The *kebabchita* is served on aluminum plates with an aluminum fork that is stuck into a piece of bread, laid on top of four *kebabchita* and not touching the little puddle of tomato sauce and finely chopped onions, and sometimes there are white beans, but on the night I am thinking about there are no white beans and I have to straighten out the tines of the fork.

Although Linda Nelson is passed on from this world, she rocked. Yeah she spoke fast and her outlines were sometimes confusing but she still knew her subject very well and was without a doubt the kindest person on the planet. I will always miss her.

Lidia and I are alone in the place and have gotten off the tram a few stops before the one for Yordan Lutibrodski where she lives with her mother. There are three people in the little room beyond where you pay and pick up the plates. A large man with a dirty white shirt and black vest. A huge man with huge hands. Craters instead of pores on the sides of his nose. How many more details? He could pick me up and break me like a match with one hand. Because of the way the window is constructed he has to bend over to talk to the customer, to take the money and give out the plates. The radio is on and it sounds like long lists of numbers are being recited. One could see two women moving around behind him preparing the food though obviously as we are the only customers this couldn't account for all their actions which seemed so exaggerated.

There is one light bulb hanging from a cord nailed to the middle of the ceiling. We sit opposite each other at the blonde wood tables on wooden stools that had soft leather like cover seats. Lidia isn't hungry, though she is cold: I am, she is saying, always cold here from September to May. I have always been cold and the teacher always yells at me that I am not supposed to wear a sweater over my school uniform. Every other week one of the teachers sends me to the school director who warns me and I go back to the classroom. Nothing happens, nothing changes… that man would like to hurt you but he won't and he won't because no reason. You will never understand any of this. Why is this room so cold? Why are there so many people in the kitchen, why is everything so ugly? We are not staying here. Medy doesn't want me to stay here. We have always been thinking about how to go away.

I eat the *kebabchita* and drink the beer. There are days when there are no *kebabchita* available but for some reason says, this place always has them, for some reason, it is never for any reason.

One could not imagine what this place looked like before since it did not seem to have a before or an after. We are just sitting there. Nothing will stop me from leaving. Nothing.

I seem to think this is when Lidia tells me she is not having any baby, no matter what. The day when I did not become a father. I have been to the American Embassy library and have brought along a record by Lightning Hopkins so we can listen to American music and I have a book explaining Jackson Pollock. I read in a low voice the back of the album cover about Lightning Hopkins and obviously I don't have it here in front of me—so remote from that *skar biera* place: Get off of my toe, he is singing and I am trying to explain what the line meant… get back, he is saying, and he picks out his toe as where people always step where they are not supposed to and they are always trying to get too close and he just wants to sing his song. It's like the life here in Bulgaria, I say or she says. People are always stepping on your toe.

So feel the cold, hear those numbers being recited on the radio, watch the man looking out from the window to see if we are finished with the plate. He couldn't understand why there is only one plate: Lidia didn't want to eat those things. They are nothing special for me. She opens the book on Pollock and there is a fold out of what I came to know was the painting *Blue Poles*. Lidia is saying: this is the life or did she say, life is this? And that man is just staring at us. He has probably never seen a book out of which pages folded… or who knows why he is looking. I am obviously a foreigner and Lidia is obviously a Bulgarian, a *Sofianka*, she will tell me, he is probably a peasant who has been moved to the city or was allowed to slip into the city because he knew someone, but I am born here.

We do not have enough words between us so I could describe a short film I saw in Patchogue about a man who I guess was supposed to be Pollock who spread paint across these great sheets of plywood and then cut them up with an electric hand saw and a guy flew in on a seaplane that lands on the lake. We see him looking over the "paintings" weighing the merits of each one and then piling all of them into the plane and the next we see of them they are on the walls of a gallery of a museum in New York City and people are talking about them and pointing in a knowing way. The last scene is the painter counting money back in Maine, I take it to be.

I feel warm for a moment from the eating and then we face the walking along the avenue for the turn into Yordan Lutibrodski and then the long walk along that street to where I am living in the winter along with her mother, who comes in later.

The Fourteenth is the Toll-House of Murder

Each day of the winter makes the street longer and longer and while the sidewalks are made of nicely fitted paving stones the streets are mud, in some cases deeply rutted and with the cold frozen and hard to walk across... it takes Medy a long time to get home as she is afraid of falling as is Lidia and no one will come to your help because you are supposed to know better than to fall.

In the house of three rooms: a small entrance way up one step from the little yard behind a board fence into a small room with a bed built into a low bookcase and display cabinet and next to that a tall metal indoor heating stove and sitting on the bed which is a sort of hard sofa during the day you can look at two doors: to the left into a small kitchen where there is a sink and some sort of stove, for sure a hot plate and a cabinet in which some dishes and pans are piled... laundry hung from cords near the ceiling. If you go into the door to your right that is the largest room: mostly big cabinets on top of which are piles of many parcels wrapped in rugs. In the center of the room under a bare light bulb a large table covered with a lace cloth... against the far wall another sleeping compartment to which eventually Lidia and I move after I came back to Bulgaria and where we awoke into the cold room as there is neither stove nor electric heater... burrowed deep under the covers...

The domestic arrangements but please no harking back, no thinking this is in anyway more interesting than years later...

I try to find the street on the map but it seems to have vanished or been transformed or the name is changed and nothing remains, as gone as anything is gone, as gone as soon all of this will be gone.

—Speak for yourself, do allow your reader to follow in the mind's eye where you are taking this person... another cold station, where it is finally understood that the child to be had to die.

There will be no washing of the hands, that single spigot of cold water passing from the brass fixture through a bit of rubber tubing.

There will be screaming, there will be drinking one glass ok rakia, one glass of gin and then a mixture of some sort of liquid into which pepper had been ground along with salt and other spices. Medy gives Lidia a pan into which to throw up, that's what she is supposed to do... if she wants to be free of what is growing inside her body.

What and if.

Now, a quick recap of the game so far…

What I learn in the camp: people had been saving bottles of liquor for weeks for a magnificent drunk on New Year's Eve, the first out in the freedom, even if it is inside the waiting…

They don't know where they are going.

Did anyone know where they are going, I probably say…

But you are American, someone says in a very clear piercing English…

There are no classes, nothing to do, no preparation for where you might be going. You just wait to see who would take you.

In Belgrade I stay at a hotel near the station… how did I know where Toshko lives… I have an address in Zemun and go walking around there and am told to go somewhere and then I am met and taken to a village on the outskirts were they are hiding out…

Six months later: meeting Toshko at the end of December in a grand café in Vienna—eating cream cakes and drinking do I even dare to remember what is drunk that New Year's—and being taken by him out to the refugee camp in Traiskirchen to celebrate the New Year's which will send the boy to New York and his mother to Australia.

I would travel out the year spending the money from my father's death.

Thirty-seven years later—who is keeping track of the

years—in restaurant Hugo in Sofia on Vitosha Boulevard, downstairs: the years remove most of Toshko's teeth and he now has eye glasses, the dark hair has grey in it: I want you to meet my friends, he says, I want you to meet my friends, I want you to meet them

I cannot find on the Sofia maps where I am living when I am first here with Lidia…

My father knows less and less after my mother dies and I think then and I probably still believe he is no longer really among the living and then he is actually dead and…

This addled sort of thinking.

Toshko is here sitting next to me in HUGO.

Why did he want us in a place like this?

Piret says to put it on the card and didn't want to see Toshko again. He is in a bad way and nothing good is happening in his life.

Of course I am remembering: No knowledge, no wisdom came from your mouth, I want Harittena to tell me. I want her to rebuke, tell me to shut up, tell me just how stupid I have been, tell me to shut the fuck up, tell me to put a cork in the bottle, put a cork in your mouth before they put a cork up your ass and stick you into the earth…

But none of that is to happen.

In Baden, the kids play us in the café. They know Toshko and his friend are from the camp. They didn't like him. We drink and Toshko is saying: they tempt us to come here and then they give you nothing or maybe it is his friend who says this, being more aware of the world, and they make you turn to doing things you wouldn't do, that's for sure, the guy is saying and these Austrians so superior to everything and still they make money off of us because they wouldn't have this camp here if it didn't make money for someone and Toshko, just let his hand move quickly back and forth—no way man, just don't interfere with my buzz, is that the word, my buzz, is that how you say it?

You are getting ready for New York. But it won't be as nice as this in New York, you got to understand.

It will not be in Austria, his friend says. They don't want me in the US, I am going to Sweden, I hope.

Milosz recalled, Tadeusz Borowski smiled contemptuously at mental speculation for he remembered seeing philosophers fighting over garbage in the camps.

Toshko has to be off. Piret and I are going to go driving around in the country. We would have a little party before we go back to New York. I hope you can come.

I want you to meet my friends. There is only one bus in the afternoon.

I'll call you. Piret goes back to the apartment on *Ul. Vasil Kolarov*. I turned and went toward the culture palace there at the end of Vitosha…

-82-

I am a man, as I walk about the city for Maple Vail… walking down Sixth Avenue. I would sit under the statue of Horace Greeley and feel the urge to GO WEST, YOUNG

MAN, while that something inside is talking about GONE EAST,

> **Linda Nelson** seems to know her stuff. However, the class is very dull, even for those people interested in History. Every class we have a lecture, in which you write about 5-7 pages of notes. Your hand wants to fall off by the end of the class.

-82-

THOMAS MCGONIGLE WALKING ON VITOSHA BOULEVARD

Yes, I know, Piret goes back to the apartment on *Ul. Solunska.* That is the name of the street now. Change is not a theory. The names are really changed. In New York people talk of Sixth Avenue when you can see on the lamp posts, Avenue of the Americas… older people talk of the IRT, the BMT, the IND subway lines. Looking across *Patriar Evtimi* at the Culture Palace in the hazy sunlight, but not crossing to walk through the park, but turning eyes taking in the KINO where I had seen KANAL one of those years… in Polish with Bulgarian subtitles… is still there but not there and still walking along Vitosha past where I live with Medy, sleep ever so briefly with Harittena, past the HUGO.. in the distance the *Sveta Nedelya* church in shadow it seems in spite of the hazy sun and the muttering: none of you know what I am seeing as I walk along… *and what is it exactly you're seeing?*

I am seeing myself walking here in 1993,

in 1984,

in 1973,

in 1990…

but who is this person walking along? Who is this person seeing the man walking along?

And still walking along Vitosha: in the distance the *Sveta Nedelya* church in shadow it seems in spite of the hazy sun and muttering: none of you walking along know what I am seeing as I walk along… *and what is it exactly you're seeing?*

Repetition as a form of hesitation.

Seeing: the Havana restaurant, the game restaurant, the arcade leading to the *advokat's dom* and a restaurant downstairs, the Russian bookstore, a Bulgarian bookstore… a photography place in front shop of the building where Medy lives in the back apartment or two rooms made into an apartment, the law courts, the history museum with the room devoted to the absence of Bulgaria, *Plastat Lenin* beyond the church or the church is in the midst of it: the tram stop and how difficult it is for Medy to hoist herself up into the car… that tram curves into the stop, wheels screeching… when you step down to your right a large restaurant that always has a band playing with a woman singer… mostly people drink but had to order some sort of food… across the way a small café frequented by students from the school of the dumb and deaf… a food store always mostly bereft of goods on the shelves… now—whatever that means—Vitosha is a pedestrian stroll with the tram running down the center and occasional taxis it seems… then cars, enough to make it seem like a major thoroughfare… is one flicking through the photographs… and so far the lack of people… but of course there are people on the streets in the summer, in the winter and what percentage can we say are now dead and what percentage are now abroad or no longer coming in to walk along Vitosha which is not even back then the most fashionable street…

Now and then. Two words, only the most melancholy of children, ever link since they are reserved for those who step over another of those lines which you are only aware of when the boat finally does sail away in old age when there is no way to…

There are photographs taken but even looking at them with the information in a few of them… the uneven paving blocks, the short skirts of the women, the faces of people the camera catches—it is a distraction from this walking along Vitosha in the present moment of memory… not a single person stopping and saying: *don't I know you*, when in fact I remember every person I meet in Sofia and I have not met anyone this time and of course I have not met any such people when I walk around in the West Village or up near Columbia when I am there a few days ago— in the moment of this writing—so why should I entertain the possibility of meeting someone as I linger on this now changing boulevard… dogs at each corner, knocked out by the heat, listless and the guys selling ice-cream are not behind their shiny bright kiosks standing as new sentinels of the change…

Faster than I can imagine the word *change* makes me

cringe. The first few times I say it and hear it, the freshness of the demand to notice a detail allows the eye to provide for observing that the policemen are no longer in their elevated stations above certain crosswalks … the ESKIMO ice cream sellers are not near the sunken passageways over from the Balkan Hotel, this now acquiring the name of the American chain now running it: in there and I am told there is no *studenski dom* or if there is one it is now closed and why are you coming in here with such a question?

A subway, I am thinking, in Sofia but it doesn't come up Vitosha as I would have thought... for me this is the center of the city: up and down I walk this boulevard, even taking the subway going out under *Stambolyski* to a far end of the city, out beyond where a railroad car is set up as a restaurant...

Every time **Linda Nelson** talks she sounds incredibly unsure of herself. The way she runs the class is utterly ridiculous (reading assignments out loud, twice). Group assignments compare to about 4th grade level (i.e. find 10 words you don't know and define them) easy, just really elementary.

-82- GALENA an introduction

As I am walking on Vitosha, I want Galena to recognize me—of this then girl, now woman, only the name remains—but with each step it seems to become both likely and unlikely I will have this wish fulfilled and not fullfilled and I can not recall if she has black hair or fair, blue eyes or green, but she did provoke Lidia, as being one of those girls who is on the look for the sort of person I am, and Lidia does not have the vocabulary to say she is on the lookout for a guy like you, but she says Galena is always looking for a man and I seem to know Galena lives off Georgi Dimitrov Boulevard, which seems impossible as Lidia knows her from school and that is on the other side of town off Botev Boulevard, but as I am stepping off the sidewalk and walking in the sun for a brief moment, in the freedom of walking in the actual street that has been stuck into my brain as full of passing cars, trucks, buses in addition to the tram, being driven without much concern for pedestrians because in Bulgaria the driver is always right and everyone knows it: if you have a car you are someone, in a fashion unlike most people, again.

Galena is probably no longer blonde as Lidia remembers her but she is unable to say more than that Galena has blonde hair and good looks, though Lidia and her mother both knew it is rare, very rare, for a good looking girl to remain like that long into her life, since the life is not easy— which is a phrase that is ever present in every conversation in Bulgaria—and not easy in particular for people like themselves *without connections* mostly but even connections can rarely stop the inevitable aging which became awful if one is away for say ten years and comes back to find the girl or the boy who is thought to be good looking in some way and meeting that person in a public place is a very tricky proposition because it is likely you would not recognize the person who you knew or know and it is far more than the little disappointments, the little shivers at the passage of time when meeting someone not seen for many years in the United States.

Galena would be in her sixties... and while there is no way to avoid using the word change... for someone like... there are only complaints most likely.

If only you could know what it is like.

I want Galena to go on about how she thought of Lidia after Lidia left Sofia. Did she for a moment try to imagine what Lidia's life is like? Medy says Galena has once come around to the kiosk but Medy did not give her the address in Dublin.

Fortunate, crosses my mind when I realize I have not to look at myself in any mirror as I walk along Vitosha. Mirrors are rare in Sofia then and now. Why remind people what they look like when they knew for sure what they look like from the tiny pieces of mirror fastened above the cold water sink in the kitchen areas of where people live, just the glimpse is enough and the tiny recollection make many a man thirsty for a *guyama* instead of a *malko mastika—guyama studeno mastika*—one of the few phrases I do know in Bulgarian but no longer do I want that so I am glad of the absence of mirrors but the memory of being caught by a reflection in a dusty store window provides a commentary of the impending end—sure of course but the ordinary then becomes more present with looking into the face caught, the nose more prominent, the eyes sinking into skull and which will be the first part of the body to be scooped out with the end: double dipping of another sort.

Is there any other way to hold on to the morbid feelings you seem to enjoy beyond the reality you inhabit is a question with no loss for an answer: my gift to be able to partially articulate... but hesitating only out of consideration as I walk up through the porch of *Sveta Nadelya* and come back on the dark side of Vitosha with the mountain to the front of me and wanting to be with Piret who might be back from her walk though I have forgotten what we are planning to do... we would be going to the mountains on another day: to Rila with Philip: but you probably already know this as it has been mentioned, I am pretty sure... only the heavenly journey of the soul, where it might begin as with the stopping at the toll-houses and naturally looking up as on my childbed I lay there in the room in the house of Furman Lane in Patchogue, looking at the model airplanes individually suspended from the ceiling by thread that gathered dust—both the thread and the planes... these tiny columns of dust as one is to be turned to ashes and then into a tiny column reaching to the heavens to stop at the B17, the Stuka, the MIG 17, the Messerschmitt, the Wright Brothers' first plane, the Spitfire, the Fokker, a Jap Zero, A Sopwith Camel, a Flying Tiger... not to try the patience or to suspend disbelief: no way to make a list of the 40 airplanes suspended from the ceiling in the child house.

And what happens to the model airplanes?

One gets older—desire to be rid of stuff, the things of childhood, comes under the fierce scrutiny blinding one to the possibility of the future when...

And no one has the nerve to set up a museum to their own childhood, saying it was like this and this and it is of no interest to me if you dare to ask what have you done with the promise or the advantages to warrant our attention to your childhood unlike the great gibbet builders with their dreams of human perfection of whom it is assumed we will be interested in every item of their snot and sputum encrusted voyage out of their mother's womb. **This paragraph is dated as between the moment of its writing and a second reading a year later Orhan Pamuk opened a museum in Istanbul dedicated to the objects that cluttered his childhood and he has written a novel which provides a narrative for this collection.**

The central courts are to my right as I turn out of the drive and part of the courts were turned into a museum once upon a time and who knows if this is still the case: in there a room is filled with books which mentioned the existence of Bulgaria as a real place during the long years of the Turkish yoke.

To exist only as a mention in a book. A territory outlined on maps that look peculiar to the modern eye, with monsters safely relegated to parts unknown. Now they are mapping out the last unknown territory, as a publicist might say, to launch a book in brain studies.

THE EIGHTEENTH IS THE
TOLL-HOUSE OF SODOMY

-48-

VISITING RILA   (incidents of tourism)

f.

Piret and I drive with Philip to Rila.

Rila is the national monastery. It is a required place on the tourist route.

Then Medy doesn't trust the departure and arrival announcements on the bus station wall. She doesn't trust what the men or women in the ticket booths say. She bought the tickets someplace other than in the bus station. I am to follow behind her as we walk around in the yard where the buses are filling with passengers and eventually she finds the bus to take us to Rila.

In the middle of a long stretch of road the bus simply stops and we wait for a couple of hours for another bus to come along. All the occupants of what we can call our bus pile on to that bus and we proceed to Rila.

We walk around the large courtyard and notice the forest covered hillsides. An old monk gives Medy a photograph of himself and shows us what I take to be the grave of Tsar Boris... I am not sure about this... one of those details... and then Medy arranges for photographs to be taken of the two of us standing in the courtyard.

We go upstairs and Medy arranges for me to sit on the chair which Ivan Vazov has sat in when he stayed at Rila.

I am a writer, she tells the monk and the monk is pleased with my wanting to sit on the chair.

We walk out of the monastery and go to our right to look for some place to eat.

We walk along what feels like a little valley.

I look into the smaller ossarium where the bones of the dead are stored which have been dug up to make room for the newly dead.

Medy finds a little *skara biera* place and we eat *kebabchita* and I have a beer and Medy drinks from her bottle of monastery well water.

You must understand Medy and I have no language in common other than her daughter in the United States.

As is said, the bus ride back to Sofia is uneventful.

A few days later photographs arrive. Such a photograph is unimaginable now. I am not sure why. The promise has gone out of me… well, closer to the final promise.

h   an incident

Philip is not a careful driver but he is concerned that Piret and I listen to a Mozart opera as we are being driven to Rila. He seems to be rushing from somewhere to nowhere and back to wherever it is he is going to and I want Piret in the front seat to see where we are going.

Really now, do we see where we are going, as if I knew where we're going beyond the destination of Rila.

But back in Sofia after that, what is it, Piret asks.

We go to Rila.

We go to Blagoevgrad.

We are driven by Philip. We have a meal with him. We take pictures at Rila and at the American University in Blagovegrad which has a startling resemblance to Pernik… but how can I tell you that? You are there too—Piret would be saying—but you never get beyond finding that wall painting for the departure of your soul. A map, you say, something you are looking for and how are you to make it available, to make it visible in a world.

And your voice would trail off because you know I just want to fuck the guy who is driving. You want him to bend me over the front of the car and pull down my pants and fuck me for all he is worth and he claims and I believe him—according to himself—to have had many many girls during his time, during the time especially of the communism before he is married and I am sure after because a man doesn't stop or maybe I would just like to suck his dick because I am sure he has a big one—you never saw it did you? do you think it's circumcised? do you think it's long and fat? do you think he likes me? why doesn't he respond to me? what is the matter with me?, what is the matter with him? and you didn't know how to respond to these questions even though you knew the questions themselves were exciting to me and I would then analyze how your answers would change from time to time and you are still able to shock me when you tell me about the guy in the Bambouk making some sort of gesture that he wants to suck your dick.

Piret read this from a homosexual guide to Sofia.

The toilets in the NDK underpass shut at 9pm on week-days and 6pm during the weekend. The best time is lunch or after work but it is almost certain that you will find action there at any point in the day. *Cruising Info/ Tips:- Compared to the rest of the public cruising spots in Sofia, most of which are now defunct, this is the place to be. An entrance charge of 0.40 stotinki applies at the door of the washroom where friendly old cleaning ladies sit all day. They are perfectly aware of what goes on inside but are totally fine with it and some are even good friends with the regular cruisers. The toilet area itself is quite damp and in places even dirty but the buzz and the sex make it all worth-while. The best thing about this place is that the crowd is so varied. You get young and fit gymnast types, old pensioners, office types in smart suits, guys from the deep province.... basically you get all sorts, but of course nothing is set in stone.

K incident

Philip leaves us off at the end Vitosha where it crosses *Patriarch Evtimi* since he is going somewhere. It makes Piret crazy as she says because he never says what he is going to do and he just has to be going somewhere and you saw him talking in that intimate fashion of his with a younger woman on *Slaveikov* and you think he touched her upper arm in some fashion but you couldn't be sure and you could tell the woman is clearly interested in Philip and she says something to his ear in the way politicians and actresses say things when they know people are possibly watching them and while it could have been nothing more than did he think it's going to rain it, could have been reminding him she had really enjoyed the good fucking he has given her a few hours ago and she is looking for him to rush over after he sees his American guests as she wants to suck his dick so he will scream to heaven even for her to stop as the pleasure is going to be so intense when I am sucking your dick and I put my finger up your ass and you tell me to keep it there and wiggle and tell me to keep my lips over the head of the penis and not to let go and you should use your tongue, go on use your tongue, are you sure she is talking to him like that… and I say I don't know if she has enough time to say everything you think she should be saying but I guess it is possible if she is quick with the words but re-member this is just a girl with long dark hair and she is thin and a little taller than Philip and I don't think she has big tits because I know that is the next thing you are going to ask is, did she have big tits? And I will have to say I didn't notice and I didn't see if they are bigger than yours as that's always the next question.

The Fourth is the Toll-House of Gluttony

-47-

The shops on Vitosha are not very interesting: dress stores, cell phone stores, bars, restaurants but nothing re-ally to detail or detain the eyes as a traveler might write home and only you have to keep walking since there are no benches and the trams came by and at the corners taxis wait and guys are hanging around… but just the very blandness of the moment right now… so that even in thinking back… back to the rooms on Solunska and Piret didn't have much interest in doing much of anything as something has come over her, really come over her and it didn't lift even when we had come back from the Black Sea and been to Rila…

One has to confuse the time a little, and even that confusion is more a shuffling of blank pages back and forth, but allow for the scratches… at least there has been no scene setting, no preparing for the revelation and once you have gotten to that point you never have to come back… and in fact the revelation was there back some pages…

> **Linda Nelson** needs to not be so self-involved. I took a summer class and she ****ed the whole time about being there. I felt the need to inform her that it was HER choice to teach that course! Maybe she should choose a new profession!

Bulgaria has not scratched Piret but Philip has and that provides the sadness even I could see in Piret's eyes. The poor girl who is happy but can't have what she wants so she is miserable beyond words, as is said in the song.

Though we are still in Vitosha and I am trying to make my way into the shops and recall the strangeness of spelling out the Cyrillic and then the allusive meaning without looking into the shops to see what is being sold. The photography shops always hold me, as when Harittena is picking up photographs at a little kiosk on *Rakovski* and I did ask her if she has one to spare so I can here include it and ask for it to be placed in my coffin to be burned or buried with me so the children will not have to wonder who this obviously now dead person has been in your father's or our father's life, as I have done when in cleaning out the basement on Grandview Avenue in Menasha, Wisconsin when my parents are leaving their exile in northern Wisconsin for what turned out to be a very temporary lodging in Upstate New York, about a hundred miles from The City, asking my father as I look through the albums when he did have hair on his head: Oh, she is from before I met your mother. She died.

So, the signs seen in magnified form: a café, signs for the upcoming fortieth anniversary of 9 IX 1944, the Moskovichs and the Ladas and the Skodas and the Fiats lining the streets demonstating a certain amount of change... but the boulevard is lined with trees sheltering pedestrians from the sun: a girl in a summer dress, wide flowing skirt, swaying as she walks, a man in an open collared short sleeved white shirt... the people walk with a sure step as they are in the capitol it could be said, they are city people either by birth or moving there, but city people... as even in New York: a certain step of authority.

Not to go back to the rooms and find Piret napping, curled into herself as sometimes things became just too much: why doesn't he like me, being said when I ask her what is the matter. She hopes for something to happen this time as we drive to and from Rila. Why didn't it happen, what is the matter with me, what is the matter with him...

I am not exactly sure, even on the written page who Piret asks this question of as I am still walking along on Vitosha, alone since I have not been here with Lidia though I have been walking here with Harittena into that one cold snowy night… a walk from the deaf people's café on *Plastat Lenin*… how lucky for you she lives here in the center, she is saying: how I wish to live in the center but it is impossible.

It is impossible. A simple phrase that echoes in every Bulgarian conversation if I dare to make general what I hear.

It is impossible.

Ne e vuzmozhno.

If I know for sure. In New York, have I ever heard such a sentence?

But I think that night as we walk along Vitosha the Havana Café seems full and there is a man at the entrance who seems … Harittena didn't want to suggest our entrance and while I am not a *negatif*, and we both know what happens when a Bulgarian woman goes walking with a *negatif* she might be saying to herself I am walking along with a little pot of gold disguised as this *negatif* and that is what you are really jealous of and he gets paid in dollars to be here a representative of his oppressed peoples in Africa and when he goes home he will be taking me back with him in a Mercedes which will be at the dock waiting for him to drive off into his future unlike you slobs—a sudden injunction of a Brooklyn accent in my telling of Harittena's understanding of what happened when *negatifs* went walking with Bulgarian girls and the bouncer at the Havana looks like he has had his fill and this is a night when even the…

However these words only distort what happens when walking along Vitosha and another person will start to tell you about another café they go to and what you experience is not like what he experiences and either you are too young or too old and fashion changes with the leaves...

Tan eyes to die for, Michael Newman could have written in a men's magazine and while I have forgotten the story I do think he writes, *violet eyes to die for...* but I am not to die for Harittina and those faces: Six girls and young women... strollers will look at those pictures as if they are strangers who they vaguely remember and how they all are crazy to find a fashion magazine from the West as each one of them knows a tailor who can make anything they could bring to him, if they have the material and each one of them probably, one hopes, has a connection to someone who knows someone who can get the cloth as close to the one in the photograph and I am outlining

how the days pass from the moment of them posing for the photographer and to sometime in another year when the tailors have mostly disappeared—just like that—and now the girls or young women would not allow their pictures to be taken and placed on display unless there is an agreement as to… no one has a right to my face except me, when I look in the mirror at night or in the morning when I see it reflected in the lust of my husband or boyfriend…

-58-

TOSHKO RE-APPEARS

Now, sadly, there is nothing special about photographs, some people might still say, but no one even rises to the argument, no one rises to any argument except to contest just how bad things have become… and you don't know the half of it, Toshko is thinking as he is in the car coming back from Greece where I have gone with my friends I really want you to meet.

Not really aware that he Toshko learned the trade from his grandmother: buy cheap, sell, sell, sell… give people what they want and you want them coming back so make sure you give them as good a quality as you can find, it doesn't matter what you are selling: buy cheap sell high, no IOUs, no credit, cash only, always a smile for the customer, but not too broad of a smile as that might be a giveaway, and remember, even surplus smiles are worth something, to store up against the day when you ain't got any reason at all for a smile, you can pull one out of storage: crap, what crap.... I am just trying to get by and trying to make contact so I can get a real job, like you said, a job on the books and become a respectable member, you need contacts, people who know people, that's how it works, now, then, here, there, forever and ever, no matter who you are who you think you are, to be without contacts, a person who can put in more than a word, who can make the word work. That's how it is, no matter what system they have, the same thing in New York, in Australia, in France in Switzerland, and here in Bulgaria with all the old and new lessons but still, you need to know someone, my friends are loyal, we help each other but everybody got his problems, I have my problems, my mother dying knocked me out of everything, I couldn't think, I couldn't travel, I couldn't talk to anyone, I couldn't do anything, it eats you up MAN, you know what I mean, it eats you up when your mother dies, you know what I mean, Man?

We go to Greece, they have so much over there that we can sell in Bulgaria, it just requires us to get up and go and we go when we get it together but then you got to drive around in little places selling stuff, like who knows, people are holding on to money they don't have, but some people have a lot of money and you just got to find them, that's what I've learned...

The Nineteenth is the Toll-House of Heresy

Did I mention, Toshko has three teeth, maybe, in his head, and his eyes have moved further back into his skull: he is saying I am under a lot of pressure and I don't work well under a lot of pressure, it's not like the old days and something happened to my teeth and I didn't have any money but all I need to do is get my papers in order and try to make some sort of contact, that's all I am asking for, to make some sort of contact, are you sure you...

On each corner there are a few guys standing around either trying out for the role of Toshko when he is just starting out, on his way, or how he ends up. The breaks are coming their way, had been by them the other day, and you should have been here in the days when things start to change: people are throwing money at me, all around me, you could walk on a carpet of the cash and no one messes with what you are doing, but Toshko is a little late for the first round, missed another round and finds himself getting back to Bulgaria after things have tightened up and he didn't have his papers in order, and getting your papers in order takes a lot of time, only someone who has been in the business of getting his papers in order can maybe appreciate what it is like: imagine, someone swipes your wallet, steals your e-mail address and password, your birth certificate and then sets you down in a country with a rotten climate and a whole class of people with their hands out and working inside a constantly changing perimeter of two hours one morning, two hours another afternoon and then there are the inevitable misspellings, letters transposed, numbers that don't agree, so you get an inkling of the difficulty, plus taking into account those three teeth in Toshko's mouth, you begin to get the idea and it is unlikely the guys trying out for his role will be any further along the road getting the papers together as in the years since the communism people have lost the knack of moving pieces of paper and with less time in which to play along since now the pretense of working and paying have come to a sort of muddled end...

-73-

ASSEN APPEARS

But Toshko, you lose me as you walk off the boulevard and yet hoping to hold our attention and those guys are there even back then with schemes for making money which rely on the remaining differences between the people who remain on the land and those who have moved to the city... here should be inserted the list of deal makings that went on... from the boy, your dear friend, Assen, as he signs his name to a letter, who would go out to the country and show people how he could take a black and white photograph and make it into a color portrait of a mother, father, child, someone dead or loved and still alive—though hard to believe—it is like those movies in which intrepid explorers would push into the jungle with their cameras and meet opposition to picture taking because the wise man or medicine man, the guy *in the know*, is telling his followers the

little box is about to capture their souls and while the peasants didn't believe it, they did have an inkling they could be
looking at a dead person brought back to life if only for the
seconds of the first seeing of the colored "life-like" and that
was enough for them to part with levas for Assen's service
and which he performs because he knows someone who
works in a photo laboratory controlled by the boys *in the
know*, as he tells Lidia... to have the ability to bring back
the dead even if only for a few seconds is still valued in the
countryside.

> About **Linda Nelson**: first of all, way too many notes. I
> write small, but I still take at least 2 pages of notes each
> class. Out of all the notes we take, only a very small por-
> tion is tested on. For tests, you have to know EVERY-
> THING about a question, otherwise you lose points. Too
> hard of a grader. TOO many notes. Gives papers back way
> too late.

People were so alone, you can't imagine it, Assen says,
and I have never, of course, forgotten those words he has
said: we all want to bring back the dead, and we want to be
brought back ourselves after we are dead for an instant after
we are gone so as to... there would be the pause as he knew
how to tell a story, in a fashion, being a few years older...
seeing their eyes made it painful to take the easy money
they push at me, even more than I have asked for or what
we have agreed to; I didn't want to use the word peasants to
describe these people but how else to explain the difference
between me, the city person, and them, though they live in
villages, they have televisions even and soon they are tell-

ing me to wait a moment and they would rummage about in the rope-bound suitcases and inevitably pull out more pictures of the same person and want me to have them coloured but I have to tell them you can only bring a person back once but if they have the picture of another relative...

That seemed to make them angry for some reason and I quietly left... I did this in the villages around Targovishte and Strazhitsa which Lidia has told him is near where her mother is from, but it is just a coincidence of who you meet or what I remember as I am sure he mentions other towns but I have no connection to them so I don't remember their names... but people forgot their disappointment and recommend me by word of mouth after I have gone and I have a nice little business you could say with bringing back the dead for a second and finally in Strazhitsa I did take the chance and agreed to do the colouring of a second photograph of a young woman who has died since these people asked me to colour the pictures of two other people and they are from a large family and I thought I should maximize my travel, as would be said later, since I am also having a lot of expenses, it is one of those times when there are things to buy and you need cash to get the best of what is to be on sale, cash only and a little more for the person who is helping.

So I have those three pictures with me in three separate envelopes. I have looked to make sure my friend had done a good job of it. I always keep the old black and white picture in a separate envelope and I probably have them someplace as no one ever asked for the original back—the process by which the black and white picture is turned into a coloured photograph is just too complicated to explain and has nothing to do with the story—I mad\ke sure the picture of the girl is there and the two other people are old people when the pictures are taken so now they were coloured pictures of two old people.

No one ever asked me to colour a picture of a person in his or her coffin.

Well I got to the house and they are sitting in a little circle: the parents I assume of the dead girl as there is no girl who resembles her and then there are assorted old people who merge into this sort of wrinkle wrapped in black... and some other people I think but I am not sure.

I hand the mother the envelope with the picture of the girl. The picture is about the size of a piece of school composition paper—here of course American readers can insert 8 by 10... who knows what it is in the metric....

As she slides the picture out of the envelope I can see the tears form at the corners of her eyes and then as the man sitting next to her sees the picture the tears began to appear and by the time they have fully leaked out of his eyes the woman is sobbing and has grabbed the photograph close to her chest. The man holds her and a little embarrassed eases the picture from her hands which fell to her side and she leans forward and I thought she is going to fall to the floor.

The picture of the girl is on the low table. As suddenly as the tears and the sobbing began it ends. The tears are wiped away. The second has passed, the girl's moment has come and gone and now the man and woman are alone with what has happened.

The people standing about look as if they should be going and that is when I put the two envelopes with the remaining pictures on the table, you remember: the pictures of two old people... the man matter-of-factly slid the pictures out of their envelopes and for some reason they both came out of the envelopes face down and lay on the table with their backs as it were to our eyes. I never interfere with how people go about looking at their pictures.

The man leans forward and flips both of the pictures over and while I could not see the expression on each and every face in the room, I am looking at the pictures as is only natural but I could distinctly hear someone saying and now that female voice is joined by a male voice and maybe even more voices and it is a terrible jumble of curses which in English do not do justice to what is said and while I don't know how to translate all of them for you, Assen is saying, but if you combine the word whore repeated over and over again with scum and shit and fuck and ass and slut and garbage and add any others you might want to think of, that might give you an idea of what is being now shouted and shrieked and then suddenly it is silent.

No one explains what has happened. Each of the photographs is inserted into its envelope. I have learned my lesson. But what the lesson is I never have really understood. It is one of those mysteries of the villages and no one is prepared to tell me what has happened. I can imagine the girl had done something. It was unclear to me why she is dead but with the two old people they are dead because they are old people but the girl is not an old person so she must have done something or nothing.

This incident didn't interfere with business as I am often back in Strazhitsa so maybe no one talked about what happened, which is good for me and I have seen that couple who had the coloured picture of the girl made. They did not acknowledge knowing me and I guess there is no reason for them to want to remember me though of course they remember me. Do I want them to say, now we know why you resisted doing that second picture since there is only pain in the past? Wouldn't that be a profound something to take from this story? Lessons don't come easy as if lessons teach anything, somehow lessons are always out there if you know what I am trying to say. But that is a way to avoid making sense of what happened.

The Fifth Toll-House is of Laziness

-78-

Sergei Begins to Arrive as Does My Father

> **Linda Nelson's** class is probably one of the most boring classes I have ever taken. There is just no excitement. It makes me rethink being a history major...We take like 5 pages of notes every class, so it's good to have a lap top.

As Assen Is moving about in the countryside Sergei would wonder into and out of the Bambouk. He is the first guy to talk with me. I never got his full story as if that is possible and since it is a small country some stories get told over and over again and I have already told Sergei's story once before and thought that I am done with it until much much later—to add emphasis as if I am about to tell you if you stand long enough in Times Square at 42nd and Seventh you will meet everyone you have ever known in this life: that is one of the things my father tells me when I meet him when coming back from college driving through the city and meeting him for lunch... that strange handshaking meeting with his fellow workers, colleagues—*guys and gals*—he always says *gals*—he works with—who you have heard me talking about, well, here he is back on his way home from college, doesn't he look like he has just come from college... and Dad didn't have an office as it is always said he is going into the office but it is just a desk in a large room and once upon a time it might have been a real office with a tiny bronze nameplate on the door or maybe it was only on a little stand on a piece of wood on a corner of his desk:

H.A. McGonigle

I hear the names much as anyone does when someone comes home from work is telling you about people at the office: they stock the day and are gone until the next day—birthdays and then they disappear from the conversation only to reappear when a death is announced, some terrible illness or accident, **just like it was yesterday:**

We go to a gin mill—but they have very good sandwiches on Third Avenue it must have been or might it have been Lexington... one of those long bar restaurants with the steam tables along one side and the bar along the opposite side and some tables in the back... we sit at the bar though at first Dad says he wants to stand as he has been sitting all morning,,. it is good to still be able to stand… he has a glass of beer and a shot of rye, a special occasion you coming into the city, he says… stopping by on the way home from college… but I wish I was able to use a phrase like, *let's go to the gin mill.*

And somewhere in that conversation is the line about meeting everyone you have ever known at the corner of 42nd and Seventh, it is like going to those dinners in the ballroom at the Commodore Hotel, one of those things from the time in New York City when people knew which side of the sidewalk to walk on, maybe when there are bowling alleys in Times Square and all the bookstores between Broadway and Sixth Avenue… and I send my father to buy FREEDOM the Anarchist newspaper from the newsdealer on the south side of 42nd between 6th and Fifth, closer to 6th… and how he put it in a large envelope and mailed it to me…

We didn't go back up to his office, Dad says he would be home at the regular time, he has something to tie up as he always has to do and is on the 6:59 in Patchogue and I pick him up, strange seeing you there I say and he laughs… he has had a couple of beers in the bar car, it is real special you came by…

I know it is awful. He seems to age in those moments as we drive down Cedar Avenue to Furman Lane: being dressed as I now knew for his end in the parking lot in Saugerties as I have seen him at his place of work where he has been by then for more than forty years: only a desk after those forty years and he will be sent into exile in Wisconsin for a final period of employment, losing the house in Patchogue, losing everything—I am sure he knows but of course what evidence did I have for this?

The office, in the city, the train, the five days a week, getting up at 5:30 every morning, coming back at seven, the train to Hunter's Point and then the subway to Grand Central coming out at the exit at 40th and Park to just walk across the street... to the office: Johnny Vogt, Leo Walsh, John Shumaecker, Anthony Sheffler, Shelby Smith, Wells Russell, Cecilia Ruscetta, Bill Ritchie, Mildred Papera, Richard Petty, Rose O'Neill, Dorothy O'Brien, Rose Miller, Horatio Miller, D.T. McFadden, Don Lemaster, Burt Lowery, Mary Kuchman, Al Kivette, Cy Heintz, Harold Dmitrik, Jim Asinsio.

> **Linda Nelson's** class was so boring. All we did every class was take page upon page of monotonous notes. If you don't like history, this is definitely not the class for you. She made no effort to make things interesting. Tests and quizzes are all written. She also takes forever to hand things back.

Sergei is like that. He keeps coming back into the conversation. He has never left but am I the only person keeping him alive?

-79-

Tall, gaunt, cadaverous, wrinkled, broad forehead, shaking hand, overcoat with one sleeve edge frayed, white

shirt—never soiled for some reason—and an English
school tie, suit jacket with wide lapels buttoning across
his skinny chest…I don't do voices but his English is clear,
grammatically correct and precise… he says he works at
the Russian embassy, he is of Russian origin and erases the
White aspect of that origin, he says of his family's ending
up in Bulgaria, but the Soviets decide he is Russian and that
is good enough, better than a Bulgarian, as I accumulate
the detail, it is letting me into his story creating who Sergei
became: and while his parental origin would ever stop him
from going back to the Soviet Union, that is always a given,
is that not how it is said: it is a given I am not allowed to go
back to Moscow and am I crying into my rum? You can see
how much I cry for this fate, if you ask me, it is better than
many people whose fates send them to North Korea in the
hopes of making some dollars or to Vietnam or Mongolia:
those are the places Bulgaria offers you for lucrative travel
if you feel the urge. But I go to my office, he says, isn't that
how Americans describe it? I see and hear them describe it
in that way as I have a pass for films not seen by everyone.

Sergei has nothing to do with Vitosha Boulevard, though
I did see him once in the Budapest—there on Rakovski—
that of course is close to the Bambouk, and am a little hurt
he did not even nod he knows me but I let it pass as when
I saw him the next day or another day, who can remember,
he is saying you did not see me in Budapest as I am not
allowed to see anyone I might know: I am incognito with
a business I can't tell you about, just yet, but it is nothing
serious if you are thinking I am important in any way at

all: I am just a man alive who has only one good memory in his life and that can never be revisited and nothing reconciles a man to such knowledge, I can tell you, but you as an American can never know what I am talking about as there are no limits on your life, as you claim but of course even those who believe American lives are all so limited want nothing more than to be given the chance to accept those limits.

My sister says our father read one book in his life—*The Spider King* by Lawrence Schoonover—and not for a moment did he ever say why he is reading about a French king in the 16th century... these remains of a life and my mother tries to read a book about Tunisian villages... Sergei says, he no longer reads anything anymore as he could not answer for himself what happens to all that reading when a person is dead. It is an idiot question, an idiotic reflection to be sure, but the bookstores all of them cater to this gluttonous fever: read, read, find out, learn, read, read, read though a person never gets to read his own tombstone unless he has had the foresight to have purchased one and supervised the stone carvers at their task: but I am not a French actress prepared to sleep in my coffin for even the French do not construct coffins to accommodate the occasional friend who might find herself in the need to share the night with me and fortunately now we transact all the contacts in pitch darkness, can I say that, pitch darkness as someone has broken the street lights on the *ulitza* where they have decided I am supposed to live, far from here around the corner from the *Septembre* restaurant, I am sure you know it, didn't Lidia mention her sister likes to go there and she has taken the both of you.

I said no such thing as far as I remember and even with the mastika guiding the tongue there was no need of my telling Sergei about going to *Septembre...* but he knew this and Lidia has told me to be careful because people didn't talk to other people in Bulgaria just to talk to other people... and this became one of those constant remarks people made about being in Bulgaria or in some of the other countries: similar remarks are to taken seriously and people are always trying to sum up any place in some remark that sounds so knowing... as in the so-called free world where the only thing that matters is money, money: Sergei would even go down that path as he has plenty of money, everybody in Sofia has plenty of money since there is nothing to buy. Have you noticed and I do not torture myself with the Corecom shops: there are humiliations I do not allow myself even with the vouchers that sometimes come my way but my woman friend uses them for things women want and you know nicer things than in the shop near the American embassy where they put on display a few garments from the West as a way to demonstrate *our people* too have access to these goods... window dressing as you know is an art form...

Hours would pass away sitting with Sergei; people came and went about the table near the front of the Bambouk. I do not know how the place is organized but I have a sense certain things happened toward the back which is not visible to the passersby: Sergei says he does not mind sitting in public, as he calls it, since I am a public man, I can't stand the walls of my room and the walls of the rooms women take me into are even more abhorrent but at least then the rum allows me not to see too clearly where I am being taken to and to be taken advantage of, you could say, though we are all creatures of our desire to not sleep alone but it is a great misfortune to not be able to sleep with much endurance.

The morning wakes me brutally and she wants me to be gone and I want to be gone. The lack of civility is disturbing and the frequency does not diminish the shock to the system as I gather my possessions and as an Englishman once told me in the pub in Notting Hill: the wits are the hardest to collect in the morning as they are the easiest to misplace. Illusion is the most efficient brainwasher in the business. It is always an illusion that leads me to these rooms and in the morning I am ready to walk to my position where as you well know the joke: we pretend to work and they pretend to pay us, and am there for the hours waiting for the first break of the morning and then the break at midday and then the two breaks in the afternoon and then the letting go for another day.

Never once did Sergei ever even hint as to what he did at the Soviet embassy though once he says they use him without mercy after he came back from London where I was at the Bulgarian embassy, a dank rancid place but they wanted my English language.

Ah London, Sergei says more than once as he adjusts the coat about his shoulders.

Can I say, I like very much the irony of Sun in Splendour—that pub in Notting Hill—which I know has some peculiar English meaning, but the idea of the sun, our Sunny Beach on the Black Sea: but in London, a pub celebrating the sun! But I could not sit in there for very long as I felt out of place. I took myself to the Prince Albert which is a large sort of place where one is always obscure though I did fancy an English person might think me exotic coming from Bulgaria but I am quick to disillusionment though grateful for the language it is offered in: hardly an exotic foliage more a variety of root vegetable, he says. We have many of these sorts about here and along the Portobello Road and in particular at the far end, have you been to the Serbian center?

Great teacher, pretty easy grader as well. **Linda Nelson** does lecture the whole class but it is all very interesting. Very knowledgeable in what she is teaching.

This man, this Jack, is my English friend who has nicotine fingers since he smokes those terrible English cigarettes right down to the calluses on the sides of his fingers. He knows someone who knows someone and goes to the Serbian center which for some reason he never really tells me but maybe he has a father who has been in Serbia in the Great War: he is of that age, a surviving son of a man who has come out of the Great War.

I don't know. We go to the Serbian center and I try to tell him about Serbian singers but he says he doesn't hear music, it has been knocked out of me... lifted up, you could say, he says, and shaken out of me as if me pockets have been turned inside out and down it comes right into the gutter, but I persist and say that music, it is true, is mostly noisy clutter but occasionally it does fill my head a little and I have known people in Sofia who claim they like Serbian music because while it is familiar in its ordinariness—the simple vocabulary, the stock figures, the very order of the stanzas—it is actually the melodramatic situations which are allowed to be sung of in another language which are intolerable to listen to in Bulgarian and while one doesn't get all the nuances the emotion of the situation feeds the Bulgarian ear.

In English, as you know people listen to Edith Piaf for the same reason and I saw records by her in the shops in London. I am immune to what is called popular music and treasure the quiet of the Prince Albert, the murmur of the human voice, the sounds of glasses being washed, even the sweep of the damp cloth across the bar top as the pub is closing for the break, how all this makes me sick for London, but no one would understand what I am saying, I am not stocking my suitcases with Union Jacks, little replicas of Big Ben or figurines of the Tower Guards or the soldiers standing in from of the Queen's Palace or the policeman in front of Number 10 complete with his peculiar helmet... but we are on our way to the Serbian center, at that far end of the Portobello and it always seems we are walking or trudging through rotting cabbage leaves if I can be inaccurate for a sense of how far away it all seems from what people here in the Bambouk might think of when I say I have been to London, something they all know and which frustrates them no end as I am not prepared to talk about what they want to hear and I am sure you have no doubts as to what they want to hear of my time in London, where they work me like a dog without a license, can you say that, a dog without a license, always waiting for the dog catcher to come and put him in the appropriate facility for, do you use the phrase, animal removal function for killing of captured animals?

Serbians are not jolly drinkers, as you well know from the time you tell me about being in Beograd… weren't you there on your way here for your first time:…I too have seen them standing in the mud drinking bottles of beer, there is something so primitive about it all, standing in filth really, the dirt easing itself over the tops of their shoes, even some dressed in suits, come from offices, right there in the center of Beograd… it must have rained, I seem to remember, maybe only the beer is available at these markets, maybe there has been a campaign against drinking which they even did in Serbia, but I am sure people are drinking other than beer, *rakia* is always available and the best is from a village, as you say, under the table but finally we are at the Serbian center, though it is in England, the comforting gloom: the bad lighting, the grumpy waitresses and Jack telling me doesn't this place have character, an undefined character to be sure, but as if someone has been reading a bad translation and decide to make a bar in homage to such an artifact: Jack is a very peculiar fellow, I can tell you, he invites me to his place once and say I will see you—I forget the time date—at Weston Towers, Weston is the family name and when I get to the address he has given me it is no tower block, but one of those little one story row houses out beyond the grand houses in Ladbroke Grove, you know where I am talking of? How visible the class structure is in England, all so obvious you could say, and Jack is at a distance from all of it, but remembering the time when he says he is living in Gibraltar and watching the police gun down these two women who turn out to be doing something for the IRA, you know what I am talking about, there has been another incident but nothing happens this time, as Jack is nobody and no one listens to a nobody about such things... did I believe him, my Jack, Sergei asks me and I reply, I believe everything people tell me and wait for them to tell me it a second time and maybe a third time, as that always happens and then I either believe or do not believe as the mood strikes me.

Take credit for an admirable distance, Sergei says. I myself do not count on repetition as a means of verifying anything. My Jack and I sit in the basement restaurant and eat the little *kebabchitas* as they are made in Serbia, unlike the large things they serve in Sofia.

—An Aside—I hear about killings in Gibraltar from Susan's first husband who is sitting at a café and watches from there::::::::::::: in slow motion:::::::::::::::::: two men::::::::::::::: go::::::::::::: up:::::::::::::::: to::::::::: two Irish women::::::::::::::::: and::::::: shooting them::::::::: shooting::::::::::: both of them::::::::::: again::::::::::: when they are on the ground::::::::: this time in the head and then just walk away.

Susan's husband is English, educated like Susan at Trinity College in Dublin and then trained as barrister in London. His testimony is listened to and then nothing ever happens. It is both the times—after all they *are* Irish and up to no good—they are not benign tourists looking to get laid or have a final fling before marriage back in Belfast...

The newspapers make something of it, but they always do now don't they, as Susan is saying when I visit her in Clapham and just living in Clapham of course is a way of ignoring what Susan is saying, one of those places inviting indifference, or, heard that done that and who cares.

—End of an Aside—

NEW YORK STATE
DEPARTMENT OF HEALTH
CERTIFICATE OF DEATH

STATE FILE

RECORDED DISTRICT 4439
REGISTER NUMBER

1. NAME: FIRST — LINDA MIDDLE — L LAST — NELSON
2. SEX — FEMALE
3A. DATE OF DEATH: MONTH 01 DAY 29 YEAR 2010
3B. HOUR 1:08

4A. PLACE OF DEATH (Check one): HOSPITAL DOA ER ☒
4B. IF FACILITY, DATE ADMITTED

4C. NAME OF FACILITY: Canton-Potsdam Hospital
4D. LOCALITY: VILLAGE ☒ Potsdam
4E. COUNTY OF DEATH: St.Lawrence

4F. MEDICAL RECORD NO.: n/a
4G. WAS DECEDENT TRANSFERRED FROM ANOTHER INSTITUTION? NO ☒

5. DATE OF BIRTH: MONTH 07 DAY 29 YEAR 1949
6A. AGE IN YEARS 60 yrs
7A. CITY AND STATE OF BIRTH: Lincoln, NE

8. SERVED IN U.S. ARMED FORCES? NO ☒
9. DECEDENT OF HISPANIC ORIGIN? A ☒ No, not Spanish/Hispanic/Latino
10. DECEDENT'S RACE: A ☒ White/Caucasian

11. DECEDENT'S EDUCATION: 7 ☒ Master's degree

12. SOCIAL SECURITY NUMBER: 508-58-9460
13. MARITAL STATUS: DIVORCED ☒
14. SURVIVING SPOUSE: n/a

15A. USUAL OCCUPATION: Professor
15B. KIND OF BUSINESS OR INDUSTRY: College
15C. NAME AND LOCALITY OF COMPANY OR FIRM: SUNY Potsdam, Potsdam, New York

16A. RESIDENCE (State or Country): New York
16B. County or Region/Province: St.Lawrence
16C. LOCALITY: TOWN ☒ Parishville

16D. STREET AND NUMBER OF RESIDENCE: 949 CR 58 P.O. Box 903 (Potsdam)
16E. ZIP CODE: 13676 Parishvil

17. NAME OF FATHER: FIRST Harold MI T LAST Nelson Sr.
18. MAIDEN NAME OF MOTHER: FIRST Rosita LAST Sheahan

19A. NAME OF INFORMANT: Harold T Nelson Jr.
19B. MAILING ADDRESS: 5611 Ohelo Rd. Kapaa, HI 96746

20A. CREMATION ☒ MONTH 02 DAY 01 YEAR 2010
20B. PLACE OF BURIAL, CREMATION, REMOVAL OR OTHER DISPOSITION: Frederick Brothers Crematory
20C. LOCATION: Theresa, NY

21A. NAME AND ADDRESS OF FUNERAL HOME: Garner Funeral Service 10 Lawrence Ave. Potsdam, NY 13676
21B. REGISTRATION NUMBER: 00654

22A. NAME OF FUNERAL DIRECTOR: Cory Varney
22B. SIGNATURE OF FUNERAL DIRECTOR
22C. REGISTRATION NUMBER: 03760

23A. SIGNATURE OF REGISTRAR
23B. DATE FILED: MONTH 2 DAY 1 YEAR 2010
24A. BURIAL OR REMOVAL PERMIT ISSUED BY
24B. DATE ISSUED: MONTH 2 DAY 1

ITEMS 25 THRU 33 COMPLETED BY CERTIFYING PHYSICIAN — OR — CORONER/CORONER'S PHYSICIAN OR MEDICAL EXAMINER

25A. CERTIFICATION: To the best of my knowledge, death occurred at the time, date and place and due to the causes stated.
Certifier's Name: Samuel A. Livingstone, MD
License No.: 199008
Signature

Certifier's Title: 2 ☒ Medical Examiner / Deputy Medical Examiner
Address: 531 Meade Street, Watertown, NY 13601

27. MANNER OF DEATH: PENDING INVESTIGATION ☒
28. WAS CASE REFERRED TO CORONER OR MEDICAL EXAMINER? YES ☒
29A. AUTOPSY? YES ☒

CONFIDENTIAL   SEE INSTRUCTION SHEET FOR COMPLETING CAUSE OF DEATH   CONFIDENTIAL

30. DEATH WAS CAUSED BY: (ENTER ONLY ONE CAUSE PER LINE FOR (A), (B), AND (C).)
PART I. IMMEDIATE CAUSE
(A)
DUE TO OR AS A CONSEQUENCE OF:
(B)
DUE TO OR AS A CONSEQUENCE OF:
(C)
PART II. OTHER SIGNIFICANT CONDITIONS CONTRIBUTING TO DEATH BUT NOT RELATED TO CAUSE GIVEN IN PART I (A).
DID TOBACCO USE CONTRIBUTE TO DEATH?

31A. IF INJURY DATE 31B. HOUR 31B. INJURY LOCALITY 31C. DESCRIBE HOW INJURY OCCURRED 31D. PLACE OF INJURY 31E

But distraction is my only vice, Sergei says. I tolerate in other words since I do not hear them very carefully, you on the other hand probably listen too carefully. This is my sole advantage for living in Sofia, news remains news for centuries as people are always surprised as they remember nothing, learn nothing except their own personal distempers they work into a system.

-82-

ALEXZ

Both my Jack and I know your friend Alexz and he true to form reminds us of his route to London and the BBC every time we meet which is no longer frequent.

I shift you notice the tenses forgetting I shall never see Jack or Trafalgar Square or probably yourself ever again, so the question remains why ever are you going to remember this impossible chattering?

It is probably beyond any claim to reason to understand what has been said, little noted nor long remembered, isn't that in some way what your President Lincoln once says about his most memorable speech which my English tutor taught me—he is then a very old man who has learned his English in some impossible way from American missionaries, when they had once come to Bulgaria...

(detail) of course I was not taking dictation back then and the notes I made were just of having met Sergei on certain days, certain drinks taken... the weather and maybe a few words were noted down, as I remember: Lincoln, Prince Albert, Sun in Splendour and while there has been a jarring of the memory—has happened when Medy and I step into see a tailor on Hristo Botev who shows me his old Bulgarian passport and the Swastika stamps marking his passage across Germany and then the stamps from the customs in New York and he is saying and I am making clearer his English: what I remember of my two years in the United States, how the sun burst into the railway cars of the elevated trains in Chicago, as if we are suddenly being painted by a large golden soaked brush—so, that is where those words of Sergei came from and where even more of those words came as I lingered near Vitosha in a little café around the corner from the KINO VITOSHA drinking an *orangada* and eating a triangle of cake (a whole other aspect for another time, maybe, cake eating in Sofia.)

Sergei is saying, when my Jack and I see Alexz it is for me an occasion of sin, if I have been raised a Catholic, but even more than a sin, since he is on a list I am sure of Bulgarians we are not supposed to see or meet in London or even know about and while no one ever recites such a list of names it is understood certain Bulgarian nationals are not to be met and if met there might be consequences which would be certainly severe and without appeal since we are supposed to know even before we have been called into that office, we would be going back to Sofia immediately in this very evening, if we have a conversation with nationals like Alexz.

Of course it is for that very reason I know Alexz and

we meet with some regularity and always he tells us of his escape from Bulgaria, across Yugoslavia, leaving behind a leg… though I never ask him how he made it across the frontier with only one leg and I know he only has one leg as one drunken evening he has Jack and me knock with our knuckles on his wooden leg, he calls it, though it is of some other material, they don't even make wooden legs out of wood anymore, he says, and no way to fake your notorious hollow leg only to be revealed to… I leave it to the imagination as to who does the discovering.

Finally, Sergei is impressed by Alexz as the story is always as gripping in repetition as it has been in the original.

And he would *leave it at that* as Jack would insist and even Lidia is impressed by the story for a short time, though her respect for Alexz did not survive the underground voyage from Tottenham Court Road to Queensway on the Central Line since as we are walking to the hotel—passing the grand shops that would in due time disappear—she is saying:

I am familiar with storytellers like Alexz in Sofia: they tell you what you want to hear and they are very convincing but they leave a sort of sour-sweetly flavor in your mouth, a flavor that is not immediately apparent but in time you always discover it as if you had been eating rotten meat and now you are aware of maggots filling your mouth.

Alexz didn't think there is room for any more Bulgarians at the BBC where he works in the Bulgarian service, they have more hands than the ship needs and while it would be interesting to have a recent arrival from Bulgaria, Lidia is too young, for sure, and they could not be more careful, but they did want a contemporary air inside the broadcasts that seem to live in a much too comfortable past with only occasional day trips into the present reality.

THAT Alexz, should have lost both his legs in Yugoslavia, it would have made for an even more compelling and interesting story.

He has you tap his wooden leg, right? He asks you to toast his good fortune, to wonder at the accident that has brought you all together and now on this evening with our recent arrival...

Now, you ask me why I got you out of there as fast as I could, you didn't want to leave, didn't you understand what he is all about: I could feel his fingers working their way into your pockets and you poor man are holding them open so he could help himself, he is calculating how many drinks he can get out of you and would ration out the story and there will be a next story, the number of relatives can be adjusted to the audience...

No wonder Sergei takes a liking to him since they are cut from the same side of the pig, as Medy would say. Sergei back in Sofia is harmless but a man like Alexz is a predator. He is the sort of Bulgarian who arrives a week before the rest of the group and is the authority as a result. We are all supposed to be beholding to his worldly experience, to the *what* he knows about the world. It is not an accident I was telling you to avoid Bulgarians when we hear Bulgarian being spoken in Venice. You do not understand, at all, no matter what, those Bulgarians are in Venice for reasons having nothing to do with why we are there. They are being rewarded for their lives in Bulgaria and those lives are part of my mother's difficulties.

Enough of Lidia, I am thinking,

back of course where I am sitting on Vitosha, the *orangada* is always chilled in that kafe for reasons I don't know, but they always did have the *orangeade* which is something you could never find in the shops. The *limonada* was again available in Sofia and Piret and I have a liter bottle of it back in the apartment.

Limonada is the taste of Bulgaria for people of my generation, if I could fake a voice for a moment, a sort of appropriate pop music reference which would suddenly appear on a page if a publisher could be persuaded to purchase the rights, *orangada* is available but never did I hear anyone say anything one way or another about that drink. The clear small bottles of a greenish urine coloured drink, not strongly carbonated, capped with a bright silver shiny cap, no label of any sort, and you bring the empty bottles clicking back for the deposit...

So, the words are moving back and forth from 2010... to 1984... to 1973... to 1967... to 2010... to—

Alexz causes me to sin by omission and commission—in the voice of Sergei—I can master the Roman Catholic catechism which is superior to the various Orthodox ones though the Bulgarians have worked out what happens to the soul after the moment of death in a far more satisfying way, if I may say so and Alexz is saying what are you going on about and I would like to now say I am sitting with

Alexz in a little place off of Charing Cross, you might know that street as filled with bookstores though I do not go into bookstores, even in England though I should have, I suppose, but do I want anything more to add to my sadness at being separated from Old London, London of my dream.

I, Sergei, am not::::::: you must try to imagine this man rising from his chair in the Bambouk, pushing up with the hands firmly grasping the edge of the chair's arms and hovering for a second or it seems minutes (would he make it?) and now finally erect and looking down his long broken nosed head moving from side to side as to engage the three sets of eyes looking at him (my blue eyes included):::::: I am not an Italian aristocrat who keeps *The Pickwick Papers* on his bedside table to consult as to what the day is to bring… just imagine that, how remote that seems from our Balkan city, here in Sofia, and in London, how would I ever read in the morning when the cold keeps all people under the covers all the night long and my nights in London are always solitary… how awful it is to have a friend join one in a bed when the room is cold, the very frigidity of the air seizes a woman and does not let go…

How jealous I am,   :::::here::: a pregnant pause about to be aborted::::

Sergei says, when he has returned to his seat after looking about the room, right back into the darkness of the far corners where the futures of pleasure are to be negotiated, of one man I am jealous and he is dead so my jealousy is without purpose and that is Bulgakov who you all know as the author of *The Master and Margarita* and who I know only as the author of *The Day of the Turbins*, the one play to which Stalin repeatedly went, to have *him* as your audience, think of that, dear friends, who of our pathetic writers can claim anyone of that authority in their audiences? And on top of that: at the end of the phone line asking if Bulgakov is happy with his life here in Moscow?

I would be waved away for remembering, but I did say it, even then in memory to Sergei, as I sit at the table, though no one might believe me and there would be a demand for its removal from these pages as being too esoteric, too remote, too interfering with the drama momentarily created: an Irish writer says, Ezra Pound spent his whole literary life trying to urge a prince into existence so Pound might have his ear for tutoring and also in truth, again that word, I have been prodding the Irish writer with Ernst Junger realizing the same inspiration in a late novel *Eumeswil.* But all of it is being held by the troubled knowing: there are no longer princes and only captains of industry or thugs in uniforms with chests plastered with unearned medals while those who might know us are in the same straightened circumstances, the same isolation, the same…

Nonsense, and none of us here will be found guilty of either speaking falsely or out of the obligation of originality.

The windows in *kafes* are never washed. Even with the

so-called changes public spaces still remain untouched and are there to be just worn down. Sidewalks are meant to decay, store fronts peel, light bulbs are not replaced, and one could go on but to no purpose...

Linda Nelson is boring. The class is lecture only. Be prepared to take at least 5-10 pages of notes per 50 minute class. Has very high expectations on assigned papers and uses a citation that no one has ever heard of before. She is very slow in handing back assignments and quizzes and tests.

-82-

Alexz comes from an anarchist family and even he cannot explain this detail about the life before and after in Bulgaria. It bothers me that I do not know some defining hypocrisy to bring the anarchists into the orbit of our constant and even true failure.

But that would be jumping ahead of ourselves as we sit in the Bambouk, for Sergei says he has read Bulgakov's story "Morphine" and just the very title reveals what has been lost in the subsequent years of our dear Soviet's rule. Now only the children of the high representatives of the people's power are so permitted to lose their lives into such a delicious oblivion. Let no one tell you anything different: there are moments of pleasure even in the most stressful of times as in September of 1944 for which we are to be grateful in two months for the forty years those Russian boys delivered us into as even I have to go along to celebrate

9 IX 44

Alexz, I miss very much and if you have known his story you would miss him also.

But I did meet Alexz, I say, since he knew the anarchists in London but it is hard to talk about those times as I am sure to get it wrong and even I have another American who came calling at Kavanagh's place in Putney and handed out his selection of newspapers which he collects from the underground as he is not prepared to pay money into the pockets of those lying owners who are always showing off their grand homes the pennies of the workers built for them by purchasing their papers. And never think for a moment there is any difference between the so-called quality papers and the trashiest of the low sheets basically appealing to a man's pecker as an intellectual's pecker is his brain and those posh newspaper people know how to lick it like an ice cream cone being worked on by a little kid.

Kavanagh and the two women friends have allowed me to stay with them for a few days when I have come over from Dublin and they have warned me another American would be coming by with his newspapers and I am not to mention the Ford Corporation as it would lead to a refighting of World War Two and how the Americans were told not to bomb anything in Germany owned by the Americans or anything they might want to own after the war is over and while he is probably correct everyone has heard it all too many times before and no one in this house is prepared to defend the Second War as anything beyond a war of gangsters wearing various stripes re-dividing the world, among themselves and don't for a moment tell us about all the dead murdered Jews since no one gave a *shite* about them one way or another until the war is over and the powers to be have to come up with some reasons for why they have done what they have done... those gangsters are just lucky one of their own had been even a bigger monster than they have allowed themselves to be... and we are not even talking about what went on in Siberia or in Hiroshima... don't get him started because even describing what he has to say just takes such a vicious turn, out of this room though he is the nicest guy you could want to know... his life in The States couldn't have been very easy as he fetches up here dazed with the loneliness of what must be the great American experience: no one to talk with who knew how to listen and reply and listen again...

The Seventeenth is the Toll-House of Lust

-47-

BULGARIANS VISITING PUTNEY

As we are sitting at table in Putney, Alexz arrives. He walks with a cane and is very tall and is similar to Sergei in that he has a certain swagger, a way of walking, a way of even sitting that has been lost. When I met Alexz I had not been to Bulgaria and couldn't have told you where it was like so many Americans though I did have some Bulgarian stamps in my albums at home, mean little stamps with bearded men on them as I remember. He says he is coming from the BBC and has been talking all day about:::::

I do not fully remember what he talks about; I could give him a few paragraphs to summarize his latest commentary and for all I know it could have been on how well English painters drew and then painted clouds. It is a skill they are supreme in, I would allow him to say, and he would then tell us he talks about such matters as they defied the expectations of both his bosses and what people are anticipating hearing. He has no interest in talking about politics but he well knows John Constable is unknown in Bulgaria and he takes a certain delight in thinking that those paid in the police to monitor the BBC broadcasts would think possibly it is all a code for some finally trivial adventure concocted by the secret services, but of course it is not. Clouds, to be able to paint a cloud and not the self-satisfied face of some idiot idler whether male or female::: and he does continue, to talk now and to listen now with no consequence since that is what freedom might be.

Alexz says he came from Sofia, but saying the city name I know has no resonance at all for you as an American though your country's air force bombed Sofia in their designs to liberate us, I am sure, bomb us into liberation. To be part of a sideshow, not a major theatre of the war or as they describe it in the Imperial War Museum: Other Theatres of the War, keeps a person inside the terrible suffocating great coat of the obscure, the place that needs so much explanation... one simply foregoes the whole attempt and as a consequence—give the story over to forgetting.

You hear it said in England, I am happy to say, I come from elsewhere and no one in London will pry since they can quickly tell you are from elsewhere and since your accent does not tag you with some particular class you really are from elsewhere and can't possibly, on one hand, be of any interest at all or on the other, it will be nice knowing you but we all well know you are not sticking around contrary to anything you might say as that is part of the formula for preparing to leave... many foreign people enjoy their stays in England, even those who hate every moment of it, because they console themselves with the thought, this visit will come to an end, one of these days.

So you hear, an anarchist from Bulgaria. In some ways as hereditary as any aristocratic face in the National Portrait Gallery: x-number of generations who have kept faith with the idea of doing away with the whole damn business or in the pure irrelevance of so much of what chains people to the wheel, all in the same way as those aristocratic noses, shriveled lips... eyes that greet the world having been able to see into the abyss from the moment of birth but carried aloft by the family just sailing on and on.

Right into the SHITTER! Marvin shouts, (finally, his name arrives, the name of the American who is there having given out his newspapers).

Alexz turns to Marvin: the wonderful counter-pointing American contribution to the evening's entertainment. More a disruption and while I suppose we should value it and his harvesting of the day's newspapers from the underground... to be attached to the day's news, already forgotten as the poet would say in the wastes of time.

So, I step back from and give you this little house in

Putney, a leafy place in London, across the river, out there— many years later=== now that is something you are dreading to read==== I go there to have lunch with Marion Boyers, a publisher whose husband, her English husband, made her a sandwich to take to the office for her lunch and she being too cheap to walk me to the nearest pub invites me to share half of her sandwich, made with that thin sliced white bread the English are fond of, you can share half of my lunch—she says with the exaggerated long A that is comically emphasized by an American passing as English of a certain type, a right triangle of two slices of sodden bread and a thin slice of ham which if picked up by itself could be seen through, it was that thin, and smeared with hot English mustard… the owner of Marion Boyars Books and formerly partner inside Calder and Boyars—

all for art I assume, you could say, but Ted and his two women friends have served us dinner and Alexz is about to say: I am aware they are cutting my leg, I saw the blade, I really did…

We believe you, Marvin is saying and we have heard this a few times before but with a new set of ears… though the weakness of you being aware of what obviously allows you to have some other feeling rather than just being aware…

A DEMONSTRATION OF THE UNCERTAIN NATURE OF EXCURSIONS FROM THE SO-CALLED STORY

The reason I have gone to thinking of Marion Boyars is the conversation with Alexz, with Marvin and with Ted and his two women friends, two women, as Marvin says later who are always hanging about Ted, each eyeing the other in the comradely way of conspirators beloved of the older novelists, neither wishing well for the other and each claiming to be a first among equals and Ted saying what is the bother all the time: worse than the tourists come looking for Trafalgar Square thinking a bookstore is some sort of stand-in for the tourist office and how ever do they find themselves lurching around in the alleyways off Charing Cross Road where that Center Point tall building is going up with the resulting shadow.

I have no interest in the good old days though I have lingered in the going into Better Books there on Charing Cross and Indica, somewhere nearby while Ted's shop is located between them, ever so briefly it seemed, and Ted was saying we are still so far behind you Americans. To show an erect penis is to invite the police in to sup off your wallet and stand you in the slammer—being said with an echo of the *shitter,* beloved of Marvin, though I didn't like the word play marking out the distance they felt from this visitor, over from Dublin, over from The States as Marvin said, why are you ever even thinking of going back, what can there be in The States that is not here in abundance and you don't have to go off to Vietnam, where mark my words, they are going to grind up all those young men, as ever and as ever...

I felt the knife, Alexz is saying, good German steel, I had the sense to recognize and at the same time knew there was now hardly much of leg beneath my knee, the communists were sadists: they didn't place large landmines on the border, they didn't want to kill you, that was their humanity showing, they wanted to create examples of what could happen if you decided to walk out of Yugoslavia, I am not kidding, this was back but not that far back, and I had been able to get across the border from Bulgaria, I knew, that was dangerous, but the Yugoslav was supposed not as dangerous so I thought this was to be easy if, but of course I was wrong, though not mortally wrong and the man with me, knew what to do as he had been a partisan in Bulgaria, and then in the army, but that is another story, mixed in with the *Slivo* and I shit myself.

Didn't I tell you, right into the shitter, Marvin says.

Shut the fuck up, it is my leg, not yours you useless sack of shit, go stuff those newspapers down your own throat, idler, the worst sort of American slime, attaching himself to the cause in the hopes of getting fucked by pretty girls who want to support the movement, themselves not having a clue which way is up but they know a stiff cock is always of some interest, even the diseased instrument of your self-abuse.

Bulgarians have never been known for the precision of their language. I use my right hand to pleasure myself. My dick is, I will have you know, in demand by the ladies.

One of Kavanagh's women stops the conversation with: he who… I do not remember what she says. It could have been the meal is served, wash your hands like the little boys you are or some such…

Marvin disappears. He is not there for breakfast and only lives in my grab bag as the guy who collects newspapers while riding the underground and is concerned about those American factories not being bombed in Germany during World War Two...

END OF THE DEMONSTRATION

Stay Connected! News: Dear Alumni & Friends. It is with great difficulty and sadness that we report to you the passing of two members of our campus community, Joe Sarnoff, whom many of you know from your days in SGA, and **Linda Nelson**, a full-time instructor of History. We learned this morning that Joe Sarnoff, Director of Retention Programs, and long-standing member of the College staff, passed away at his home. Joe has been part of the SUNY Potsdam family for nearly 40 years and was a tireless advocate for students and student programming

-33-

ALEXZ Who Leaves Bulgaria

Alexz is no longer lying on the ground with his friend cutting away his destroyed leg, tourniquet fastened and both of them ending up first in a hospital in Trieste and then a dark room overlooking the grand canal in the city. A candle would have provided more light than the bulb hanging from the ceiling as if they want to stage our suicides for us, you could say, you have come to this and do you think

226

it is going to get any better when you leave here, so why go on with this foolishness of hope, hope is a debased slogan of the days of the fascism to be replaced by the day of the communism.

Alexz is saying, living is more of a whim, I can tell you and it is the only thing I have learned, as death is a whim so is the life and when we go walking—I really didn't walk in Trieste—more pushed along in a cart-like contraption my friend arranges for me, the American soldiers walk around looking for fun, I remember learning that expression from one of them: just looking for some fun and if that ain't the most innocent thing in the world, you can kick me to the gutter, he is saying, most people don't like people looking for fun, they don't understand a guy looking for some fun, it seems sacrilegious or something almost, when you think about it and too many of the officers have no sense of humour or see how lucky they are to miss the fighting, years ago a guy told me no soldier, no real soldier envies any soldier who has been in combat, no solder who has been in real combat is ever really going to be demanding everyone have the same experience knowing it is mere accident and all those who escape even those who cheat, lie, fraud, it doesn't matter: anything to have to... that is if a man has really been in combat...

Alexz is saying, this American fellow seems a voice from another universe and I know I could never go on to the United States as so many hope, England would do me quite nicely, England would be full up for a short period of time: Estonian corpse washers, Bulgarian gardeners, Russian flower sellers, Polish mechanics... Armenians who ran clubs in Soho, where things went on I can tell you, during that time, if only for a mere few seconds.

The Tenth is the Toll-House of Envy

Kavanagh sits across from us. The girls to either side of him. Each is drumming the fingers of a hand on his chest. He is wearing a tattered Irish sweater, which his granny aunt had knitted for him, wanting to be able to ID my corpse, she would be...

But these are all stories of so long ago, today Bulgaria does not intrude into anyone's mind, unless you are going across it for Istanbul, and sometimes everyone I meet is making for the pudding shop, they call it or some hotel nearby... setting up the rides for Teheran, Kabul, Katmandu: a regular caravan to forgetfulness.

> **Linda Nelson's** voice is very monotone, puts you to sleep. She talks so fast it is impossible to write down the 10 pages of notes she gives every day. I do not recommend at all, ended up dropping the class.

No one in Bulgaria would go East, never to the East as we have enough of that within our own borders... next week I will talk on the radio about going East and how people avoid Bulgaria, it has a reputation for not being... but maybe Bulgarians could think of the East in another way.

Do you know there is a cast iron church in the center of Istanbul, shipped down from Austria, piece by piece, on barges down the Danube and across the Black Sea... but the Turks have ruled us and when a ruler loses his teeth dinner turns away to be devoured by the more powerful, glowing white fangs that sink deep into the willing flesh, we have always ever wanted to be devoured.

Shall we go out, one of the women by Kavanagh asks and it is commanded.

Alekz says, we should go because of the hour a club off Charing Cross, he knows, from his first days in London, you will find it interesting.

The same place he takes Lidia and I to when we turn up in London around Easter in '68, missing Paris, and unable to be part of the French class *soixanthuitiyards*, though Lidia might be described as being part of the very much smaller class of '68 who left Bulgaria for the West complete with a red leather passport from the Народна република България (НРБ)

All the waiters are bald. You sit on a backless stool around a table that is below your knees. You could stretch your legs out under the table and as the evening wears on you find yourself bending forward as if you want to rest your head on the table, but it seems designed to encourage some sort of conversation requiring a certain intimacy.

-43-

PIRET WANTS TO FUCK maybe IN SOFIA

Do you want to fuck me, Piret is asking from the other room in the apartment on Solunska, when I get back from Vitosha, from all *your thinks*.

229

Well, do you want to fuck me? I hear her say obviously now for the second time. I am sitting in the glass enclosed balcony watching a man shower in outline through the thin curtain, across the way. A woman is sitting on a chair waiting her turn or not…

Disoriented?

…as am I during these moments in Sofia, when the sadness at the center of Piret's being eases itself out and as we are standing outside the Vardar subway stop wondering as the song might have: which way to go…

Philip is nowhere about, and we are trying to find a veterinarian who takes care of stray dogs… a wide boulevard, large apartment complexes, the shops on the ground floor… bright sun, exposed…

I have gone into the room following my voice. Piret is turned away, I don't feel anything… I feel everything, it's so unfair, to feel everything, all the time and not have the vocabulary to describe it in English, in Estonian, in Italian, in Hebrew, in Bulgarian. How many more languages should I try to wallow in before the time's up?

Piret is lying in the darkened room, on her side of the bed, away from everything, waiting, or not waiting. With Piret it is always hard to figure out what is to happen next, that next thing… it always arrives, and the moment is gone, as if it has not existed and it is only in the thought of what has happened, so the wiping out of the memory is sufficient to allow the mystery to reassert itself: we are together, here in Sofia… as the result of the long march of history—the lights well turned on and the clothes neatly piled for departure—more a slithering into that which we have no choice, really, in the matter… the drapes have been pulled back and the shadowed light fills the room where Piret rests on her back, by now her hand has moved lower down and she knows what to do to take care… whatever, as the current slang has it.

-72-

OUT OF THE HOUSE INTO SOFIA

Getting out of the modern subway built by the Koreans or Japanese, it is unclear, or I just didn't know, it hasn't been built by the Bulgarians that is for sure, Piret says.

It isn't beaten up yet, it has not begun to fall apart and the finding of money for repairs, even in the capitol, but that is off to the side… you walk up from this international situation and are on the sidewalk of a very wide boulevard going out from the city center and all about, apartment buildings, with dim shops trying to make a go of it…

A boring necessary reminder. We have come out to this place because Piret is interested in the abandoned dogs on the streets and here was a man who ran a shelter for them in his free time. People donate money, materials and he takes care of the dogs and a few cats and others try to find homes for them.

Somewhere out this way is the road over to Nadeshda but that is another story.

Piret is a little scared by the people just standing around near the entrances to the apartment buildings. The grounds all about are waste lands. No one gives a shit, as it didn't belong to them. When you look at the façade of the buildings you notice some of the apartments have been refaced and others are as shabby as they have always been and always would be. Some people fix their places up and others sit midst their complaint. An abandoned tramway or at least an infrequently used one… garbage heaped at random, parts of machines dropped off… those waste areas in New Jersey you drive through hoping never for the car to break down.

Philip is saying, in a socialist country public properties are there for the taking and abuse, the dereliction is a conscious result of what people think of the public place: they are superstitious materialists to their inner cores and express this by keeping hidden any remnant feeling… when in public they slash, tear apart, spit, vomit, defecate upon the public spaces: it ain't mine… orphans are lined up and beaten for the bad luck they represent, a man is down, kick him to protect your own good fortune, trip the blind, burn the retards, steal what can be detached, disfigure what remains…

-72-
DOGS

There is no end to these stories, Piret says. Let's look at the dogs and be gone. We have gone to the shelter to look at how they save dogs from the street in Sofia and the man is there smiling in a sort of embarrassed way at how primitive the shelter is. A small building with a sort of operating room and storage space and some cages outside with a lean-to and area for the dogs to run around in… against the far fence a couple of abandoned cars under which some other dogs shelter from the sun…

We are welcomed as *honoured guests* and the doctor has large bottles of Coca Cola and orange soda and if we want something to drink he has that also… a hint of formality to what is…

Piret and the Vet talk about the dogs and the Vet's English is okay as long as he didn't have to explain—a volunteer is supposed to come and help with this part of the visit.

During the communism dogs either work for their food on farms or in the fields and only communists have dogs

233

which you could say are pure bred and they brought them back from abroad along with the bicycles which are a fashion back then… and then with the changes people decided they want to have pets and then when things got bad the dogs are released into the streets…

Of course there are always lessons to be learned depending on the politics you want to support.

But, Piret says, the dogs are what matters, the what which can be done. They live and die on the street, much like people do but at least the dogs don't turn on you unless you are too pushy with wanting to help them. People take anything that is not nailed down.

now, something not expected at all:

Piret is saying, everything is broken in Sofia and if it is not broken it's on its way to being broken and not repaired. Every piece of sidewalk is cracked, broken, pieces removed, and people look at you, have you noticed this? they look at you, through you, their eyes glazed and stupefied by a something, not resembling—strangely—being drugged or high on drugs or drunk, vacant as if expecting blood to gush out of your eye sockets and not able to scream, not able to have any possible response at the ready, though there is a hint they are calculating how long it is going to take you to die with the amount of blood being lost, for no apparent reason, and with no way to stop it, easily at hand, or even thought of it because that is what they are wishing would happen to you, something bursting behind your eyes and just flowing out of you, but at the same time they are waiting to strip your body clean, avoiding the messy reality of how blood soaked the clothing will be but what is a bit of dried blood on your clothing, nothing is really ever clean in Sofia,

You don't see starvation or hideously crippled people which is something I am surprised by, though the peculiar way people stare at you, is disturbing enough, but no desperate hands out other than an occasional gypsy woman with a hand out but the arm held close to her body for if you did drop a coin into the hand there is the possibility the hand and the arm would instantly strike out and grab you close to the skinny bosom and there in contact you would be absorbed, so as to disappear.

One sees only the sad potentiality to only lie with other dogs at the corners waiting to rouse themselves to hunt again for food of some sort of food and then surely people think these stupid foreign people with their bags of dog food feeding the abandoned dogs, abandoned for good reasonable reasons, now don't these people get it, they are preserving what should be wiped away.

What can foreign people be thinking, Piret is also saying, Bulgarians are saying to each other, feeding these animals no one wants and which serve no purpose at all and they never look at their own lives of course, looking only at the abandoned dogs and cats, let's not forget the cats which do not lounge as you say, you saw in Venice, where cats lounge and have a public place in the life of the city, you say, I am thinking of the display in the Hare Krishna storefront of Second Avenue depicting the cycle of life, the baby to growing up, responsible and then the falling over with old age and reappearing as a baby... the temptation of such a belief, though I have never seen old people at the storefront as what old person wants to be reminded about what is about to come knocking them over...

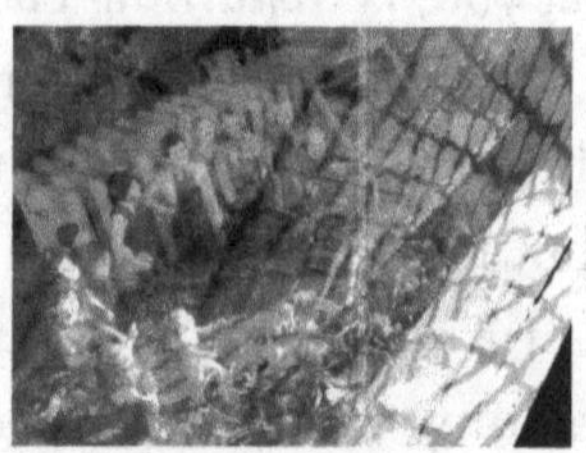

Did I notice the Hare Krishna boy near the tram stop on Vitosha? as Piret has noticed and he seems quite at home, though he is not chanting, but he has the line of paint down the ridge of his nose, Bulgarians are falling into every sort of explanation of the world but they have long been going along with anything other than what is right in front of their noses as it is simply too terrible to constantly be reminded of anything that takes one away, even for a moment, even knowing one could feel one's self being moved along by the wish.

-44-

The Seventeenth is the Toll-House of Adultery

Harittena Reappears by way of MARINA

Again thinking of Harittena who is now old, don't you get it, she is an old woman, and if you can imagine that she is remembering a winter fuck, even a winter fuck after a drink in the deaf and mute café in *Plastat Lenin*, you must not be living in the world where we are at this moment, Piret is saying: just get me out of here.

We are not lost, there is only the one subway line, and you will know where you are when we get back there. You can't get lost in Sofia… of course I know only a tiny part of the city and that has been de-populated, there is a sort of freedom walking about and neither a single person to be recognized nor will I recognize anyone…

Harittena did get to go to Italy but it is only after the fall of the communism. This is the sort of information that is not supposed to arrive without adequate foretelling, shadowing, suggesting while coincidence is not applauded as it used to be or at least over-looked.

So, an update: I had an email from Marina in Milan saying she had been to a small concert at the Brera and she had walked past the self-portrait of Boccioni

remembering I noticed it on our visit there before going on to Sofia....and I imagine, Marina is writing, places like that are all about in Sofia, empty spaces with ugly buildings or falling to ruin though they were only recently put up and you are finding yourself at an angle to it all, and when the concert is at the intermission—it is a concert of Gyorgy Kurtag and his wife playing piano music or rather little dabs of piano music, these two very old people leaning towards and away from each other as they play their duets at the same piano, we fell into a conversation with a Bulgarian woman, of all nationalities, and I say my friend is in Sofia at that moment and to make the usual long story, which continued after the intermission over coffee, she says she thinks she remembers meeting you as she sang in the choir at the cathedral and when she met you she is hoping to go to Italy which is not meant to be until so much later, but she remembers meeting an American in the winter and she didn't know much English but you and she walk around in Sofia and she knows you would not write letters as she told you about a Swedish boy who wrote her letters until he wrote to tell her he is getting married to a girl in Sweden and he hopes she would be happy by meeting someone else and she says you have told her you would not forget her but you have not promised to write to her or anything and… though she gave you an address she didn't remember if you ever wrote as all of that is a long long time ago.

-45-

MARINA is in Contact with Harittena.

As in the note from Marina: Harittena is alive at the moment in Milan and we are to be brought together at that café in *La Rinascente*, looking down at the Duomo and who will say it first:

could one ever believe

and she will turn to Marina who will put into Italian and add she has known him pointing at me since that summer when I met him as my teacher in Dublin, that summer after the events of May in Paris, which is a strange parenthesis, Harittena says, as it matters not at all in Sofia where there is a large celebration for world peace and all the usual communist slogans and everyone has a good time, for some reason but no one claims to be a veteran of it later on… I am saying to Marina she could tell Harittena I remember reading the Irish Times with Marina and there are two Czech students at the school that August and they didn't know what to do and I remember only the fact of those two Czech students and we read the reports in the Irish Times and the boss of the school is telling me he had to cut back on the hours as parents are calling home their children and there just wouldn't be enough au-pair girls to fill up the classes and even the nightclub is not having a good time of it and…

Both Piret and Harittena have heard all of this before and why am I going on about it now, for these few minutes we would all be together and Harittena has things to do as her time in Milano is short and Piret and I are flying back to New York where nothing changes except inside of my head and again there is no way of being able to give this story over to just one other person but that is a lie, I am not interested in just one other person, though no matter how many people knew this story and couldn't figure out why this story held them even for a second… none of this would postpone my translation to another category of being as a guy in a Flann O'Brien novel might say and Marina, did I take you to the Brazen Head to see the highwayman's name scratched into the old glass and all of the city being torn down all about that sheltered pub just down from Eve's and Adam's church as Mr. Joyce would have… the most desolate bit of road in all of Dublin…

Harittena tells Marina, she no longer sings… it has been a brief minute in her life and while she had tried in all the usual ways, official, unofficial ways, there is no path for her to Italy to allow her to learn to sing with Boris Christoff: that has been one of those dreams, those hopes one held on to and tell people about just as I have told him about it—in the winter in Sofia—and there is nothing he could do and the places to be filled near Boris Christoff in Rome are occupied by the children of people who have the power within The Party and who express some sort of an interest in music—that is, they could hum something, hum anything is the only additional required qualification for a place abroad if you are a child of the Power.

Not for a moment did it matter if they have any talent or no talent, it did not matter and that is the most difficult thing for people who are not from Bulgaria to understand: what matters is your connection to The Power.

I have no connections and even the one I think I have tied myself to with a month at the Black Sea is forgotten even before he has come back to Sofia and it is a lesson not even worth talking about, as I should have known, people help those who can help them—is the expression in English—one hand washes the other and it is not unlike those gruesome green hands of Soviet-Bulgarian Friendship placed over the entrances to the school in October: hands reaching out from beyond the frame of the poster and always a sort of greenish shade to the ink that is used, for some reason, and I can't be the only person to notice this, but noticing this aesthetic detail and the reality of who got what did not give you even a tiny advantage, it gives you nothing… so you end up in an office where you are cheaper than buying an adding machine to add the long lists of numbers coming from some other office and are to be sent to another office where the addition will be repeated by another person who is also cheaper than an adding machine.

Marina mentions it is getting late and it is near the time for her to meet Giovanni, as he will be coming from Pavia, as he had been in Rome this morning, if you want: can you come to dinner with us—she draws two little maps from the Duomo to the outdoor restaurant—and Harittena is saying she can only stay for a short time and hopes it would not be thought rude of her if she leaves early as she would like to come to dinner, she has been too long with Bulgarians in Milano and Marina says she did not know there are Bulgarians in Milan, she has been more familiar with the Polish people who have come to work, never to play music, for some reason or it might just have been who she has met and Piret and I went back to the hotel and Harittena went back to wherever it is she is staying, still husbanding the money as is often the case back then when it is possible to leave Bulgaria…there really are times when it is easy to get a visa, for no reason at all, you must remember and there is no telling how long this would last, or if it would be repeated or, just the fact: visas are available to leave Bulgaria and you could almost see the border guards wishing you well with the food wrapped in the car and in the sacks on your back, knowing somewhere you have hidden the dollars that have been accumulated, one by one in ways no one is proud to even mention but it is always assumed the dollars did not come from the thin air but through some method not to be talked about as it is not worth talking about, no lessons in the life, no lesson for the future… just a few dollars that did not go very far and the two other people have to have the money for the petrol…

Nothing remains of Harittena except the tan eyes in my memory.

The walking along on Vitosha and then she turns off the boulevard before we get to the courts…

Then the maps change or rather they change the names of most of the streets named for Communist heroes or for the dates in the communist calendar.

Harittena lives on 8 MART in Nadeshda, Sofia.

THE FINAL MOVEMENT

I couldn't stand **Linda Nelson's** horrible filler word habit when she gave lectures. UGH! It was like listening to a woodchuck choke on a block of oak!

-46-

The Hint of HARITTENA

a

If you want, you can go without me, Piret is saying, you have things you want to say and hear and I would only be in the way and no one wants an observer at such moments, an extra person not part of this resurrection, this parody of Easter though I do think the boulders are too easily rolled back and we only get sad when we look at what is our past.

b

Whatever, do you really remember of meeting Harittena and why would she want to remember?—as there has been no contact for is it almost 40 years or are you? always in contact with her since she lives on inside your head, as a mystic I am sure would tell you.

e

Giovanni has been to his English language class and wants to work on the future tense. Is there a way we can talk for hours using the future tense? He asks and he is not doing this in some way to show what he is learning but to allow Marina to shine in her English language.

Will and shall are about it in English, I say. Will Harittena show up and I would suggest she will not. Piret is not feeling well the whole time in Bulgaria and she thought she will be better once she gets back to Italy on our way back to America and then in America will it be any better?

But you have control over neither the past nor the future. Will you ever be able to say I have control over the future let alone will I have control over the past?

f

Nonsense, really, Marina is saying. You will be finding yourself spinning in a room with Leopardi, spinning to postpone the reality of the grave opening before you.

-47-

Be glad Piret is here in Milano with you and you will be seeing her in a couple of hours.

Harittena will not be coming to dinner with us.

You have no need of such memories; will you allow the present to fill up your days?

So to Pernik

So, you are holding in mind we are in Milano.

So, you are holding in mind we are in Sofia, never having left Vitosha Boulevard.

Of course it is only in the books Piret reads—where a reader is always able to sleep through the reading—as it were—the writer is constantly marking the pages like a dog going around the block, but all those books are easily available and why would I forsake the pleasure of the new train to Pernik.

And telling Piret:

> Leaving the train at five o'clock in the afternoon,
> found love dressed in a black uniform.

See where that gets you! But I should be grateful, isn't one supposed to always be saying these days, be grateful, while sitting on a new train, will it break down, for Pernik. With VV to meet us and show us about his town, city really... not far, really, I'll meet you at the station, he is saying, though I have to look into the hospital to see how my brother is doing, but I should be finished by the time you get there, you can see where I live and visit with a friend and we can have lunch and I'll put you back on the train

-92-

LAST WORDS FROM THE STREET

-92-

IN PERNIK

VV comes from an anarchist family, an uncle has been in the camps, has been released, has been sent back, been released...

VV has fled Bulgaria and comes back after the change.

Your friend from Hollywood in New York, VV is saying, is always telling you how narrow is the circle of people you know in Bulgaria and all of them agree with you and you end up parroting their comments, their experiences as if they are your own and you can't realize how narrow a view of the world it produces... which of course is how she herself sees the world and really, it is how anyone sees the world: we are caught in the paragraphs others have contributed clause upon clause to lengthen the sentences en-

247

compassing the world: none of the mean subject verb object reductionism…

ON The First Aerial Toll-House The Soul Is Questioned About The Sins Of The Tongue

The center of Pernik has been ripped out by the communists who built a square around which they could march their power on the necessary days commemorating the people's power and its organs for enforcing it.

Coal mining has been the central industry in Pernik for many years and has declined as the time went by… one says these things, VV is saying, but they are sentences no human voice could articulate, the eye reads them and tries harder than it is worth to think them spoken by anyone we might know.

In Finland, VV is saying, if the communism had continued in the Soviet Union, every village in Finland would have a subway as that is about the only thing the Soviets are able to build which actually seemed to work.

(This is here to provide some sort of shading while being in Pernik)

VV takes us to a restaurant, under umbrellas and trees, attached to the culture center, eventually every village is to have culture center: poor Platonic something or other of their cousin in Sofia … and I am telling VV about being on a boat going up the Bosporus while the French tourists are telling each other, when we get back to Paris you have to come over to my Dolmabachi… and VV is asked how

he escaped from Bulgaria, you ended up in Rome, right?...
yes, but are you alluding to the grand Palace of Culture in
Sofia, as vandalized as the Coliseum in Rome, though to
make the comparison realistic we must acknowledge the
impossibility of catching a Henry Jamesian disease in the
Palace of Culture in Sofia, though in the underground passageways more contemporary delights are on offer, midst
the excrement and piss...

I walked out of Bulgaria, VV is saying, just like that,
people are always saying, I walked out of the movie, I got
fed up with the talk, I had enough of meetings, I just walk
and the man who put me on the path got in trouble not
only for not telling his superior he has known I am going
to walk out of Bulgaria, but for not trying to stop me... it is
both easier than that and harder, near the border they have
shopping days when people, who of course have relatives,
on both sides and vice versa, of the border—that line on a
piece of paper—go back and forth, in spite of what almost
fifty years of having a now fortified and armed frontier to
keep hostile elements out so as to protect our people, you
remember we often talk about the plural pronoun, our people who are always in need of protection and there are always people who know best and the people are to know
they are being protected... and no humor is allowed as to
who will protect us from those protecting us: I just walk out
one day and have an identification card stating I live in the
village and it is all you have to show and if you time it right
and they have a new *militizia* man there who didn't know
too well who is who, so you could just walk—no one looks

like those photographs, as you well know, which are on the passes and the guard... they didn't go looking for whoever it is who has walked out that day, and by then no one is really keeping track of these things though my friend at the institute got in trouble since he had not reported knowing he thinks I am going to walk out of Bulgaria... the communists always feel it personally, they are like dangerous little children who have been rejected, imagine, someone left our country, you know the old joke when Zhivkov is asked why they made it so hard for people to leave the wonderful country of Bulgaria, replies, do you want me to live here by myself?

VV is saying, I put it out of mind, how I packed for walking out of Bulgaria—did I ever say, I am walking out on Bulgaria, that curious way you can say this in English, walking out on Bulgaria, you want to take this, take that and then there is the other stuff and thinking about other things, but you decide to take nothing and I didn't take a map because if I am caught with a map, it is a thing that is considered a dangerous weapon of aggression against the people's power, of course I take underwear which didn't show where I am from, clothing is what gives you away before anything else, I take socks because I don't like wet socks and I am sure my feet would get wet.

I did have an empty notebook. I didn't write in the book until I get to Italy.

And now VV is back in Pernik to attend to the brother in the hospital, who is in and out of the hospital: something wrong with his kidneys, he only has one but that is another story: you still have one, the doctor has consoled him the last time he is in the hospital a few years ago, and they can't seem to find out now what is wrong with the brother and VV is getting tired of the run around since the doctors go on vacation at this time of the year and it doesn't do any good to say, well, illnesses don't go on holiday at this time of the year because there is bound to be some clever young doctor about to serve up numbers showing people don't get sick for whatever week we are talking around, it is always another week...

I have the apartment my mother lives in after my father died, there is a lot of work to be done and I am not here when she dies so there is a corner of the apartment taken over by her stuff, by herself, which I don't touch because not enough time has elapsed, you know a person comes to inhabit their clothes and after a person dies, one can still have the sense he or she is still in the house when we see the clothes hanging from a peg on the wall, or the sandals, now dusty, that pathetic glimpse, by the door, did I tell you I thought I would know many people when I came back to Pernik, but that is not the case, I don't want to meet young people as they seem to be from another planet and I don't want to meet the old people, the few who are left, who since they stayed here, through thick and thicker, as they like to say, or thin and thinner, look on me as a sort of traitor, and they know I want to ask them for something or other and I know this and I know they have prepared their rejections, their clipped words for putting me in my place: I have escaped my place here in Pernik. for a few moments, and places are not being held for anyone, which you under-stand, just as I understood there is a reward for Bulgarians who are caught in Yugoslavia, I escaped before that country fell apart, a reward paid upon delivery for Bulgaria's little errant truant returned to his home, to his real home—why ever have you thought to even wanted to leave your home—to be firmly—they always use that word—reprimanded and they no longer send you to prison but you have to pay for the reward and the transportation and you have to write a letter begging to be forgiven and they would refuse to give you back your job and you have to find some other way to survive and they ask you to report to the local police station where you have to wait and wait until the guy who records your visit would feel like seeing you, as he always has more important things to do…

but I escape, I walk out of Bulgaria and across Yugoslavia, just like that, you could say and did not have any problems until I have been in Rome for a few months and someone steals all my documents.

I am like your poor Toshko: a man without papers in Rome… but you know all that and then came for me the life in The States and like everyone I too think things would never ever change, but they did and I am now back in Pernik along with all the people who stayed and who also never thought anything would change, but of course just because people talk all the time about change, doesn't mean there has been change, but it is hard to argue there has been no changes, VV is saying, as we walk by the in-flated slide, similar to the one we have seen in the village in Italy and which appear on 10th Street near Grace Church School in Manhattan once a year in May for the annual fun

fair fund raiser, but changes like the slide and the appearance of McDonald's and Kentucky Fried Chicken and the
Irish pubs in the

   narrow streets behind Solunska is hard to argue against
though but you must mention McDonald's with a knowing
smirk or a disdainful strained out gasp of a laugh, as if you
have yourself never been in one of those places if only to
use the bathroom or to be there with a child, as this seeing,
which you have

   found, will be ignored, if you fail to loudly smirk at the
mention of certain American brand names, absolutely ignored, by those who pride themselves in seeing what is re-

ally important and the smirk is the essential and required code for entrance into the precincts of their imaginations which are so lucrative, for themselves, and which bear little resemblance to reality, though they like it that way, because it allows them to understand the world, so fully, and as a result every day they remark to themselves on how intelligent they are when compared to the sea through which they are forced to wade on the way to collect their little pots of gold. Your friend from Hollywood in New York well knows this even if she is not prepared to agree with me, as if only natural.

> My only issue with **Linda Nelson** as a professor is her inability to work with technology. We had so many technical problems because she didn't know how to use the equipment or would break it at the beginning of class… it was a FILM class and we couldn't watch the films! Otherwise a decent professor.

In Italy, they have no real fear of a sinking ship of state, I think VV might say if he had seen the inflated slide in the town where we have been staying, but he is telling us he could not find the necessary words for his own town. He has thought to describe a man, bowed down by the heat and the humidity—you can feel it closing in even on a day like this, and his arm sweeps about the cool restaurant, you can see the steps of the people begin to slow after the invigoration at the arrival of Spring, and the forced march through winter which holds their steps to a firm forward motion, as if with every step they are pushing back the heavy load of the cold, but with the spring is that, VV, said later, enough of the weather, I am told in a lecture on Park Avenue in Manhattan, a writer is to avoid in his prose if he wants his reader to keep on with the reading and not question the investment in what is turning out to be a weather forecast—better visualized and transformed on the Weather Channel, of course, so no need to go into the proverbial mammals falling from the sky...

the steps pick up and one cannot detect obvious purpose, so one is given over to pagan ruminations—can I say that?—but quickly the heat makes itself known as you can see and be glad you will be gone from Pernik and Bulgaria before the heat takes people by the neck, so I am going to give a man a piece of ice, wrap the piece of ice in a clean handkerchief, an object Bulgarians still use, for some reason, and will have him rub it back and forth across the back of his neck as he walks around the town of Pernik, following, ever so discreetly one person after another because I think a novel could be constructed by the accident of who I see, who turns to look at me and where has this happened? would become the locale and my way into describing Pernik which would allow the town to join other literary towns, to replace the reality with my version and as he is talking VV is seeing a man in his youth who has been rubbing the back of his neck with a piece of ice he has gripped with a scrap of newspaper but the ice is leaking the ink from the pages and he is smudging his neck, VV suddenly says to us, the way a young boy is trying to erase a mistake and no matter how he rubs the mistake with the eraser the virginity of the paper has been forever lost and the evident mistake is permanently present and here this man is carrying his mistake on the back of his neck as if the executioner had smudged the goal of the axe.

I remembered the man since he is always subject of talking and is always known as the man who has gone to Paris when he is young and came back and look at him now! It is always unclear to me about how we are to look at him. Is it: one, here, is a man who has gone to Paris or two, here, is a man who has come back. Of course Paris is a suspect place. There have been men who have gone to Berlin, I remember that very distinctly, and the success or as is more likely failure of their lives is never ascribed to their going to Berlin but in the case of this man with the mark of the axe on the back of his neck has gone to Paris and he has come back.

Some of the bitterness in the descriptions of this man has to do with the fact that it is as a young man he has gone to and come back from Paris and people remember why with shame how they themselves have not gone somewhere when they, hard as it is to believe, have once been young.

But he gets what he deserves, an uncle tells me with a decisiveness I have never heard in him before or since. As a young man I couldn't ask why this man has gotten what he deserved but I know also this man is special in our town. He has been to Paris and he has come back and he has done it as a young man and that is no longer something which is possible for young people to contemplate in the socialism we are living through in our preparation for the perfection of communism which would foreclose all necessity of going to a place called Paris and soon enough there would never be a necessity or occasion for some to have even an inkling that he should be thinking about going away...

The man with the piece of ice is walking forth and back in Pernik, holding the melting coolant, as he may be thinking, conscious of the new words constantly being taken into the living body of Bulgarian: to the main square and with his back marked by VV's eyes and who knows if he found a reason to ask this man for directions, there is no way this man would believe that he is dealing with someone who is lost.

I have thought to follow a woman but that is more perilous for reasons no reasonable person could question... children are beyond thought... the old did not move fast enough and I am aware that in Venice I have seen a woman walking about imagining she is following a famous philosopher, but she is pretty in the way of earnest French women who require just a little abuse to be really interesting, but I have no experience of France or of French women... my uncle claims the example of Yavarov is enough for any man: France equals botched suicides, it is a country to unsteady the gun, the swipe of the blade, the strength of the rope or the...

Italy does not encourage lingering for people coming from the East, it brings out that habit in the English and the Americans... I was on to Denmark, following my one friend who has walked out on Bulgaria before I did, VV is saying, and he ends up as mailman in a small town near Copenhagen, with a young wife, two children and his distemper at ending up in a happy situation, beyond—as the cliché would have it—his best dreams—and he decides Pernik and my being from there is a reminder of the shade in his life: why has he not been able to dream of being happy? Why have his dreams never foretold of any happiness in his life? I have no answer from him and realized I am not to make Copenhagen my home, though the sorts of *free republics*, as I am told they are called are very inviting with young beautiful women wanting to experience… I don't have to tell you what they want and they would see me as a means to that pleasurable end or beginning since they have decided to expunge the word *end* from their vocabulary as they have done from their lives and while I do stop by, as Americans are always saying: why not stop by sometime, do you notice how Americans are always saying it, but never does that time arrive: never in my experience in New York has anyone ever stopped by, just like I don't know what…

So, people are sent spinning out from our conversation—dervishers of words and remembering, what is happening and what might happen and…

I think she hit the back of her head—Linda's **cousin intrudes**—maybe she couldn't see the wound, her skull cracked, you could say how was it cracked? the edge of a table, a chair, but how is her body sent in that direction? coming back late on Wednesay afer a long day of teaching, I think it is, in the first week which is both easy and hard in that you are meeting people, she told me once, many people and all you have are lists of names and their faces for a moment when you call the names and they are looking at you when they can pry themselves away from the electronic devices they now all carry, eyes ears glued to them—I know—an effort to draw them away which she did not bother to make rules about, why bother? and yet hoping her vocal annoyance might carry the day along with some of them at the interuption that is always inevitable with a sudden sharp call tone which was, no matter the sound, always a cause for some laughter but since the course is an introductory course there are no familiar faces though famliar types are present to be sure and she could make a list of them but she chose consciously not to as she wants to be fair really fair to everyone and she gives out a verbal preliminary syllabus since the regular one would be given out next week as she puts the title of the book on the blackboard—the chalk scratches, as it always does, for some reason and she tells the students they should go sooner rather than later as there might be secondhand copies and they could save some money but sadly, she says, the cost of books has gotten very high but she could think of no way around this for this course and she does say she really did use the text and it is not one of those books she would only refer to but it is a book that is really used and so they need to have their own copies of the book because you can't really share such an intimate thing with room-mates or friends who might not really be as they say on the same page and if they were on the same page you could not be on the same page because a page can only have one set of eyes looking at it at the same time and all of that was the easy part of the class and the hard part came from the the fact that she is listening to herself and hears herself repeating the same lines and paragraphs three times today echoing all the other years she has said the same things as the clock dictates what is said no matter if it is American history or European history: the first day or days of the class are the same and that is what is hard and her body is not being found until Friday... the dogs are still locked in the bedroom, it seems they are always kept there, the mess... their excrement and **Linda's** blood and stuff there, you don't want to know or hear and that is where she keeps her papers—such as they are—all those papers and books from Bulgaria and the writing no one can understand what it is and it is all soiled beyond any... and the dogs are all over the papers and frantic they must have been and then in the room where **Linda**... flailed... did she? did she move or was there just a flinging one last time or is that word too strong? So, just the mess and the state policeman says people don't commit suicide by banging their heads against the bathroom sink and there doesn't seem to be any evidence of anyone coming in and his voice is so matter of fact, these things happen, all the time, all the time but that is just the way it is and I nodded to him and he nodded to me and I wasn't going to argue with him as how can one argue about such a situation... I didn't want him to leave and I didn't want to stay there either and I hope the men who I hire to take away the stuff won't think badly of **Linda**... but they are trained for this sort of work but I wonder how you train someone for this sort of work? though I guess someone has to do it and the landlady wasn't going to burn down the trailer or get rid of it since it is firmly on the cement blocks and there are only a few places around Potsdam to rent so she is sure she would find someone to take it... but she didn't give me back **Linda'a** deposit but I didn't ask for it... (**LINDA'S** cousin left Hawaii for Arizona as he wanted to be near a hospital that might not kill him as he thought the hospitals in Hawaii might do)

VV

is drifting as he is talking and he is, like ourselves back in New York wondering when would we next be in Bulgaria and there is **the man in the corner**, you can never forget **the man in the corner** and everyone wants to be this person or know him since he has to be a man who seems to know something people who sit in the middle of a room are always deciding they must know and it is the sort of wisdom not passed on in the middle of a wide street, in the center of a room or walking across... did you notice, VV is saying, in Venice, no one talks as they cross the Piazza San Marco, unless they are tourists convinced they are going surely in the correct or wrong direction without a moment's hesitation: never do they muddle, they walk with a firm step, unless stopped by the need to appear in those photographs that have been taken thousands of times, before, and one can feel those fingers pushing the button to re-appear forty years later on a grey Monday afternoon in the spring in New York City, there on East First Street.

But in Pernik, there are no walls in the restaurnt where we have been sitting with VV, so as a result we are bereft of the possibility of there being a man in the corner. He would be found:

no doubt about it and having exhausted: what is there to see in Pernik now that we have been to the mining museum, met with VV's cousin, been given copies of the drawings of a man who has been imprisoned in the mines, back when having a relative in Paris is of course a mistake that can not go unpunished or unrewarded depending on your understanding of the human condition, but as we walk through the galleries of the museum... mostly from the days of the communism: on a wall some drawings of desolation which seem so out of place with the pictures of celebrations and explanation of the how's of coal mining in Pernik...

The Sixth is the Toll-House of Theft.

A windowless museum, so the idea of being underground, down there... a bank of great red flags and banners the workers carry on May Day, on 9 IX... those golden profiles of Lenin, Dimitrov, Blagoev and other founders... the gold or yellow thread and the now fading red silk or satin of the banners... I should linger unfurling each banner to watch the march of history, seeing if they have retained banners from the day of Stalin, and then the subsequent leaders of the Bulgarian Communist Party, subsequent to the death of Dimitrov...

No pictures of mining disasters as they no longer happen since the mines are no longer run to profit the capitalist class.

The photographs report on your being here, actually being here and devoid of people, the absence of the satisfaction in surviving all those people, who once alive, as Francis Bacon would say, looking at pictures from the Nineteenth Century, full up of life, they are, he says, as you and I looking at them and soon enough someone will be coming along looking at pictures of us looking at these pictures and now two levels of people full up with the life and naturally, heavens permit a good thing, the perfectly leaky boat and the necessary heavy seas, adrift and wiped out, as fast as his bruiser's hand slicing through the air of the French pub in London as we walk by the portraits of

heroes of socialist labor, heroes of bossing around socialist labor—ties in place, hair combed, posing with firm chin marching into the future from this building put up by the capitalists to glorify their exploitation of labor and the land

And now, Piret says. No gift shop.

Lead about by a guy in sunglasses, some sort of cousin or relative of VV who has a black wig on, badly fitted as it should, the more artificial the better when wearing a rug, as Piret calls it, 1960 ratpack lingo from when as we lounge in the Bar Trinidad in Palm Springs… how did such a thought arrive, no stranger than any other, though there are sure to be detractors, casting aspirations: a rather grand fellow though short of stature, grand in mind and bearing, if you can follow and the only guy in Bulgaria, in our time, really here—what you see is what you get—a walking Bulgarian talking homage to Roy Orbison not unlike VV who keeps his own face creams in the refrigerator just as girls learn what they have to do to stay fresh and young and he is the living the dying epitome of Roy Orbison, right there on the stage in Dublin: shorter, slighter and not speaking a word of English except to repeat *Pretty Woman*, yes, *Pretty Woman* and the tune is being hummed as Marielle Minke listening in the balcony of the Adelphi Cinema in Dublin, in the still winter, verging onto Spring, 1965, being seen by the same eyes as when I look to Piret, who gives me her far-away expression... as we are listening via VV as to what Kiril

KIRIL SERGINOV

Born in 1946, Pernik, Bulgaria. Graduated from the Art Studio of Vassil Valev (Sofia, 1972-1976).

Personal exhibitions: Interfolk Art Gallery (1983, Pernik, Bulgaria); Olga Gallery (1984, Moscow, Russia); Museum of Fine Arts (1985, Radomir, Bulgaria); Art Gallery (1986, Tashkent, Uzbekistan); Art Gallery Cultural Information Center (1994, 1996, 1999, 2000, 2001 Pernik; 2000, 2001, Sofia;). Has been taking part in art exhibitions since 1972 (Bulgaria, Belarus, Austria, France, Russia, the Republic of Macedonia, USA, Canada).

Works are kept at museums, galleries and private collections in the USA, Bulgaria, Russia, Italy, Macedonia, France. A member of the Bulgarian Union of Artists. Lives in Pernik, Bulgaria.

is saying, which is available in the book he gives us as we are leaving the headquarters of the mines in Pernik:

THROUGH THE ALTERNATIVE
DIMENSIONS OF KIRIL SERGINOV.

The beginning of each easteuropean story, dedicated to certain alternative artists always begins with the history for his individual impact with the local tradition and the political system. Just because the destiny of the East European artist is different. It is connected with impact which is based on personal intuition, but also on the influence of different prototypes of the modern eastern art of the time. The "story" in this catalogue is the same, although even partly, it will try to show and give life the presence of Kiril Serginov in the development of the alternative Bulgarian culture, which even today is out of the professional critic's sight.

Kiril seems—I am saying to VV and Piret—to be one of the few people in Bulgaria, really hearing as the cliché might have it, a drummer banging away on a tune only he is hearing and seems in some way to be happier than any other person ever met in Bulgaria, now and then, and VV is a little annoyed, as another cliché might have it, that I might say such a thing as what finally is the point of saying something like this and surely **the man in the corner** would have something to say about it and while we still have to see where VV is living, what four thousand miles from the Grassroots in New York City, which is, as if he has walked in, only the other day, and we are always there up near the front, when a person walks down the few steps from the sidewalk and opens the door to the darkness of the shabby room, as one can hear said by a guy telling his friend from out of town as he is explaining where they are going: to this old bar, with George who in so many ways is the perfect man as candidate for being the man in the corner, though Piret is not prepared to go anywhere near the possibility of seeing the guy in the sunglasses, again, no: Kiril what's his name? just creeps me out like any guy who would dress in homage to… why didn't people decide to dress in homage to you name anyone but a guy like Roy Orbison, ask your daughter if anyone knows his name who is not pushing themselves along in an imaginary wheelchair going on about what great music they had back in the day, as is said now when a person is talking about the ancient times of those people who look like they have time engraved on the face and it can be real scary seeing those lines deepening the closer you get to a person like that and how easy it is to fall into the falling into what has been, and is just that: what has been.

Of course, I know, to call Kiril a happy man is to exaggerate him into being an impossible person, a man who does not exist as flesh, blood, as having the potential to be dumped into the city cemetery, to take the train into Sofia and appear at art galleries playing musical instruments of his own design while claiming to fasten what he has been doing to the Beatles and the Japanese woman who survives John Lennon, though there is no denying we have been to visit with Kiril and he walks us through the galleries eventually to the offices upstairs where the director is not in so we can sit in the conference room and then sit in the director's office in his chair, much as has been done in the

room in the Rila Monastery, when Medy asks the priest if
he can sit in the chair where Ivan Vasov is sitting when he
is writing his first book about being

in the mountains.

LINDA NELSON is a nice lady and not afraid to have
fun in class. The note taking can be a bit boring after a
while, so I advise you to only take 50 min classes with
her. Good grader though, just study the notes and read-
ings and you'll do just fine

A Pause.

Piret and I came to visit VV in Pernik. We have been
walked about the town. **The man in the corner** insists on
this moment to allow everyone to catch up. Soon enough
we would all have to be heading back to Sofia to be on our
way. VV is staying behind, whatever that might mean.

Upstairs in the meeting room next to the director's office a spiral bound album of reproductions of large drawings by Nikola Tanev which define bleakness, if it has ever been done, not a grabbing by the lapels of your coat and shaking you: look at this, in the manner of Kathe Kolowitz, or there are the myriad squadrons of sleeve tuggers: see how sensitive I am, see my eye in action… no, these drawings, spare of detail: individuals move midst over-head ore conveyers, carts being pushed, roads being trudged upon, cottages huddle, a lot of empty space as if the effort to draw is too much. A few steps before the gestures of Cy Twombly, just so impossible, Piret is telling me and VV, who can care so much, who cares: we each carry these names, these pictures, these streets and snapshots from seconds without order and to impose order produces an order to roll the stone over your grave, you will be saying next, roll that stone and stamp on top of it so it better be flat so with each thudding stomp of the boot: forget, forget for our own sake and **the man in the corner** is itching to set everyone straight which is probably impossible to say these days when we are to be setting everything into the required crooked lines.

We never did see the mines either above ground or underground, so a typical modern experience, better always the depiction rather than the actual mine, while Kiril's sunglasses didn't fully disguise the lines of age from inching relentlessly out from the corners of his eyes.

There the severe guard of "spirituality", does not like to snick out, and the treatment is possible only on the individual level or in the small social groups. From the

bacteria of the postcommunism few people are saved and their thin boat passing away from the stinky "chalgadjisky", island in direction to sky fields of mental hygiene. Because the ground on which we walk is again covered with dirty shroud and this makes us invisible again.

—prof. phd. Svilen Stefano

VV has no way to describe Kiril, isn't it as they say in Brooklyn you get what you see, there is nothing more or less, but I could do with more or I could do with less.

He has always been like this.

I suspect **the man in the corner** is saying and he might as well be saying as thinking, such a demarcation is an obvious device, as almost to be beneath contempt, a total failure, and what else does a person want to be sometimes, and maybe being in Pernik, is a way to possibly understand how it must be to find as **the man in the corner**, looking on, as these foreign people come to Pernik, invited by VV, who has become something of a foreign person, though not having fully been taken possession of by his new language and still thinking, dreaming in Bulgarian, though also feeling, of course goes without saying, in Bulgarian or he is always saying: he is walking these people about "his" city but it is "his city" as a person who is saying, I grew up in Brooklyn, I grew up in Patchogue, I grew up in Menasha and I can hear voices calling me back and the proper rejoinder would have to be: what sort of hearing gadget are you using now since your ears have been shot to shit.

We walk, VV is saying and we all agree, yes, we walk and we walk and we are not walking up the hill to see the

remains of some sort of fortification. The hills have shadowed our walking and rain threatens, Piret is saying, while
she does not like to carry an umbrella, she is scared of getting soaked: as if I am about to be dissolved, she says, and
don't you tell me there should be a little dissolving about
the edges, but of course you are thinking this, I can tell, as
I always can tell, when a man says he is not thinking about
the connection between a woman and her fear of the rain
and her physical shape, how certain things creep edging
into every aspect of what might be called normal conversation so even the statement: it might rain, becomes: and the
man who has found a way to protect himself against two
sides is still open to the diagonal created by the imaginary
line going from one side of the corner, this is your conventional 90 degree angle, to the other side of the corner,
well mostly, there is a certain wobble to the line, since it is
built back in the years when building is *the all* and such is
the nature of things, a sort of danger within the perfectly
formed corner, however, in the recent past and in the present of Pernik there is no real danger of being found in such
a perfection: as Kiril has at times felt the need to explain
what he is attempting to do, but the brass instrument on
display reminds one and all of the urinal displayed so many
years ago and once Duchamp's object signed R. Mutt is not
immediately removed from the wall, no amount of forgetfulness could be gathered and VV takes us to his rooms left
to him with the death of his mother and he can understand
the dilemma arising when I say, now suspended between
Bulgaria and Estonia, you think, suspended between two

obscurities which have nothing in common beyond the impossibility of holding them in mind if you are standing at 57th and Fifth in New York City on a Spring afternoon around 2pm, they seem so remote and isn't it Wayne who explaines he didn't want to die in a country where three hundred people can die in a sort of disaster and it would rate only an inch of space in *The New York Times*, how nostalgic can anyone get, VV rebukes us, how nostalgic and even Wayne dying of AIDS now becomes a reminder of when no one **knew**...

THE EIGHTH IS THE TOLL-HOUSE OF USURY

No one knows anything, knew anything and then everyone says they knew all along, even in Pernik, VV is saying, welcome, welcome, to my abode, never thought to see you here, never thought to get you to come to visit, how will you remember it?

Let's don't go and say we did, Piret replies, since bereft of imagination or should it be, not given to fancy, we are here with you, VV, looking down to the waste lands surrounding the housing

blocks, areas given to the public so as to provide space for the blank slate upon which the neighbors can describe their preparations for the ordeal of the bed by way of the scars they leave behind, though mostly unseen by the casual passerby, as if the creature known as the passerby exists in today's Bulgaria because he, and sometimes it could be a she, is an unknown voyager upon the streets of Sofia and of Pernik, VV has told us, but if you look closely into the work of Tanev you can glimpse ever so briefly a passerby within his painted memories of Sofia… but such shades are the victims of the communism, difficult to commemorate, but which did ever so briefly appear in Sofia when Yavarov is living in Sofia, but all of that requires such fantastic explication though standing at the balcony looking down to the land about the block Piret understands the secret labors of VV and you must, she says, poking her pointing finger into my chest inching toward my left shoulder, not allow it to pass away, scars, you say, she turns to VV, scars of the failures repeated night after night upon the hard folk beds inside this block.

If you want to say so, can I offer you a coffee? VV is measuring out the Nescafe into cups, the ultimate luxury, you remember, he turns to me, and I held it for your visit or at least Piret will join me, I wish I had a *limonada* to offer you… I am sure Piret doesn't understand the concept of Nescafe.

You can save that for another time, please, Piret says.

You can't be serious, the scars of having memories, thinking of those who say they have bad memories, do they cultivate their poor memories or are they only lying to torment those of us…

VV as before suddenly stops, runs out of the words: he is thinking of his brother with the one remaining kidney, and the doctor is saying the kidney specialist is on holiday in Cyprus and people with kidney problems just have to wait, their problems just have to wait, there is only one man in Pernik who knows where the kidney is located in the human body, he is on holiday in Cyprus and can't be disturbed, even if we knew how to disturb him, as that is how it is, now, in the new Bulgaria, doctors go on holiday, they really do, new regulations come from Brussels: conditions, illnesses and sickness and so many other aspects of human health now disappear from view, they go on holiday, since there is no doctor to record the condition, to make a diagnosis that is medically sound, of course nurses and other doctors could make a diagnosis but that is not the point, the man who knows the human kidney is on holiday in Cyprus.

I got the sense **Linda Nelson** is a Russian studies prof teaching a general European subject which I felt made her subconscious about being out of her element. The lectures were ok. Just didn't project authority to the class.

A certain disturbance, to be sure as we are on the train station platform saying goodbye to VV who will remain behind in Pernik as we return to Sofia.

He: Kak si?

He: Po-dobre ot utre.

HOWEVER, we have jumped ahead of ourselves as we are still walking about in the rooms, square by square meter, VV is, as the saying would have it, making it his own, though he is not saying this is where he is planning to die. That is a statement he does not allow his mind to evolve into a question, probably no one is to suggest asking as we have entered these rooms and well knowing at a certain point a person of course wonders: with this move will it be my last and while I won't be rehashing much of anything from the wisdom of this move in particular having been translated to the region marked by the necrologues ever so briefly tacked on the wall near by the mailboxes in the entry way, but with my sons in The States it is unlikely they will be taking care of this traditional obligation and is it possible there will be even one set of eyes which will linger longer than a second at the necrologue and recognizing— how this will happen is beyond me—this is for the guy who is usually seen hobbling alone, worried by the shadows, worried about **the man in the corner**, about another man carrying a piece of ice in a wrapping of newspaper, how will someone see in the smiling handsome—I must say: I am a handsome man, a real handsome man as one or two women say—photographed man, for how to reconcile the before as surely represented by the photograph and the now of seeing the photograph and the trying to focus the eyes from the photograph and the eyes full of this man who we would see every day walking into the town center, worried, he always seems and once when I stop him he is talking about **the man in the corner** or a man he has seen who is carefully rubbing a piece of ice back and forth on the back of his neck: you do remember that moment, I am sure someone must be saying to another of the tenants but didn't that guy move here only after someone has died and: who is he really, does anyone know him and you see Piret, how complicated it gets and I am shown photographs of school mates who are pictured just before the lid of the coffin closes down that life, another life, erased up here above the six foot deep repository and the moment when both

are now gone to the place marked by this piece of paper
with a final lie in the photograph... that tries valiantly to
replace the actual old guy who must have come back to
Bulgaria to die, why didn't he just stay and die in America, I am hearing them saying, VV says, why ever has he
bothered to come back here, this place from which he flees
to live, he is probably thinking and we can all hear him
saying in Rome: I fled that place, that Bulgaria, to have the
chance to... and they would pause duplicating his dramatic
pause which they would say as one person, this is always
required in the West, people in the West expect the pause
so as to participate in the ritual of another person fleeing
the communism, the necessary pause: be free, to
breathe the free air of the West and NOW he comes back
here to die, what is that supposed to mean? Bulgaria is not
just a depository of the dead, for those who find themselves
making that turn, for the last time, down the street, one or
two, over from the central *gropshta,* didn't he know foreign
people find our country a place for sport, for pleasurable activity and some of them invest in property so now Bulgaria
is really part of the world: people hold in their portfolios
Bulgarian real estate, but you might be thinking, Piret, VV
says, these voices are mere fiction, that word *mere* always
attached to the noun of fiction though there are some who
believe only fiction can possibly tell the truth as everyone
at the same time both believes the newspapers and disbe-
lieves the newspapers.

What can they be thinking about and while that has
the appearance of a rhetorical question with the change we

have grown away from the making of such and now no longer listen to such questions but are always posing them for ourselves: as in Why am I here? Why are you here? What will you take away from here? What is there to take away from here?

When I as a young person, VV is still saying, I thought it such a confusing moment when someone would take a picture of a dead person in the coffin, but when I was going through my mother's possessions, probably the most violent action I have ever performed in my life, can it be described, the violence… no, that would have to be for another or another time. I have the feeling, can I say it, I often wonder in English, I have the feeling this apartment is very empty because I did that to my mother, but I only began and stopped, but the beginning is enough: this apartment is empty, believe me, please.

I do not know who takes the picture of my father in his coffin in New Jersey, Piret says, I feel as I have been found with soiled panties, is that graphic enough, and those pictures are sent around the world to all his friends and colleagues—if ever the pictures are being shown of my father in his casket together with assembled surviving pastors coming to attest to his death or rather his passing as is now the way to say my father is dead, I would be unable to ever meet any of these people, I would feel the coffin displaying my father has replaced my face as they look at me, poor girl whose father is dead, dead in public and not away as it should be, but you, she turns to me, know the man in a bar who carries his dead in his wallet and when the drink really has him opens his wallet and looks through the photographs of his dead, trying to remember who they are and why he is looking at them and why, why, is he still walking around since his whole family is now no more, nothing remains of them as the pictures have been taken just before they had been burnt up.

Yes, that is in The 55 on Christopher Street, he is probably gone like all the people I saw in that bar which remains, but that is all it does: remains, I never took you there, as I no longer know anyone, though on occasion I will walk by and almost go in but resist, just too simple…

Enough, VV is saying, don't you admire the view from my window on the world: hazy through

windows I can't wash—one of those design flaws—as who is to be proud enough of where they live so they would wash clean the view because didn't the view never changed and who is to be looking out the window anyway, my mother is too small of a woman to be sitting in her chair and looking out the window, everything she cherishes is within this room and out there is only outside which has taken her husband, taken her sons and given her this apartment with windows that are not meant to be looked out of, only in Bulgaria, you could probably say or I am just unable to imagine another place, I am too caught by this apartment and the rules it imposes upon its inhabitants, unlike both of you...

You might be wrong, Piret says, he never washes the windows of the room in New York and I do not insist as I am never to be a person who would sit by the window looking out at... what would I see by looking out of the windows of the house in New Jersey? In New York, as you know you can go to the tenement museum, imagine a museum for slum housing and they have a permanent exhibition on how to look out of the window in a tenement in New York City, the Lower East Side, back when… the women have pillows they would lean on, decorated with embroidery, a free show, I guess, playing out down on the streets, in Estonia, I saw a woman leaning on one of those pillows in the housing block next to the place where we are staying, but she might have been Russian, I am not sure, my mother never talks about looking out of the windows of the house she grew up there in Tartu. Windows are to be kept shut, the drapes drawn depending on the time of the day, curtains open only so far and never would a child go near the window, someone might see you, is how she would say it, but he never looks out the windows on First Street, now, unless he is looking for the mailman.

Albert Speer is going to write a history of the window, is said, once I remember reading, after he is released from Spandau, since for twenty years he looks out of the same window, I guess it is, all those twenty years, but maybe not really the same window because reality is not as neat as a casual anecdote would want us to have and Speer never got around to it as he never got out of the Nazi years, even after twenty years in prison, that's all people want to know: those years when he knows Hitler.

On First Street, the window only gets dirty when you wash it. The other window has the air conditioner and there is no way to wash it without removing the air conditioner.

When do we laugh, VV says. Are you having me along for a ride somewhere or other?

Why should you think that, Piret has been to the museum, I would never go to something like it, my sister became a member of the museum, what to do with people like that, I think your mother has the right idea, and she is probably telling you there is something unnatural about living up here on the tenth floor, isn't it? And you would be telling her I should not be flying back and forth to The States because if God means us to fly he would have provided us with wings and she might also have said if you did not fly so much, if people did not fly so much and hunger to fly so much, and it is the hunger which is the great fault, the hunger to be flying, people would actually be able to fly, isn't it so…and I am hearing in the *isn't it so*, something Piret's mother always tags on to so many statements about her comparisons of what has happened to the condition of the life in the United States when you look around today and try to think back, try to remember, what it was like when we—she would always use the plural pronoun, having been fully incorporated into the family unit arriving: of herself, her mother and younger brother, the other brothers left temporarily behind in England, Germany—arriving in this country in 1951, just as I have learned to say, from being around people like VV, around Piret's mother, around Lidia, statements about *the life*… and they are not making allusions to women who prostitute themselves in what is said to be taking up *the life,* but we are talking about the life in the hopes of keeping ourselves in the present moment so as to avoid falling back into the past which is just another way of falling into the grave head backwards as opposed to forward.

if u like to have your work from a class back sooner than a month later do not take **Linda Nelson's** class. Not only does she not grade your work she cancels class time to grade it. She needs to make SUNY Potsdam more of a priority and quit teaching at Clarkson and pay more attention to us. Her quizzes and tests are easy but like i said u won't know what u got.

Taking a real header, Piret says, but VV turns to the window, seems lost as his English remains just over the line from requiring him to ship every single English word he hears into some sort of dictionary: ENGLISH/BULGARIAN and then BULGARIAN/ENGLISH, I never hit her if that is what you are saying, a son would never hit his mother, no matter the provocation, I am not some fellow in the bar who is talking about the accident of breaking his girlfriend's jaw when the words got away from him and her.

She isn't saying that, is said and they could both feel the farewell is coming on quickly, the time to rush for the train, to get back to Sofia, to get ready to go to dinner, to get ready to see who are we seeing tonight, how the time flies away, how the visit comes to the end, or the beginning of the next visit if, when, if and we don't need the mournful tones even before we have left, you can save them, momentarily, is soon enough and we will be flying back to Milano for one more tiny taste of Italy, almost more time to be spent in airport, train station, on the bus to and from airport, all that dreary business of connecting, waiting…

But, we are still here in Pernik waiting to walk to the station, think of ourselves as reverse commuters who have been out here on business and we or rather you just want to prop up your feet, you can't loosen the tie as no one wears ties, Piret is saying, while VV will soon enough be writing us back in New York, I just came from the cafe at the cultural house. Walk a lot. We'll talk about my books back in NY. There is a Russian movie (action) in the Mines Memorial in the center of Pernik. I'm not sure, maybe I'll go...maybe not, enjoying the cherries and the strawberries and lonely, lonely in Pernik. All my friends are gone. The man in the museum is on the Black Sea. You have his best regards. I go also to the sea but I don't know when. Then, Rhodopa Mountains. Soon enough I shall be scattered to the Bulgarian four winds.

The Sixth Toll-House
is the Toll-House of Unmercifulness

For the longest time, is said, I have thought I want to be buried in Tombstone, in the regular city cemetery out at the end of West Allen Street before it turns into the road going to the Schieflin Monument, going to... nowhere, actually.. the road just stops, eventually and then I thought, the cemetery in Douglas, but it seems rather conventional but with VV's hint could one ever expect survivors to cart the ashes to Bulgaria, rent a car and drive to Shipka... pick a day just after a rain has stopped, end of day where from the heights one can see clouds off in the distance dropping rain on some place, but here where the rained-on grass glistens, to imagine the children, the survivors walking around the great monument strewing the ashes out on to the hillsides falling away, where how many years ago, Bulgarian and Turk struggled hand to hand, strewing the ashes though it is also possible when going through customs the ashes got dropped and literary folk will remember the dispersal of Murphy's ashes on the Dublin pub floor, midst the sputum, the discarded cigarette butts, the mud as it would have to be a rainy day, none other would do for the final mixing.

The delicious morbidity, Piret is saying, can't you, VV, taste it in your mouth?

Ash is too dry for me, when I can still walk into town, sit in the café, under the trees retaining some coolness midst the staggering heat, thinking of those who are not here and might be here if I only could concentrate, that is all one has to do in Pernik, concentrate and it wipes out the loneliness.

Not for a moment do I believe you, is said, to think is to be alone, to remember the touch, the glance…

Of course you are romantic, I didn't want to suggest it. I am thinking of my father who is sent to the Belene camp… for some reason he survives, they beat him, they beat him, but he is meant to live, there is no accounting for it, some live, some die… he says it is the only thing he learns but he knows it is a useless thing to learn, everything you learn from life is useless, and you learn nothing from death since it always happens to someone else, the cliché has it, no one comes back from their death.

Dueling morbidities, Piret is saying, should we be going, down the elevator…there will be a death notice near the mailboxes, VV will not know the woman pictured, he should have known, but has not really lived in this building that long, but these notices add something to the building, in New York you think the buildings have no past, though of course you know they have a past but there are no signs, no indications who came before beyond sometimes they forget to update the bell names, the names on the mailboxes, but more and more people don't put their names on the bells or the mailboxes… no dedication stones: the buildings all just arrive, like that, they are built, they are, when I lived on 30th Street, someone, A. SMITH had been penciled into the space for the name, next to my apartment bell downstairs, I put a typed piece of paper with my last name on it, I should have just put the apartment number, redundantly, since it was already there engraved on the metal frame, people would ring the bell and say my last name, but I learned quickly, not from anything awful happening: but who was A. SMITH?

The delivery guys would hurry in and scatter their menus and ads for the restaurants, supplying the suppers for the people living alone, never cooking just ordering out, their lives, eating alone from plastic bags and plastic containers, night after night coming home from work, the hard day, turn on the TV, see what's been checked off in the give-away newspaper: the tiny violins all sawing away some cloying Beatles song, you people, how you could listen to that music, didn't you think to hoot them off stage, the mechanical tears, wrinkled face of sadness and loneliness, what a pathetic generation, getting your feelings from pop music.

Hold your breath and down we go, VV says, as the elevator with no door closing the front of the descending compartment, just drops to the ground floor where a door is pushed open. You have to be alert. Many people don't take the elevators. They are not afraid of getting stuck or anything like, but it is more they have the idea something is going to leap out and scrape their faces off as the car falls down to the ground floor... I don't understand the mechanics of these fears, we are a materialistic people who believe every weird idea you can imagine, nothing is too strange for any of us, didn't George tell you, when he came back in '93 he was surprised by how many psychoanalysts there are in the country... it is easy in Bulgaria, to be a psychoanalyst, all you have to do is say you have read some Freud and he is the father of psychoanalysis and as a result you are a psychoanalyst, while the only trick is how to get paid for what you did and you only have a vague idea what a psychoanalyst does but it is so easy back then as no one knows what a psychoanalyst did... they help people and they talk about sex or want to listen to the patient talking about sex so they have to start talking about sex which is something that is never talked about under the communism, there is never any nudity in films, never any suggestion of what really went on and there is no birth control most of the time, but after the change, the former communists got into the sex newspaper business and printed these cheap newspapers filled with stuff you don't want to know about or do you? and Piret is nodding her head yes and trying not to be obvious about it as this is the first time the three letter word has been spoken and while she has been told by a former politician in Bulgaria that during the communism people fucked, like they say in English, rabbits, is it the correct expression? and yet they didn't reproduce like rabbits so Piret asks, did the guys always pull out or did they put their penises, which is not the correct form for the plural of that most singular of words, into the mouths of willing girls or did they put into that dark place only homosexuals like to talk about with loving attention to details of wrinkles, numbers of tiny wrinkles ringing the abyss, radiating as spokes about that dark, dark... of course you think I am some sort of slut but I was in college during the height, that's not the best way to say it, of the AIDS crisis and an awful lot of time is devoted to the necessity for and use of dental dams... at which point a person would look away and VV is also looking away and sometimes one just walks along... happy midst the devastated landscape, and VV is saying, it looks all rather grim in its way, but it could be worse, it could be deserted like many of the country plac-es are in Bulgaria or it could all still be running like back in the days, but that maybe is even worse because we are always being told how prosperous Pernik is, how valiant our miners are, how good every damn thing is so you could imagine if you listened only to the radio and are blind and a little slow of mind you are living in a sort of paradise, but a unique paradise ever vigilant, ever strong in defense of the motherland always endangered by agents of the subversive power who wants to take away from you dear workers who have labored so hard in the building of the socialism, have I the lingo down, VV asks? you do, could be the only response, yet, Piret says, why do people in Bulgaria shy away from talk of what is on everyone's mind and I am not about to hear I am the only one who looks first to what a man might have underneath his belt buckle or the way his face is covered with hair or his eyes or…and do not deny any of this as I still remember the politician, prude that he has turned out to be, after as he said "fucking like a rabbit" during the days of the communism, and now nothing much though his hand had a good feel of my…

VV says do you see that the river is actually running clearly now, for some reason… while in other days it is filled with unnatural colors no one wants to think about as the origin is not far from where the water comes that we drink.

And as a sort of conclusion...were any lessons learned or has all this been again in vain...and with that, thought.

Call to the poet:

Sun setting
eventually
I am leaving
sun remains
always

While it is certainly hard to decide whether the train is coming or going, Piret and I return to Sofia on a modern train like this one, leaving VV to his, as is said, devices, and as a result sending him to the desk to record our visit in his day book, mostly blank as we are the first to visit him this summer. He does not ask himself if there would be others and he then turns the pages and began to make a list of possible articles he could begin to write in preparation for a new book that would take its heart from another photo that while reduced to the paper near where this is being read exists only in his memory of why was he walking across the road to take a picture of VV and Piret standing in Pernik?

A last thought: VV has talked with me in New York and we have gone to parties together and talked about how we both miss George, and that might be an article: the fate of a Bulgarian psychoanalyst in New York City... but how would he explain all the background a reader would need to know?

BULLETIN—SUNY POTSDAM ICON MOURNS TWO LOSSES IN LESS THAN A WEEK; SARNOFF, NELSON EXPIRE

THE SUNY POTSDAM COMMUNITY IS MOURNING THE LOSS OF BOTH A CAMPUS ICON AND A WELL-RESPECTED SCHOLAR; TWO DEATHS IN LESS THAN A WEEK'S TIME.

99 NEWS HAS LEARNED JOSEPH SARNOFF HAS PASSED. SARNOFF HAD BEEN ASSOCIATED WITH SUNY POTSDAM SINCE 1970. HE WAS HIRED OUT OF COLLEGE TO BE THE FIRST DIRECTOR OF THE STUDENT UNION AND ACTIVITIES, A POSITION HE HELD FOR MORE THAN 30 YEARS BEFORE TRANSITIONING EARLIER THIS DECADE INTO THE POST OF DIRECTOR OF STUDENT RETENTION SERVICES WHICH HE HELD AT THE TIME OF HIS DEATH. SARNOFF HAD A LONG AND DISTINGUISHED PUBLIC SERVICE CAREER. HE WAS DEPUTY POTSDAM VILLAGE JUSTICE FOR MANY YEARS AND HELD A NUMBER OF OTHER APPOINTED POSITIONS ON GOVERNMENT BOARDS AND VOLUNTEER GROUPS. HE WAS A RECENT MEMBER OF THE POTSDAM TOWN PLANNING BOARD. SARNOFF WAS ALSO KNOWN FOR HUMANITARIAN EFFORTS OF VARIOUS KINDS, TAKING TRIPS TO SEVERAL FOREIGN COUNTRIES. HE WAS ALSO AN HONORARY BROTHER OF THE ORDER OF PROMETHEUS. JOE SARNOFF EXPIRED AT HIS HOME; HE WAS IN HIS EARLY 60'S.

HISTORY PROFESSOR DR.LINDA NELSON ALSO PASSED AWAY IN RECENT DAYS. NELSON WAS PERHAPS BEST KNOWN FOR HER WORK IN RE-SEARCH AND TEACHING EUROPEAN HISTORY, ESPECIALLY RUSSIAN HISTORY. NELSON ALSO TAUGHT SECTIONS OF US HISTORY. LINDA NEL-SON DIED AT CANTON-POTSDAM HOSPITAL SAT-URDAY AT THE AGE OF 60.

And that photo of two people on a bridge with the wom-an looking away from the river at what looks like near end of day and that smokestack ever suggestive

WHAT CAME... AFTER OR BEFORE...
—Yes.
—"And eternally so, all our lives in hand! Hurrah for Karamazov!" Kolya cried once more ecstatically, and once more all the boys joined in his exclamation.

—And this is the only immortality you and I may share,
my Lolita.

—I dont. I dont. I dont hate it. I dont hate it!

—...and nobody, nobody knows what's going to happen
to anybody besides the forlorn rags of growing old, I think
of Dean Moriarty, I even think of old Dean Moriarty the
father we never found, I think of Dean Moriarty.

—*It was the devious-cruising Rachel, that in her retracing
search after her missing children, only found another orphan.*

—We can exist at the highest degree of intensity as long
as we live, so Roithamer (June 7). The end is no process.
Clearing.

—In the present case, it is as essential to surmount a
consciousness of an unreal freedom and to recognize a de-
pendence not perceived by our senses.

—: go and see for yourselves if you are loathe to believe
me.

Readers give themselves to fiction and naturally wonder what happened to the characters they "have lived with"
while reading and the same with those watching a play or a
movie. Of course it is the suspension of disbelief, a knowing forgetfulness, that the "lives" they have been reading
or viewing have not ceased when the last page was turned,
the curtain came down, THE END appeared on the screen.

Of course a book can be re-read, a play read or viewed
again, a movie watched again and those lives are there: all
now revealed yet back we go...

Of late there are sequels, and even prequels though no one has written for instance a sequel to WAR AND PEACE... but there is a HIGH NOON Part Two and characters from previously published works have reappeared in fictions written by other writers...

Through EMPTY AMERICAN LETTERS you already know what came after and even... but I also thought how predictable so it became necessary: thusly, what came before this voyage along the Aerial Toll-Houses, THE VARNA CRUSADE or the Crusade of Varna...

As the fight increases in fury, both the troops of Islam and the infidels display such zeal that, in the marketplace of death, father could neither recognize son nor son father, and the angels in heaven and the fish in the seas wonder at the fury of the fight.

The shades whisper a Bulgarian witness is beginning.

I hinted at this to Denis D. who does not hold with such hocus-pocus but we'll see... as even he has talked of the necessity in providing approaches to avenues for words... but is it strange for a 15th Century Bulgarian to be speaking English, to say the least, though in Patchogue where all such things were fixed in solid material form, upon remembered thought, stronger than granite—one had seen too many buildings of brick and wood pulled down or gutted by fire on Main Street—thus, on the screen at the Rialto or Patchogue Theatre... everyone spoke English or if according to the dictates of imagination it might be understood in *movie* reality they might be speaking in a foreign language—though I personally never actually heard a foreign language come from one of these screens—we properly assumed these very strange historical figures wearing clothing never to be seen on any street in the village might be speaking in their so-called native languages but as we listened to them while sitting in our seats we heard them in English and of course understood what they were saying.

Like many things happening on or near Botev Boulevard in Sofia—the most interesting street in Sofia because it had been now more than forty years before, the first street upon which I walked in that then night in September after leaving the train from Beograd which was continuing on to Istanbul—is the site for how this book will come to a conclusion in the meeting with Ivan.

No, this is not Ivan, the *Darzhavna sigurnost* agent, but another Ivan and you can think of him as the other Ivan or as the interesting Ivan or as the Ivan who told me about the Varna Crusade or the Crusade of Varna which came to an end on 10 November 1444, just over five hundred years before the 9th of September 1944 when another beginning fell upon Bulgaria.

Like most people in Patchogue and I might as well use that village as a reference point as to say, like most people in New York City or London or Paris I thought that the Crusades were all about Richard the Lionhearted and Saladin and then the strange crusades lead by men such as Peter the Hermit or the Children's Crusade or the Crusade that sacked Constantinople since that was easier done than going all the way to Jerusalem… but here was the last crusade, hundreds of years later and ending in Bulgaria of all places or maybe not so obscure…but remembering Bulgaria had disappeared from history in 1396.

Resistance continued in Vidin for three more years but it was eclipsed in 1396. Bulgaria as a state was not to exist for almost half a millennium. *A CONCISE HISTORY OF BULGARIA* by R. J. Crampton.

What comes after: "Many were crippled by frostbite many more died in smaller follow-up battles, and most European prisoners were killed or sold into slavery"

The voice is interested in those few days…the bodies gathered, stripped… separated according to religion.

The weather could be talked about.

There could be a chorus, of course, a chorus insisting on the significance…

God, there has to be significance… it all has to mean something for why is the reader bothering…

After Varna is a phrase appearing in the chronicles and is now, even for us, *long ago we were* in Varna but being neither Polish nor Hungarian we were not taken to the museum.

During the time of the communism there was an initial suppression of all the history from before 9 September 1944 which did not feature the heroes of the communist party… but somewhere along the way the beach was discovered and a tourist industry created and as a result souvenirs had to be invented along with sanitized folk music and dance… and as the industry developed museums began to appear and the Battle of Varna was discovered… and small reenactments began to be staged… but a defeat is always a problem though since no Bulgarian armies participated— since there was no longer a Bulgarian army or a Bulgarian state though the people remained, the people remained not speaking Turkish…but having to try to understand it, yes that's a question, asked by Frederik as he rose slowly from the chair he was sitting on in front of the cabin on the hillside near Madara:

Frederik—of course you remember him—with the three passports: an American since he was born in Boston: and if things get really bad in Europe I can always go to The States, be miserable of course as only you can be in The States since being miserable also comes with a hopefulness, the awful hopefulness, you know what I mean? I'm sure you do and know why I keep the Irish passport because my mother was Irish and going to Ireland is easier than to The States when living in the utopia of Sweden, as too many people like to fancy it: you are living in a utopia, isn't it grand as they would say in Dublin, isn't it grand to be living where you don't… so with a dead Swedish father and a dead Irish mother and myself born in Boston… has himself living on the side of a mountain near Madara.

But you said you were going to hear Ivan?

And Frederik is telling me, use me, use me as you will. It would be an honor to be included in your…

FIVE

at the Battle of Varna (near the Black Sea fortress of Varna, Bulgaria). The Ottomans won a decisive victory despite heavy losses, while the Hungarians lost their King and over 10,000 men.

SIX

In November Murad arrived in Varna with a considerably larger force than the Crusaders. In a hard-fought battle, Ladislas was killed charging the Turks and word of his death put the Crusaders to flight. Most of them were killed, though Hunyadi escaped...

They come here and kill each other. No way to run away. If they see you: how to be invisible, how to disappear…

But where are these words   —coming from?

Desperation   something happened.

Words come from where they have always come from: there's not much of a secret there.

SEVEN

1pm, 9/11/01. The Chinese guy who owns the hardware store on Second Avenue had broken up the packs of the dust masks you use when house cleaning or scraping old paint from the walls. Usually, they sell three for a dollar now he was selling one face mask for a dollar. We all thought there would be smoke and dust clogging the air that day and for the following few days but the wind blew away from the north as we were north of the site. However, we could smell something.

There was only one television channel instead of the hundreds.

Is there any difference now between 11 September 2001 and 10 November 1444?

EIGHT

You're maybe expecting to hear me tell you, when Ivan came back from wherever he had gone to, he would be bringing something to link him—this short man standing before me as I sat on the straight back chair with my face to the inside of the room, away from the boulevard out there beyond the window across which a crack had developed and been repaired with a piece of white cloth like tape—to the battle which had taken place near Varna in 1444.

You have to imagine, he said, what I had heard as a young man, once when I had gone to visit a friend on the hillside near Madara, in a house without electricity... not really a house more a shelter for the shepherds but my friend had gone there to think, as he said... I had argued with him saying you can think anywhere, the motions of the mind do not require such a re-location.

Frederik, as you remember has been found on a mountainside near Madara, over at an angle from the park and buses and the wooden pathway up to the caves and the looking up at the figure on the horse. Ivan didn't know Frederik so this is not an allusion to Frederik but it reminded us, Ivan was always trying to be friends with us, a friend so we would forget and really turn him into the shade you require for this thinking about the Varna Crusade...

But in order to think away from this moment sometimes requires a going away...

Madara is a special place, Ivan is saying, as here a few of those who had escaped the slaughter at Varna sought refuge. The Turks... as superstitious as all people are, think this place is... I do not know what is inside their heads but I do know it is a place these young men flee to or fell upon and noticed their pursuers turning suddenly away.

You know there was this man on a horse carved into the side of the mountain. Turks turn away from a carving depicting the human form, but a glance is sufficient to keep them turned away and that is the respite.

I do not know why they have not been taken by a fit of iconoclasm...

It would be a lie to tell you anyone recorded any of this.

We are not as well organized as I have heard the Irish have been in recovering the stories, those stories that...

These men who did not speak our language and we did not speak their language: all these utterings, human to be sure.

These men arriving with hands as empty as Ivan's coming back with from wherever he has gone but it is obvious the only place he has gone is the toilet though it is possible he has been to the place where he did some cooking, that I know is back beyond the curtain and he must have washed his hands ever so briefly at the tiny sink but they are not fully dried, as there is sheen of wet on the back of both hands that moved as he talks of how is one to understand what has been happening after 10 November 1444... we only have to remember what happened here after 9 September, 500 hundred years later...

but you should try to exclude the word *later* and its companion *earlier* as the listener is trained inevitably to exclude anything hinting at what has been.

So, we are sitting in this room in a building with no real idea of its actual origin though I have been able to trace its existence back a certain number of years, but please, we are sitting in this room and in that wooded area in front of the great horse at Madara and we are trying to understand what held certain responses back with the appearance of these strangers, blonde strangers from someplace, which held clubs, fists, ropes from being...

I have sat where you are sitting and try as hard as I can to call into being one face, one human face and have failed. I do not hear any voices. There are no smells or feelings or intimations.

I do know I want to imagine such men and possibly that is a beginning. There can only be men standing now where I have placed them. To add women or children is to complicate before we have even begun.

However there has been no discussion of what is the present moment or is that something to be left unclear? Will everything be in what might he said to be the eternal present since a human being—so obviously you for instance or I can only he sitting in this exact moment in this room on this boulevard... we cannot be at the same time sitting here last year or in the coming year.

I haven't even visited the museum, I am telling Ivan,

who replies he has heard of it though he never has much interest in going there. We didn't go to Varna to go to museums, as you know, maybe to the aquarium on a rainy day but even that required too much get-up-and-go for a look at fish swimming around in tanks.

In Gibbon's *The History of the Decline and Fall of the Roman Empire* one can read: the Catholics marched through the plains of Bulgaria, burning, with wanton cruelty, the churches and villages of the Christian natives their last station was at Varna.

While it is not hard to imagine such events while sitting on Botev Boulevard in Sofia… here in New York City, though with more frequency, than one might care to admit, departed bodies show up in the garbage and everyday people are killed in random acts of…

The burning of a house at the beginning of the winter, the stealing of the sacks of saved up grain, the driving off of the pigs and other animals… and nowhere to turn and not able to walk that far…

How far can a man walk living on grass and what he can grab or find already dead…

Frederik is found by them. They are found by them. Two of them and many of them. The two have known each for a year. They come from the same village. All of them came from this place. The two of them could not understand what is being said. The two have not been in this place on the way to where they had fought. They have heard at home about battles they have not seen and they have not seen a battle before. Everyone is being killed. You could not run away, it seems. They were on horse but our ones on horse raced away and they went after them.. Their men on horse did not bother with us on foot, just then…

But something happens and they have got away or some got some place who were not in the battle or dead already or ready to be dead as if they know what is happening since they have no words in common, but no one is calling after them as they keep walking and walking and are now surrounded by them but these men just look at them and they now stare at the grass. They look down at the grass or the earth if they knew the difference, but they looked down and looked up to the sky which was a bright blue.

But where are these people? Outside some sort of fencing, trees cut down to keep out who might be there to prey upon them but how do you prey upon someone when you have nothing in your hand and are not on a horse and are not wearing armor?

What will they do?

Frederik finds a copy of the treaty… the treaty. The monument of Christian perfidy, has been displayed in the front of battle; and it is said that the sultan in his distress, lifting his eyes and his hands to heaven, implored the protection of the God of truth; and called on the prophet Jesus himself to avenge the impious mockery of his name and religion. Some Christian writers affirm that the sultan drew from his bosom the host or wafer on which the treaty had been sworn. The Moslems suppose, with more simplicity, an appeal to God and his prophet Jesus…Ivan should have found the treaty In the National Library, but he didn't

have the permission to make a copy on a photo-copying
machine of it from a book.

John Hunyadi flees north, which is more than these two
men would have known, Ivan says. Knowing this we always stand superior to them and that is not something people read with ease. These two men who we have discovered,
unburied you could say, now present, at least a few lines
present or words... but as of yet, no face, no height, no
color of hair: it would be easy to make them fairhaired, but
that would be giving away a hand... they are both seeming-
ly healthy, about the same age though neither one of them
could tell you their age as that was something that is not
part of their lives... of course they know that they have
been born and have names and once a year they go to the
church on the day of their name's saint... to have a day for
their own individual birth is not something,
But, Frederik might ask where is an insistent sort of
need to tell anyone this is coming from...
Trying to gather an authority, Ivan says, that is all any
one person can do... I can show you how to hammer a nail
by my own ability to hammer a nail into a piece of wood
without bending the nail without splitting the piece of
wood but some would jump to the conclusion: he knows
how to saw a piece of wood after demonstrating my ability to a hammer and a nail, but they wait: the day divides
into night and day and with no bells in the church—did or
do they have bells in Bulgarian churches Frederik asks...
where would they have been made?... who has heard a bell

ring? At least that is what they have experienced so far on this voyage to this place. They have not heard a bell ring or bells ringing.

But, there are nagging questions.

Why would a person make room for a stranger?

Strangers brought bad things to a place though today we look upon strangers with curiosity, a breaking of the monotony, but if a village has been burnt to the ground, all the animals driven off or killed…

The how to begin again and again?

The appearance of a stranger, not a maker of miracles, not a priest or monk or holy man…

When does a stranger cease to be a stranger and become a man or a woman?

These two men arrive on foot.

Clichés demand: *the unbearable violence of the times.*

Men on horses doing what they want.

The difficulty of pulling a man down from a horse.

They carry lances, swords, maces.

They tie heads to their saddles and feel them hitting against their legs as they ride?

The winter empties the fields and the hillsides…

What is gone does not depend on the number of years between the event and the ever present moment as on this day, 2 December 2014 reading: Kortenhaus, Carole Carole Mary Kortenhaus, 75, of Sea Girt, New Jersey and Orlando, Florida, passed away on Friday, November 28, 2014, at her home in Florida. Carole Mary Kortenhaus was the oldest child of John and Verna Cronin. She was born in Newark, and was a resident of Mountainside, NJ, before moving to Spring Lake in 1972. She later moved to Sea Girt, and also maintained a residence in Florida for many years. She was a graduate of Monmouth University and employed for 22 years by the US Dept. of Defense supporting Army programs at Fort Monmouth, NJ and 10 years at the Army Program Executive Office for Simulation, Training and Instrumentation (PEO STRI) in Orlando. While in Spring Lake, she was actively involved in St. Catharine's School, which her children attended. She taught art classes, and assisted Sisters Rose and Linda in the classroom. She would even drive the school bus when needed. In 1979, she took several nuns to Disney World. Mrs. Kortenhaus is survived by her children, Lynne Kummer, Frederick, MD, Katherine Harris, Orlando, FL, Robert J. Kortenhaus, Howell, NJ, Sue Campia, Falmouth, MA, Michael B. Kortenhaus, Howell, NJ, Daniel J. Kortenhaus, St. Petersburg, FL, John Kortenhaus, Plano, TX, and Andrea West, Bayville, NJ. She is also survived by 14 grandchildren, 4 great-grandchildren, and her siblings, Dan Cronin, Dennis Cronin, Pat Sloan, Katie Bevins and Mary Konikowski. She was predeceased by a sister, Claire Hicks. Visitation will take place at O'Brien Funeral Home, 2028 Hwy. 35, Wall, on Tuesday, December 2, 2014, from 2-8 PM. The funeral Mass will be celebrated at St. Catharine's Church, Spring Lake, on Wednesday, December 3, 2014, at 10:30 AM, followed by interment at St. Catharine's Cemetery

COMMENTARY: who is not mentioned in this obituary for an obviously pious woman of the present moment?

WHO, so you get an idea of the cast of individuals who are named:

King Vladislav

John Hunyadi, Voevode of Transylvania

Cardinal Julian Cesarini

Murad II

… ENOUGH, Frederik says. Enough as you are moving too fast for anyone other than the very young who are able to read quickly forgetting as they read… so they must keep reading as they—as they say—love reading and only reading as long as they are not asked to describe what they have been reading.

Episodes on the fringes of the Ottoman Empire encourage the Crusaders.

A Moslem preacher appeared in Edirne claims Jesus was superior to Mohamet… he is executed and his followers are gruesomely punished.

Hunyadi and Vladislav set out in full certainty…

They cross the Danube and make for Sofia which they burn and where they slaughter all the Turks and leave and for four days burning everything that lay in his path and around…

The crusaders set fire to the fortress in Shumen and the defenders jump to their deaths…

Frederik is forced to say: reminds anyone who was alive in New York City on 11 September of those jumping… so the chronicles are hardly accurate: they just want to draw a line under the incident.

At Varna: at first the Hungarians defeat the Anatolians

killing their commander then drive the Rumelian cavalry from the field.

Vladislav sees Murad standing alone midst his Janissaries and other soldiers… it is said Murad sits idly like a lady in a grandstand watching a mere soldier gaining glory from his victories… combining victory with personal glory…

Ivan says, there should be a pause as the so-called story is now lurching backwards to provide the narrative with a bad guy, at least according to the historical memory. They all of them go out in triumph to greet and honour the new Cardinal. He is received with reverence, and at once expert preachers and qualified priests are chosen to leave at once and go throughout the two kingdoms proclaiming and preaching the crusade. They are to carry graces, indulgences and pardons which everyone can acquire through the campaign, either by going in person or by donating their possessions, in accordance with the means and ability of each contributor.

When the preachers broadcast the marvelous graces of the Holy Father, they move the hearts of the people, as the chronicles recount, to such devotion a number of them personally and at their own expense take up arms to fight the infidel Turks and to defend the Holy Catholic faith.

Meanwhile, such of those faithless and accursed men as have been spared the sword somehow or other find their way with great difficulty to Belgrade. They limp along groaning and moaning, some blind, some lame, bareheaded and barefooted, hungry and thirsty, creeping from valley to valley and peak to peak. Now the accursed men who live in Belgrade were watching the road expecting good news from their king...

These accursed and faithless men have departed in fear for their own lives, leaving their prisoners behind. When, by the grace of God, they are freed every one rejoices as they find their sons, daughters and wives. Mothers find their sons and sons their mothers. They bleat like sheep and lambs as they embrace one another: all of them like new-born babes.

The infidels who are as low as the dust raise the white flag and call out, begging for quarter... then the Padishah decrees that there can be no mercy in these realms for infidels and so after enslaving the fresh-faced lads from the infidels who are as low as the earth they put all their grown men to the sword.

Praised be to God and again praise.

-85-

In Madara—how always coming back to a few places, that mattering little at the moment, take root... even the drive to and from Madara, actually four times... it is the going through the little towns, not closed up and abandoned towns, under the bright sun of late June... though Piret is waiting for that man to re-appear and nothing can dissuade her from this terrible expectation: she cannot see those two men who have found their way to this place...Piret talks with Frederik in Estonian as that is another of his languages but that does not make the man from Strazhitsa disappear while Frederik is trying to convince her the the world is full of such people like the man from Strazhitsa and you might see him when you go to those villages near Lake Peipsi and standing in a church of the Old Believers you will notice a man crossing himself with two fingers and you will ask if that has a meaning and you will turn to … later and he will say in the Catholic tradition you touch your forehead with the four fingers of your right hand... it is the little things… and to hold the little things like the glance of the man from Strazhitsa and can Ivan embellish what has been embellished: imaginatively watching Hunyadi 'a mere soldier' gain glory by his victory against Karaca Bey and then against the Rumelians, while he, the King, 'sat idly by, like a lady in a grandstand watching the feats.'

Ivan says, here again is *the bad guy* as the Americans like to say: The exact fate of Cardinal Cesarini remains unknown. Dlugosz reports a Vlach boat man killed him as he ferried him across the Danube on his flight from Varna and his body was later retrieved from the river. The boatman notices the boat was unusually unbalanced so the Cardinal must have been weighted down with what anyone could not fail to resist.

But there is another story Ivan says, according to Hans Maugest, the Turks took Cesarini to Edirne where they intended to flay him alive. The stripping of flesh from the staked out Cardinal is a refined pleasure, a real crowd pleaser.

Hunyadi—this is the guy who survives everything, the one who will die in his own bed, is able to gather his men and leave the battlefield in good order. Having crossed the

Danube, Vlad Drakul captures him and holds him for ransom for having pillaged his lands on the way to Varna.

As to the Christian king:

ONE. The Hungarians never recovered the body of the King.

TWO. Murad had his body buried in a Greek chapel but without the head.

THREE. Turks in Gallipoli showed Loredan a severed head which they claimed was the King's.

FOUR: Maugest states that Murad sent the head to the Mamluk Sultan in Cairo.

Maugest says 12 knights and 12 squires were sent to the Mamluk Sultan in Cairo.

Twelve knights and 24 squires are sent to the Khan of the Crimea. Six knights and six squires are sent to Karaman.

In March 1445 the Hungarian captives arrive in Cairo to be paraded around in their full armor. A few weeks later they convert to Islam.

The remaining captives who escaped execution are sold as slaves.

A few were ransomed in Constantinople.

Hunyadi acquires a lasting reputation first as a Christian hero and later as a national hero of both Hungary and Romania. He's what will be called a survivor

… but aren't they always saying that, Ivan asks, no one remembers anything anymore and never did for that matter. So again it is reported the King has said, When the Osman is defeated and takes to flight, you should be careful not to pursue the

Turks. When the Turks are defeated and put to flight, you must be wary of leaving what you are doing in order to plunder their goods. First, you should destroy the bees then you can eat their honey.

Both sides are caught up in a melee as prefiguring the Judgment Day. Zupan Yanko is clad in steel and exerts himself more powerfully and energetically than words can express.

On our side Sahin Pasha girds up his loins and drives forward the seven ranks.

These, it is true, did not take flight from the infidels, but the infidels who are as low as the dust have come clad from head to toe in iron. However hard the warriors strike with their swords, it makes no impression on the infidels who are as low as the dust. When the warriors of Islam see this, they all take up maces, clubs and batter the infidels with zeal and heroism.

For a time it was such that father could not recognize son nor son father.

Then the accursed man called Zupan Yanko takes his lance into his hand and says, Come on now let me see how you strive for the love of Jesus. For each of you I shall get great favors from the King.

As he was galloping and urging on the infidel troops a warrior on the Moslem side takes up his bow and arrow and aims at the pig Yanko. However it is he fires it, he does not miss. The arrow plants itself straight into the accursed Yanko's eye, so he is stunned and falls in a faint.

A little later he comes to his senses mounts his horse

and leaves the battlefield to have his head bandaged so he can return to the fray.

By now the Padishah is left with about three hundred Janissaries and he immediately dismounts from his horse, rubs his face in the earth and at the same moment raises his hands in fervent prayer to God, taking up a handful of dust and passes it through his collar into breast and rubs his face with his hands. He takes up his sword and the troops of Islam fall upon the Infidels.

The King of the Infidels has no idea what to do. However hard he tries it is impossible to restore his line. As he is galloping up and down a strong armed warrior from the army of Islam struck the evil-doing King several blows with a mace and knocked him off his horse. The Janissaries and Arabs fell upon the King and struck him with their axes...

Innumerable Infidels are put to the sword on the field: many and great praises be to God!

Now on that day they wield the sword until dusk, and did the same all night until morning and on the next day they slaughter the infidels until the time of the afternoon prayer.

Some of the warriors of Islam took the infidels who are as low as dust prisoner and brought them into the presence of the Padishah, who ordered them to enslave the young infidels and put the adults to the sword.

The Padishah rides to the field where he sees corpse piled upon corpse and bodies awash with blood. So many infidels have been slaughtered only God can count their number.

From there he proceeds to the camp of the King's tent. He goes inside and drives his sword into the King's throne and sits down giving praise and thanks for the favor and guidance of God.

Frederik says, let's go up and look at the Madara Horseman on the side of the mountain. The fleeing sun will animate him, more than our words and let this be the final word.

MARCH 2018

THOMAS MCGONIGLE was born at 110 Willoughby Avenue, Brooklyn, some years ago. His patriotism is divided between: Patchogue, Dublin, Sofia and a base on East First Street in Manhattan. His books: *In Patchogue, The Corpse Dream of N. Petkov* (in English and Bulgarian), *Going to Patchogue, Diptych Before Dying* (in Bulgarian), *St. Patrick's Day another day in Dublin.* Reviews and articles by TM can be read at *The Guardian* (London) *The Washington Post, Chicago Tribune, The Los Angeles Times, Newsday. The Hollins Critic* etc.

abcofreading.blogspot.com